IT WILL END LIKE THIS

Delacorte Press

IT WILL END LIKE THIS

KYRA LEIGH

Text copyright © 2022 by Kyra Williams
Jacket art copyright © 2022 by Elena Garnu

Visit us on the Web! GetUnderlined.com

Educators and librarians, for a variety of teaching tools,
visit us at RHTeachersLibrarians.com

Library of Congress Cataloging-in-Publication Data
Names: Leigh, Kyra, author.
Title: It will end like this / Kyra Leigh.
Description: First edition. | New York : Delacorte Press, 2022. |
Audience: Ages 14+. | Audience: Grades 10-12. | Summary: When their
mother suddenly dies, sisters Charlotte and Maddi begin to suspect that their
father and his new girlfriend played a part in her death, and they spiral into
paranoia with horrifying consequences.
Identifiers: LCCN 2021017820 (print) | LCCN 2021017821 (ebook) |
ISBN 978-0-593-37552-5 (hardcover) | ISBN 978-0-593-37555-6 (ebook) |
ISBN 978-0-593-48706-8 (export)
Subjects: CYAC: Sisters—Fiction. | Death—Fiction. |
Belief and doubt—Fiction. | LCGFT: Novels.
Classification: LCC PZ7.1.L4443 It 2022 (print) | LCC PZ7.1.L4443 (ebook) |
DDC [Fic]—dc23

The text of this book is set in Janson MT Pro.
Interior design by Jen Valero

Printed in the United States of America
10 9 8 7 6 5 4 3 2 1
First Edition

For my sisters

I always went to my sister, because she was older
and had the care of me after my mother died.

—*Lizzie Borden*

Lizzie Borden took an ax,
And gave her mother forty whacks.
When she saw what she had done,
She gave her father forty-one.

—*American skipping rhyme*

Do you ever stand in the kitchen and look at the knives? Do you ever wonder what you could do with a meat cleaver? What about a butcher's knife?

It could cut through flesh so fast someone might not even feel pain.

Might not even bleed.

Dark thoughts fill my head.

I tell myself not to think about it.

But then myself tells me to.

Dark thoughts.

They fill my head like water. They fill my mind.

Sometimes it's like they fill my soul.

Charlotte

"She's dead."

A woman in black stands at the foot of my bed. Her hair is long and dark and covers her face. I don't know who she is or why she's here, but she keeps saying the same thing.

"She's dead. She's dead."

My body is stuck to my bed. I can't move my arms or legs. I turn my head and look out the window. A crow sits on the sill and looks in at me through the glass.

"She's dead," the crow says. Its eyes are huge and dark green. And when it speaks, it sounds afraid. I can sense its fear—it washes over my body like a cold shower.

"She's dead," the woman cries again. Only, each time she says it, her voice cracks more and more, and I hear tears, and something else, hiding in her throat.

It's so dark I almost can't see the woman. But I can feel her. Feel her presence.

Who is she? Who has died?

I look back at the crow, and a tear falls out of its big green eye.

"Wake up, wake up!" the crow cries. Loud and familiar in my ear.

I try to move my body, but can't.

"Charlotte, she's dead, wake up. Wake up."

The woman in black comes close to me, and then reaches down and shakes my shoulders. I'm paralyzed. Unable to move away. I see that she's covered in blood. She reaches out to me again, and I close my eyes tight.

"She's dead," she whispers right into my ear.

That's when I wake up. But the voice doesn't stop. My eyes focus, and I look up and see my older sister, Maddi, standing above me. She cries when she speaks.

"What?" I say, my voice hoarse with sleep and nightmares.

Maddi sits down at my feet and puts her face in her hands and sobs. Big loud sobs. It reminds me of a dog howling.

That dream.

That dream felt so real. So vivid.

"What's going on?" I shout.

"She's dead, Charlotte. Mom is dead. An ambulance is on the way to come and get her," Maddi says. I don't recognize the look in her eyes.

What?

What?

I sit up fast and grab Maddi's arm and shake her. My head spins for a moment, but then stills when I look at my sister. She sits there, like she's lost all ability to move. Her arms limp and thin.

"What are you talking about? How? What happened?"

This must be a joke. I just saw Mom before I went to sleep. I hugged her before bed. She was fine. She was breathing. She was alive.

4

"Out by the beach. Dad found her . . ." Maddi can hardly finish the sentence. I've never heard her like this before. Frightened. Scared. Heartbroken.

No.

No.

After the baby died, Mom started having fears. Weird fears. Fears that made her believe that something was eating her from the inside out, that something was killing her, but that's all they were, fears.

Sometimes I would worry about her. But after months of dealing with it, I decided to let it go. Pretended I didn't care that she was afraid.

How could I have been so stupid?

How could her fears have come true?

"That's a lie. You're lying. She's asleep," I shout, and get out of bed. Then I run out of my room and down the dark hallway, to Mom and Dad's room. I'm dizzy with sleep and the feeling of sick hits my stomach, but I ignore it.

"Where is she? Where's Mom?" I scream when I open the bedroom door. But no one's there except Mom's assistant, Amber. She's making the bed and crying.

There's a lamp on by Mom's side of the bed.

Dad isn't here.

Is he out there with her? With Mom?

The light from the lamp washes the room in yellow. There's a shadow on the wall from where Amber stands. She drops the pale blue comforter in her hands when she sees me.

"Where is she? *Take me to my mom.*" I try to hold back the scream that's building deep inside my chest.

"Charlotte," Amber says. She opens her arms for me and I go to her and hug her. She smells like flour and sweat. She holds me tight.

"What happened?" I say into her shoulder. My head feels like it's going to explode, and my heart has shattered. To bits and pieces.

This isn't true.

This is just another bad dream.

Another bad dream that I need to wake myself up from.

You don't just die.

Wake up, Charlotte. Wake up, you're asleep.

How can someone just suddenly die?

"I don't know. I don't know," Amber says. She holds me tight in a hug for a long time.

I blink as many times as I can, but I know this isn't a dream. That I'm living this moment, right now.

My mother isn't here.

"How?" I pull away from Amber and fall to the floor. I touch the soft white carpet, to make sure I can still move my arms. Move my hands. To make sure I'm still here.

How.

Why.

Over and over and over I think this. Over and over I ask myself.

"Is she outside? Can't I go check on her? Just to make sure it's her? It's actually my mom?" I look up at Amber. I hadn't realized how much taller she was than me. Not until now. Not until this moment.

"An ambulance is on the way, Charlotte. You can't go outside right now," Amber says.

I try not to picture Mom out there. But I can't get the image out of my head. Her body, out by the water. Bloated and cold. I'm going to puke. I know I'm going to.

Where is she?

It's not her. She can't be dead.

It's not my mom. It's someone else.

She can't be dead.

"She's gone. Your mother is gone."

Charlotte

"Charlotte, get up. We're gonna be late for school."

I lie in bed and stare up at the ceiling.

It's been four months.

Four months since I've gone to school, yet every morning Maddi pops her head into my room and tells me to get up. I try not to let it get under my skin, but it does. Because she knows I'm not interested. Knows I don't ever want to go back there. To show my face there. And to be honest, I'm sure no one wants to see me there, either.

Maybe she wants things to be normal again, but I know that can't happen. She *must* know that can't happen.

Nothing will ever be the same.

She needs to leave me alone.

She needs to go away.

"Charlotte?"

My door squeaks as Maddi opens it and walks in. She's wearing a sundress. It's pink with white flowers. It reminds me of raspberry sorbet. Mom bought the dress for her a few years back. I remember because Mom bought my favorite white dress for me then, too. The one I wore to the funeral. It was the only thing she ever did that was remotely religious, buying us Easter dresses.

Maddi brings spring and life into my room even though I know it's cold and dark outside. I can hear waves crashing against rocks in the distance.

The perks of living in a beach house.

That sound used to give me comfort. Used to soothe me to sleep.

Now it makes my skin crawl. A constant reminder of Mom. Of where she was found.

It's cold in my room today. Winter is just around the corner, but Maddi hasn't packed her summer clothes away yet.

I wonder if she will.

They remind me of Mom. I wonder if they remind her of Mom, too.

Maybe that's why she wears them.

"You look nice." I sit up. My room's a wreck. I haven't folded my laundry in weeks. There are empty soda cans, glasses of water, and candy wrappers scattered about. Sometimes Maddi will come in and clean up for me, but mostly my room just stays the way it is.

Messy.

Disorganized.

I've been wearing the same sweater and leggings for the last couple of days. I can smell myself, but it's easier than doing laundry.

I'm such a slob.

I don't even care that I'm a slob.

"Let's go to school together today. Please?" Maddi is just

eleven months older than me. I'm sixteen and she's seventeen. We've always been really close, but the last few months we haven't spent as much time together.

It's my fault. I know it. She does too.

"I can't," I say.

Can't.

Can't go back there.

Everyone knows what happened.

Everyone thinks they know what happened.

Mom.

According to the police, her heart stopped and she died.

How can your heart beat one minute and then stop the next?

Her heart was broken.

Can you die of a broken heart?

I'll never forget that day. Trying to get out to where she was. Maddi and Amber kept me away from her body. An ambulance came, but it didn't have its lights or siren on. I begged and pleaded with Maddi and Amber to let me go to her. But they wouldn't.

I looked out the window as the paramedics brought Mom up from the beach and left. They had her zipped up in a black bag.

Don't think about that.

Maddi walks into my room and sits at the foot of my bed. She has a sad look in her eyes.

Maddi used to glow with happiness. All bright and sunny mornings. But lately I can see in her eyes that she's losing it. That she's driving full speed down the tunnel of sadness. The same one I've already crashed and burned in.

I glance around my bedroom and try to look at it from Maddi's point of view.

What does she see when she looks at the state of my room? Even my appearance?

Same thing you see when you look in the mirror. Trash.

Don't think like that.

Trash.

"Why do you make me go alone? Do you know what it's like walking around those halls? I hate it. I'm sick of it."

This is the first I've heard of her hating school. Usually when Maddi comes home in the afternoon she fills me in on the latest gossip. When she comes in and chats with me, I make a real effort to pretend to care about what she has to say. And sometimes I really do.

It's too early, so I haven't had time to put on my "I give a fuck" face. The thought of going to school makes my skin crawl.

"I didn't know that you hated it there." I look down at my hands. My nails are bitten so short it makes me sick to look at them. The skin on my fingers all chewed up and bloody.

I used to grow my nails long and paint them pink.

I used to do a lot of things.

"It's uncomfortable being the only one, that's all," Maddi says. She softens her voice, and I wonder if she feels bad for snapping at me.

Do they look at her the way I know they'd look at me?

They must.

My therapist, Nancy, tells me it's not healthy to mind read, to assume I know what someone is thinking, but sometimes I can't help it.

Sometimes I just know.

I grab my blankets and throw them over my head. I'm safe in my bed. I'm safe in my room. Away from them.

Maddi crawls up next to me and gets under the covers.

Does she notice the smell of unwashed sheets? Does she feel the crumbs buried in the bed?

"I can't go by myself again. Please," she whispers.

I think about before. How her and I did everything together. Best friends. Inseparable. And now we're worlds apart.

I reside on my moon of sadness, and she's stuck on the sun, trying to fill the rest of the family with light and joy. But I know that deep down she just wants to be back on the moon with me.

Mind reading again . . .

"Just skip today. Stay here," I say. I used to ask her all the time to stay home with me, but eventually I gave up. I think that she only goes to school because it makes her feel like things haven't changed as much as we both know they have.

"I'll stay tomorrow if you come with me today. Please," Maddi says. I hear the desperation in her voice. A stab of guilt hits me.

You're not allowed to feel guilty.

Have I abandoned my sister?

Have I left her out in the darkness to fend for herself?

Maddi

I've been best friends with my sister ever since she was born. I don't remember that moment, but Mom told me when Charlotte came (on the exact day she was due) that I crawled up into Mom's lap and kissed Charlotte right on the face. I was almost one. After that moment, we were inseparable. There isn't anyone I love as much as I love Charlotte, except Mom.

Sometimes it's weird to think about our lives before.

Before death. Before sadness.

Was that a life I actually lived?

When I think about *before*, it's like I was in some sort of dream state. It was *real*, but looking back on it, it doesn't feel like it was real.

I would go to school with my sister, we'd eat lunch together, or skip third period to get coffee, or meet up at one of our friends' houses. We'd film stupid videos of ourselves dancing in the mirror.

Was that my life? Was that real?

Before Charlotte stopped being Charlotte, and before Mom died, before all of that, there was some normalcy in my family.

Mom and Dad weren't "in love," but they got along. I wasn't great in school, but I was getting by with the grades I had.

When I look at photos from that time in my life, I don't even recognize the girl I see. She was happy. She was confident, or at least as confident as a sixteen-year-old can be. We were whole. Our family. Whole. Together.

Charlotte

Cheer squad captain.

Basketball star.

Thriving businessman.

Property owner and happy mom.

Money.

Money.

More money.

All things that make a perfect family, right? All things that keep you loving one another.

This is what I used to think. This is what I used to believe. As long as we kept up our routine, as long as we did what made us appear normal, then things would stay perfect.

Ignorant.

Blind.

Stupid.

I was stupid. I was stupid to think that that's all I needed to stay happy.

Charlotte

"You're gonna do great. Cat has been asking about you and, of course, so has Stephen," Maddi says.

We're on our way to school.

Four months, and I've finally let Maddi win.

I caved. I fucking caved.

Getting out of bed was a blur. Putting on fresh clothes was a blur. This whole ride is a blur. Maddi told me I should wear my favorite white dress, for luck. But I left it hidden in the back of my closet.

Instead I threw on a ratty old sweatshirt and some faded black leggings. My classmates won't recognize me.

Don't kid yourself.

At least I'll feel hidden away.

What will I tell Stephen? What if he asks me questions? What if he ignores me?

I haven't talked to him since everything happened.

"What has Stephen said?" I ask. We drive past an old smoke shop. It reminds me of my first cigarette. One I stole from Mom. She nearly killed me when she found out.

"Smoking is for dying adults, not growing children," she'd

said. She was always certain she was dying. Even when I was certain she wasn't.

Mother knows best, I guess.

I glance at the console in Maddi's car. Plugged into her charger is her Juul.

Not so perfect.

I wonder what Mom would say about that. Early death on its way to Maddi, too. Just in a new form.

Outside the sky is gray and stormy. Typical Massachusetts weather. Off in the distance, behind the smoke shop, I know the ocean hides. Probably getting angrier and angrier the colder it gets. The harder the wind pushes it.

I know what it's like to be pushed like that.

"Just asks how you're doing. He misses you. And so you know, he hasn't been seeing anyone else." Maddi glances at me and gives me "the face" after she says this.

The face that says, *He's still yours if you want him to be.*

Do I want him to be? I'm not sure anymore.

"I don't know if I can do this." I try to push the last time I saw Stephen out of my head, but it's crowded in my brain and I only have so many places to hide memories away.

Maddi rolls down her window even though it's freezing outside. I flick the heat up a notch and put my hands over the vent. It helps.

Sort of.

"That's too bad. Because you already are." Maddi reaches over and grabs her Juul from the charger and takes a puff. A cloud of mint-smelling vapor fills the car for just a moment and then disappears.

"For the stress," she says, and then puts the e-cig back on the charger.

I sigh as loud as I can, just so that Maddi knows I'm annoyed. But she's right, I'm already in the car. I'm already on my way. Why bitch when I already agreed to it?

I glance down at my pants. There's a hole in one thigh the size of a quarter. There's also dust and sugar from the powdered doughnut I had for breakfast. I should probably care about my appearance today, but I don't. I stick my finger in the hole in my leggings and tear it bigger.

"I miss Mom," I say.

Miss her more than ever.

Miss her more than anything.

"Hey, I've actually wanted to talk to you about something," Maddi says. "Have you been able to find the last journal she wrote?"

Mom's journals.

When she was alive, she wrote in a journal every single day. She'd usually leave them scattered around the house, in the kitchen, the living room, even the bathroom. But now that Maddi mentions it, I haven't seen one since before Mom's funeral.

"That's a good question. I haven't," I say, "which means Dad probably stored them somewhere."

Do I really want to know what her last thoughts were?

"Maybe the cops took them," Maddi says quietly.

"Maybe," I say.

Her heart stopped. Why would the cops need her journals when they already knew everything they needed to know about Mom?

Your heart doesn't just stop.

Maybe.

Or maybe Amber has the journals.

Stolen the journals. Stolen so we can't read them.

Does she think we'll forget about our mother?

Does she think she can swoop in and pretend to take the place of our mother?

"We should find them," I say.

Maddi nods and then makes a right-hand turn and we're here.

The shithole we call school.

Charlotte

After Mom died, it was pretty obvious that Amber and Dad had been seeing each other.

Amber had already been living with us well before Mom died. So it made it easy for her and Dad to sneak around, I'm sure.

I remember telling Nancy that Amber was acting like she owned the place, not two months after Mom was buried deep in the ground.

"Maybe she's just trying to be a support," Nancy had said. Always the optimist. I guess that's her job. To help me not to assume the worst, to find a way to process things in a healthy manner, even though I knew none of my life was healthy.

Nancy's office was painted mint green, and for some reason the color made my eyes hurt. She also had all types of plants scattered about. Maybe to give the feeling of life whenever one of her clients spoke of death.

Every time we met, Nancy would sit in an office chair directly across from where I sat on the couch. Even though she had a large desk, I never saw her behind it.

"She's been flirting with my father, I see her doing it. He

lights up whenever Amber walks in the room. Doesn't he feel any grief about my mom? They were married almost twenty years," I said.

Nancy shrugged. "This may be the way he grieves. This may be how he's coping." She tried to give me what I imagine she thought was an encouraging smile. But the look on her face just got under my skin, and I wasn't sure why.

I felt like that was an excuse. Always an excuse when it came to my father. Maybe that's not what Nancy was trying to do, but that's how it felt.

"Well, I'm sure they're sleeping together. Dad never kicked her out after Mom died," I said.

That was partly me and Maddi's fault. In the beginning we wanted Amber to stay, until we eventually realized what was going on. But by then I guess it was too late.

"Just try to have an open mind. Give your dad more credit," Nancy said.

I really had wanted to give my father more credit. Maybe he and I had grown apart over the years, but that didn't mean I thought everything he did was bad or evil.

At least not until I got home that night.

I still remember walking into the house after that therapy session. I was drained from head to toe, and all I wanted was a cup of hot chocolate and a bath. When I walked into the kitchen I caught Dad and Amber kissing. Dad had his hand on Amber's bare stomach, and I could see a small butterfly tattoo she had on her waist.

I stared at them for a moment and then nearly lost my fucking mind. Screamed, shouted, broke half the dishes in the cabinet. It felt like the beginning of something, and the end of something else. It confirmed that my life would never go back to normal. That Mom really was gone, and that my father didn't give two fucks about me or my sister.

I stopped going to therapy after that. Despite Maddi begging, even my father begging.

I didn't want to talk to someone who would give my dad an excuse. I knew no matter what Nancy told me, I was right about everything. What was talking to her going to do for me?

Soon after I stopped therapy, Amber moved out of the guesthouse she rented from us and set up camp in Mom and Dad's room. Nothing else to hide. I'd caught them in the act, so why keep pretending we didn't know?

I wanted to ask Dad why. Wanted to ask Amber how could she. But I didn't. Instead I locked myself away and wished that Mom would come back. Even though I knew that was never going to happen.

Charlotte

"I don't feel well," Mom had said.

We were sitting out in the garden. We sipped rose-flavored herbal tea and watched nothing but the sky as the sun set. It was warm out. The sun cast a gorgeous pink hue all around our front yard. I could smell the flowers in the air. That was one thing Mom hadn't given up on, her garden. Her love for plants and flowers and herbs. Everything around us practically singing in color. I'd hoped so much that the garden was helping her with her sadness. With the loss.

"I can take you to the doctor, Mom," I said.

I was annoyed. She was ruining the sunset, ruining the moment. She was always complaining about this type of thing, and I was getting tired of it. Of hearing her complain. If she wanted to figure out what was wrong, there was only one way to find out.

The pinks in the sunset started to turn into oranges and golds. The humidity was dying down, and I could smell in the air that fall was on its way. Soon the sunshine was going to be replaced with a cold dreary sky and the flowers would be gone. The green that surrounded us was on its way out.

"Doctors don't know anything about anything. You know they can't help me. Besides, sadness hurts. From the inside out."

Mom always struggled with her mood. Even when I was a kid. But the complaints of constantly being in pain? This was new. This only started after the baby.

It was true. She was always a little wary of doctors. She felt like they forced people to take medication they didn't need, made illnesses worse, and almost never helped. But after she lost the baby, she lost all faith in them. Still, a late-term miscarriage wasn't a reason to completely blow off medical science.

"A doctor can't fix how I'm feeling," Mom said.

She said it felt like something was eating her from the inside out. Something was scratching in her belly and wouldn't go away. No matter what she did, ate, or drank.

Dad had said she was being dramatic or that she was still getting over the postpartum depression. So he never fed into it. And Mom probably *was* being dramatic, but it still stressed me out. I hated the thought of her going untreated, even if it wasn't anything physical.

It all mattered.

I had also read all kinds of horror stories about the body after a late-term miscarriage. What if something was happening to her? Something life-threatening? I had to push those fears out of my head, otherwise I would drive myself crazy.

"I'll keep taking the herbs," Mom said, more to herself than to me. "Plus, I love this new tea." She held up her mug. That was her new remedy, tea and herbs.

She thought herbs were the cure for everything.

"What if it's something serious, Mom? If you're in this much pain, it could mean it's something bad." I used a harsh tone even though I hadn't meant to. I glanced at Mom and saw a little bit of hurt in her expression.

"I'm just worried," I said, trying to be nicer. If there really was something wrong with her, we'd never know.

"Don't worry. I think I just need rest," Mom said. She finished her tea, and then gave me a kiss on the cheek and went inside. The smell of rose petals and herbs lingered on her breath.

I picked up my phone and texted Stephen.

My mom is being a stubborn idiot.

He texted me back with a smiley face.

If something is wrong with her, how will I ever know?

Don't worry so much about her. She's fine.

I hated when he told me not to worry. But I couldn't help it. I hoped so much that Mom's illness was just in her head. But something told me it was more than that.

Charlotte

The school smells like shit.

Nothing has changed. Dirty halls, old food in the vending machines, and that god-awful smell.

Nasty, sticky, stale, and wet, all at the same time.

Total shit.

Maddi and I walk down the hallway to our lockers. Even though we're in different grades, Dad somehow managed to get the school to give us lockers next to each other.

Right now, I am grateful for that.

At least he could do that for us.

At least.

As we walk, I hear whispers.

Or maybe I don't.

When you live in a small town, there isn't a lot to talk about. We're just outside of Fall River, Massachusetts, so you'd think we'd have a bigger school and a bigger town with bigger topics and better secrets. But we don't. Especially when someone in one of the community's most privileged families falls apart.

I glance at my classmates. They smile at me, or they don't look at all.

What are they thinking?

I think I already know what's on their minds.

I've almost made it to my locker. I'm almost to safety when Catherine hunts me down. My best friend.

Damn it.

"Charlotte! Oh my shit, you're back." She walks straight for me. Looks just the same as always. Nothing's changed about her, not in four months, not in years. Her dark hair almost glistens, her skin is the same nice bronze shade. She has a tanning bed in her basement. It's supposed to be some big secret, but I know her secrets. And anyone who saw her strawberry-blond roots would know her secrets, too.

Maddi grabs my hand and makes me stop walking. She waves at Catherine.

"Cat, you found us," Maddi says, putting on a huge fake smile.

Cat.

I forgot she likes being called that now. She gave herself the nickname right before my mom died. I've never cared for it.

Because it's dumb as shit.

"Why didn't you tell me you were coming back?" Cat shouts. Even her whisper is a borderline screech. She's probably the loudest person I know.

It used to be something I liked about her. In fact, a ton of people seem to like that about her. She has thousands of followers on Snapchat and TikTok, and the majority of what she posts involves that loud screeching voice.

Used to be something I liked.

She throws her skinny arms around me and squeals, I swear, just like a pig.

A spray-tanned pig.

Don't be an asshole.

"How are you? How is everything? I haven't seen you since the funeral. How's your father? Have you run into Stephen yet?" She talks a million miles a minute, and it makes my head race.

This was a mistake. I should not have come here.

How could I have let Maddi talk me into this?

It's loud, and someone nearby smells like BO and cheap perfume. Is that Cat? Or is that me?

It's you.

My Native deodorant is failing me.

Oh well, time to switch back to Dove.

"I'm fine. I just needed to take a break. It's good to be back," I say. I wonder if the lie shows on my face. I glance at Maddi, and she gives me another fake smile.

We wear masks, Maddi and I.

Masks to hide what's really on our minds. What we're really feeling.

"I've missed you guys so much. Seriously, it's been so boring around here without you. I did hear about your dad and Amber. Is he for real?" Cat folds her arms across her chest and looks me straight in the face. The gossip in her couldn't stay hidden long.

Is she really asking me this now?

Of course she is. Don't be so surprised.

Would I do the same thing if the roles were reversed?

Maybe before, I would have.

Cat leans in close to me and whispers, "Is it true?" Cat says this, and then she raises her eyebrows.

Of course she's heard about Dad and Amber. She's known

our family for years, and so has her mom. I'm sure someone saw them somewhere doing something that only couples do.

Listening to Cat talk makes me feel sick. Maybe I have something eating me from the inside like Mom did. Maybe whatever it is will strike me down and *my* heart will stop and I'll die here in the middle of the hall. Then people would have something new to talk about.

Is this how people speak to each other? Is this normal? I mean, I'm not the most sensitive person on the planet, but Jesus.

Is this how I spoke? Is this how I am?

"Could we not?" Maddi says. Her tone is sweet, but I can hear the harsh edge to it. I wonder if Cat notices.

"Sorry, sorry, sorry," Cat says. "I've just been curious. We all have. Well. I'm gonna get to class. See you later." She leans in and gives me a peck on the cheek.

To think that she used to be my best friend.

Just feeling her that close to me makes my stomach turn. My head starts to ache, and suddenly the fluorescent lights in the hallway feel extra bright.

Just breathe through it.

Have I always felt sick around Cat? Or is this something that comes with grief and sadness? Feeling repulsed by everyone in your path? Is this what Mom meant when she'd tell me that sadness hurts on the inside and out?

Maddi and I head to our lockers.

"Is that how it's been the last few months?" I ask. I almost feel bad for leaving Maddi here alone, to deal with all the talk and whispers.

29

Almost.

But she didn't have to come back. And she didn't have to bring me with her, either.

I guess I didn't have to come.

"It's been much worse than that," Maddi says. She opens her locker and throws her books in. They land on the bottom shelf with a loud bang. The sound hits me in just the spot I'm already getting a headache.

"But it'll be better now that you're here," she says. Somehow I know that she and I both know that's total bullshit.

I fucking hate school.

Maddi

The first few weeks back at school after Mom's death were hard. Almost unbearable. But being at home was worse.

Watching my father slowly try to remove the memory of Mom got under my skin, and oftentimes just walking into the kitchen was enough to make me burst into tears. I knew that toward the end of Mom's life that Dad and Mom weren't as in love as they once were, but after she died, Dad's feelings toward their marriage really started to show. I started feeling anger that I didn't know I had. Anger toward my father. Toward Amber. Even toward myself.

At school, people spoke to me like I was a stranger. Even the girls on my basketball team acted like they didn't know me. Teachers looked at me like they felt sorry for me. But the whispers were the worst.

Mom was a big part of the community. She ran for city council when I was younger, she donated money to local businesses, and she had friends all over the country. Our family was one of those families that people looked up to. Not just because of the money but also because of how awesome Mom was.

"I can't do it," I said out loud. I was driving myself to school.

It was my first day back after Mom's funeral. "It's too hard," I said to myself, but also a little bit to Mom.

Sometimes, I pretended she was still there. Just listening.

When I got to school, I was in a daze. Wandering the halls with sad faces directed at me. Like I was the first kid in school to lose a parent (I wasn't).

My friends Mandy and Ellis stopped by my locker with cards and flowers but wouldn't eat lunch with me. I don't remember a lot from those first few days; I retained nothing from class. The only thing getting me through was the thought of Mom and whispering to her throughout the day. If I thought about her, I knew I could do it.

Yet even my little whispers to Mom didn't change how sad I was.

But it helped with the loneliness.

Without Charlotte there, I had no one. I knew my friends would come back to me eventually, and it would all calm down. But knowing that didn't make it easier. And I knew things wouldn't be like they had been and probably never would be again.

After Mom died, we got letters from all over the community. People stopped by with homemade bread, and casseroles. When Dad wasn't home, which was more often than not in those early days of Mom's death, I tried to visit with people when they came, whoever they were. I'd fake conversations with them, make small talk, send thank-you cards. I did the best I could, but it was hard.

"Who are these people?" I'd asked. But Mom never answered.

Charlotte couldn't fake it. She couldn't even pretend for a

second when *anyone* stopped by. And honestly, I didn't blame her. It was hard to hide my feelings. Hard to hide the anger. The rage I sometimes felt toward everyone. Everyone who pretended like they cared about Mom.

Where had these people been before she died?

Mom stopped running her business at least a year before she passed away. She stopped going out with her friends months before that. And the community? She dropped off that map almost as if she never existed right after her miscarriage.

Why hadn't they stopped by then?

I wanted to ask. But I never did.

It didn't matter how many times they told us they missed Mom, how things wouldn't be the same without her. They were telling us that like we didn't already know. But what they didn't care to mention was how things had changed long before she died. And no one came then.

So why come now?

Charlotte

"Charlotte, welcome back! We've all missed you so much. Take a seat wherever you like."

This is the greeting I get when I walk into math class. Miss Brush puts her arms around me and gives me an unnecessary hug.

In front of everyone.

She's probably not even supposed to do that.

Shouldn't she ask my permission before she touches me?

I glance around the room and see Stephen.

My heart jumps when I see him. Jumps from sadness, and maybe excitement? I don't know. But he looks better than ever. His dark hair has gotten longer, and he's wearing a gray sweater that shows his collarbones. It's everything I can do not to run over and fall into his arms. Tell him how sorry I am.

How much I miss him.

Did he see me in the halls? Did he know I was coming back?

Maybe the gossip queen tipped him off after she saw me.

There's an empty desk right next to Stephen's. I stare at it, but don't move.

"Sit anywhere that's available," Miss Brush says, sounding

slightly annoyed. I guess she was only happy to have me back for a second.

There's another empty seat in the back row by the window. I wait a moment longer and then take the seat in the back.

A front-row view of the doom gloom that is the outside world. The window looks out onto the school parking lot.

Stephen turns around and stares at me. His eyes are hurt.

I know, I'm a bitch. But I can't be close to him.

It hurts too much. It's self-inflicted, and I know it. But pain, nonetheless.

I look down at my desk and focus on the little cracks in the wood. Anything to keep my eyes away from Stephen's. Anything to distract myself.

The desk is chipping on the side and there are pencil drawings all over the top.

The word *ShitHole* is scratched deep into the surface. It's small enough that it's not terribly noticeable, but large enough that I can feel how deep the wood has been scratched.

How old is this thing?

Did Mom ever sit here? She went to the same school. This desk looks like it could have been from her high school years. Maybe even before that.

The heat kicks on in the classroom and it brings in the shit smell from the hallway. I wonder if anyone else notices how bad this place stinks.

While I focus on the words and scratches that are dug into the wood, I can feel eyes. Someone is looking at me the same way I'm looking at this desk.

I glance up and see the girl next to me. I've never seen her before. Or at least I've never noticed her until now.

She has maroon hair that falls to her waist, and she's wearing a long red dress.

My mind splits in two and decides to have a debate about this chick's clothing. One side reminds me of my old self, the self before Mom died, the self before everything happened.

The other side is lonely, confused Charlotte. I try to focus on her. She's the nice one. She's the one who keeps me from being angry. She's the one who keeps my head on straight.

Why the hell would anyone wear a dress like that to school?

She can wear whatever she wants. Plus she's kind of gorgeous.

If you think that looks cool then there's no hope for us.

I mouth *Hi* to the girl in the dress. I'm not sure why, though.

She gives me a smile and then waves. But she doesn't turn away. Just keeps looking at me like I'm some prize pig.

What the hell is her problem?

Maybe she thinks she knows me.

Or maybe she's a nosy bitch who needs to keep her eyes to herself.

I grab a sheet of paper out of my notebook.

Do you have a problem? I write on the page and hand her the note.

She looks down and scribbles something on the paper and hands it back to me.

I think I can help you.

Help me? How can this chick help me?

I don't know, but she's the first person to offer.

I pause a moment, and then write back.

Help with what?

36

I pass the note to the girl, trying to look like I don't care, when really I do sort of care. Though I'm not sure why. I'm not supposed to give any shits about stuff anymore, yet here I am, giving a shit about some stranger and what she has to say.

Great.

She unfolds the piece of paper and looks back up to me. Then she leans in close. I can smell her perfume as she gets closer. It's peppery with sweet undertones.

"You know," she whispers.

When she says this I feel my stomach do that flip again. That scratchy feeling on the inside of me comes back.

I look over at her and give her a nod.

Maybe I *could* use some help.

After class, the girl in red follows me into the hall. Her dress drags on the floor. I notice that it's lace and almost completely see-through. She's wearing a black bra and panties underneath.

Is she even allowed to dress like that here?

She looks like a freak.

She looks cool, and brave.

"Hi, I'm Lana." She holds her hand out to me. Her nails are painted bright orange. They are shaped like claws. It reminds me of candy corn.

Where does someone get nail polish like that?

Probably a Halloween store.

The smell of shit in the hallway still lingers, but looking at this girl dressed in Halloween clothes, it's almost distracting.

Just a few feet from where I stand is one of the many dumpsters overflowing with trash.

"I'm Charlotte," I say in a quiet voice. I'm sure she already knows my name.

Everyone knows my fucking name.

Don't be so self-involved.

"I've wanted to meet you since I moved here," Lana says. I walk toward my locker and Lana follows. Her dress drags on the floor behind her. I glance at the ground and notice how dirty it is. Because it's been rainy, there are clumps of dried mud everywhere, and Lana's dress drags right over it.

How dirty.

She's kinda cool.

"Where are you from?"

A couple of girls from my old cheer team walk by us. Jenni and Jennifer. Both blond, both pretty, both terrible at cheer. They glance at Lana and laugh out loud. It echoes in the hall.

At least I think it echoes in the hall.

I try not to look at them as they pass. But I do.

Would I have laughed at this girl?

Don't act like you're some angel. You know you would have.

I would have.

"Oh, I'm from up north a ways. About three hours from here," Lana says. "Just got settled in like, four weeks ago?" She speaks fast and confident. I bet she didn't even notice the Jens laughing at us.

How could she not notice?

Maybe she doesn't care. Doesn't give a shit, just like I'm not supposed to.

"Do you like it here?"

Why are you talking to her?

"Does anyone? This place is a dump. My mom's boyfriend hit her one too many times, so she decided to move back to her hometown. She actually knows your mom. Well, *knew* your mom. They were friends."

Lana says this without skipping a beat.

Talks about Mom in the past tense.

For some reason it doesn't bother me.

Why doesn't it bother me?

"Oh, that's cool," I say. Not sure how to respond. I try to picture my mom walking the halls with this girl's mother. Getting coffee. Being a teenager. I'd seen photos of her when she was my age. She always looked happy.

"Yeah, my mom said that your mom was super successful. That everyone knew who she was. A real Girlboss!" Lana says, and then laughs. "Sometimes I wonder what would have happened if Mom had stuck around. Maybe they would have opened a business together or something."

What the hell is she talking about?

She's making small talk.

She doesn't know anything about Mom.

I see Maddi at our lockers waiting for me and a rush of relief runs over me. I pick up the pace and walk faster toward her. Lana keeps up with me.

"Is that your sister?" she says.

"Yeah. Maddi, this is Lana," I say. Maddi gives me a smile. But I can't tell if it's a real smile or not.

"Hello. I've seen you around. Where do you get these amazing dresses?" Maddi says, touching the collar of Lana's dress.

Dresses? How many of those awful things could exist in the world? It's nice.

Who are you trying to convince?

"I actually make them. Would you like one? It's kind of a hobby," Lana says. Then she laughs. A loud laugh that actually makes me giggle, though I'm not sure why.

"I would love to buy one from you," Maddi says. I can't tell if she's being serious or just trying to be nice.

I'll have to ask her later.

The heat kicks on and the hallway starts to get hotter by the second. I feel my sweater begin to itch under my armpits, and I know for sure that I'm part of the reason this place stinks.

"Cool! I'm gonna head to class. Charlie, would you like my number? Maybe we could hang out or something," Lana says. It surprises me when she calls me Charlie. The only person who ever called me Charlie was Mom. I try to ignore the sadness that hits at hearing my nickname, and smile.

She's nice. Maybe we will have something in common.

She's probably a stalker.

Stop being so dramatic.

I hand Lana my phone for her to put her number in. She does, and then calls herself.

"Great. Well, I'll see you around," Lana says, then walks away all dramatic. She's practically floating.

"Good. You're making friends again," Maddi says. "Hopefully she's as nice as she seems."

I just shrug.

Friends?

Charlotte

When we get home from school, Dad's Porsche is in the driveway. Parked behind it, Amber's BMW.

Mom helped her pay for that BMW. I still remember when they went to test-drive cars. Amber had only been Mom's personal assistant for six months, but I knew Mom was attached to her. She'd already moved Amber into the guesthouse above our garage, given her a credit card, and treated her like family.

I thought for sure Amber would have gotten rid of that car by now. That there would be no way she could afford it without Mom paying her bills.

She doesn't need Mom anymore. She has Dad to take care of her.

He has all of Mom's money now. To do whatever he wants with.

"Great, Amber's here," Maddi says. We've done pretty well avoiding Amber and Dad the last few weeks. Mostly because they don't hang around the house during the day.

Right after Mom died, Dad took a leave of absence at work and hired someone to manage the last few rental properties he and Mom owned. But after a while, he began going back to work a few days a week. Some days he gets home after dinner, other days he doesn't go to work at all. On the days that Dad is gone, Amber tends to stay away from the house, too.

"I don't know. But if that woman tries to talk to me again, I swear I'll lose my mind," I say.

Amber used to be a part of our life.

Now she's like a stranger. Someone who makes me cringe every time I see her.

I know Maddi feels the same way I do. Even if she's not as loud or mean about it.

How dare she park in the driveway.

How dare she.

"What should we do?" I ask. Maddi parks the car in front of our house but doesn't shut it off.

Usually Amber parks in front of the house, but seeing her car in Mom's spot in the driveway hurts. And I don't know why.

The house looks haunted. It reminds me of that old movie, *The Addams Family.* I used to think our home was the greatest place in the world. Now I hate looking at it.

Haunted with the heartbreak of all the people who live in it.

Maybe by the person who died right outside of it.

"We should probably talk to them, try to be nice. We haven't spoken to her in over a month," Maddi says.

Maddi is the peacemaker. She tries to make things right, even if they shouldn't be.

"I don't give a shit. I don't want to see either of them," I say. My voice comes out mean and angry.

What could they be doing in there? Usually Amber is out this early in the day. At Pilates or with her friends getting her nails done. She works for Dad a few days a week, but I wonder how much "work" she's actually doing.

The heat in Maddi's car blasts onto my face; it feels warm and cozy. She's stuck an air freshener in the vent. It smells like pine and vanilla. The smell reminds me of Christmas morning. A cheaper version of Christmas.

I don't want to get out of the car. I'm safe in here.

What do they even do together?

How can they stand to be around each other?

"They aren't getting down, are they?" I say out loud. I don't know why I ask it. The thought makes my stomach turn, and I want to squirm out of my seat.

"That's disgusting." Maddi sounds more tired than annoyed. But I still know I've grossed her out. She shuts the car off and the warm Christmas air goes away. She gets out and slams the door shut behind her.

The wind blows and her hair flies wild. It's cold—I can tell because her face has already started to change color. Her cheeks and nose are red.

It's supposed to be fall. But it's icy cold with no ice. Soon enough, though, I'm sure.

I roll the window down just a crack.

"What are you doing?" I shout. Maddi walks around and opens my door. The bitter breeze hits me like a smack in the face. It *is* colder than it looks. The ocean crashes against the shore, and I wonder how mad it is today.

Mad at the wind.

The cold, maybe.

"There must be a reason they're both here, and I'm betting it has something to do with us. Let's get this nightmare over with," Maddi says.

I hesitate for a moment, and then get out and follow Maddi into the house.

This is a nightmare. A nightmare you can't wake up from.

When we get inside, I hear Dad and Amber out in the garden talking.

Mom's garden.

Mom's beautiful garden that she loved more than almost anything. I don't get why they'd want to hang out in it. All the trees we had have been cut down, and it's cold outside. The hot tub Dad recently had installed isn't even working.

That fucking hot tub.

Mom would have hated that.

I try not to think too much about all the changes Dad has made to Mom's garden in such a short amount of time. That just makes me angrier. It's freezing, and all of Mom's plants have withered up and died. I wonder if they'll come back next year.

They won't be back.

They're all gone, just like Mom.

"Do you want to go back there?" I look at Maddi. We're both standing in the kitchen. It smells like fresh bread. All warm and inviting.

Amber's cooking again. She used to be such an amazing cook. She'd make cookies and danish. Three-course meals for dinner. All kinds of stuff. She was well beyond an assistant.

We can't touch anything she makes.

Now I refuse to eat her food.

44

"Or we could do this," Maddi says. She walks over to the stereo and turns it on as loud as we can stand. Music blares out of the speakers. The bass is so heavy I feel it vibrating off the walls.

It only takes a few beats before the porch door swings open and Dad comes storming in.

Only he isn't storming. He has a huge smile slapped across his face. Behind him is Amber. She holds a glass of wine in one hand and a bag of chocolate in the other.

She's drunk.

Or maybe she's pretending to be drunk.

"Girls, you're home. Turn that crap off and come sit on the porch with us. It's a beautiful day," Dad says. His voice comes out loud. He's also drunk. I can tell. His beard doesn't hide his rosy cheeks and glassy eyes.

Beautiful day?

He must be more than drunk.

He's seriously lost it.

Dad walks over to the stereo and clicks the power button. Silence crashes into the room.

I instantly feel even more alone without the music.

"Dad, it's three-thirty in the afternoon. Why are you drinking?" Maddi has her arms crossed in front of her chest, and she does not look happy.

She looks furious.

She looks like she knows something bad is about to happen.

She has that look on her face, which is almost a mirror image of Mom's. Dark eyes, dark hair, and a frown. By the end of Mom's life, the only real expression she had was that same frown Maddi is wearing now.

Before the baby, Dad never drank like this. Sometimes he'd have a glass of wine with Mom in the garden, but never more than one.

Now he's drinking every day. Well, at least the days I see him.

"We're celebrating!" Dad shouts. Then he grabs Amber and pulls her into a hug. She looks shy and timid. And, of course, beautiful. Long dark hair, slender legs, the clearest skin you've ever seen.

The exact opposite of my mother. Who liked to keep her hair short and wore baggy shirts and torn-up jeans.

"Celebrating what?" I say. I push as much bitch into my voice as possible. No need to sugarcoat how much I can't stand to be around them.

Probably celebrating their new love affair.

Probably celebrating their happiness in our grief.

Amber holds her left hand out and shows us her ring finger. On it is Mom's engagement ring.

Mom's. Engagement. Ring.

"What the fuck is this?" Maddi grabs Amber's hand. When she does, I feel my stomach do another flip. It always surprises me when Maddi swears or raises her voice.

Amber pulls her hand away fast.

Who does this sort of thing? Is this normal? Probably not, but has Dad ever cared about what's normal and what isn't?

I used to love that about him. I used to love that he didn't follow the rules, just went his own way and acted however he wanted. Now I can't stand it. Can't stand him.

What's right and what's wrong. He never cared.

"Maddi, watch your mouth. This is a happy day," Dad says. His voice booms, and I swear it's going to shake the walls down.

"That's Mom's ring, Dad. Why is she wearing it?" Maddi says. I can hear she's fighting back tears.

Why did I think that her ring was buried with her?

Of course Dad wouldn't bury a diamond that big.

I feel tears fighting their way out, too.

What. What. What!

He's gone too far. How could they?

"Your mother is gone. She would have wanted Amber to have it. She left it to me in her will," Dad says. He talks to us like we're children. Like we don't understand what's happened. "She always said if she died she wanted me to remarry. You'll understand when you fall in love."

We understand more than he does. We know more than he thinks we know.

Maybe he's right about Mom saying that, but that doesn't make it any better. Doesn't mean I'm going to accept this.

"Shut up, shut up!" I shout. I walk close to Amber. She flinches, like I'm going to take a swing at her. Or worse.

I could take a swing at her. If I was braver, or dumber, I could do it.

Around her neck is a rose-shaped pendant made out of rubies.

Mom's necklace. She got it when she was a teenager.

She's just taking everything of Mom's and making it her own.

"Why? Why would you do this? She treated you like you were a sister, or even a daughter. Why would you do this to her?

To us?" I yell. "You take her husband, and her house, and now you're wearing her jewelry? Getting married and wearing her engagement ring? Do you not see how fucked up that is?"

Mom treated Amber better than family. She took care of her. And this is how Amber repays her?

"Your mom wasn't so perfect, Charlotte. You need to realize that everything isn't always about her, or you and your sister," Amber says.

She was the perfect mom for me.

"She loved you, Amber. She was kind to you." I'm crying now. And Amber is too. I don't want to look at her, but I do. I stare into her eyes until she turns away and cries into Dad's shoulder. He puts his arms around her. I hear him whisper something, and then they both turn and walk back out to the garden.

Together. Like they're in love.

And maybe they are. But either way, it sickens me.

I could end it all.

I could.

No more pain, no more anger, no more lies.

I would pretend Mom was there, out in the garden. I could do it out there. End it all, and everything would go back to normal. The garden would bloom again, the flowers growing strong and bright, and the feeling of love would return to our home.

Forget what sadness is. Forget the pain. Pretend none of this ever happened, so everything can go back to normal.

My sister would be happy again.

And maybe so would I.

Charlotte

"I don't get it, I seriously do not get it," Maddi says. We're sitting on her floor. Maddi's face is red from crying. Her hands shake a little when she talks. She's more emotional than I am.

At least it seems that way.

"Money. She's marrying him for money. There's no way anyone her age would even consider someone like Dad, unless money was involved," I say. And it's true.

Dad isn't an old man. But he's a lot older than Amber. He could be her father.

Mom was eighteen and Dad was twenty-four when they got married. They built a business and a life together.

Amber is a twenty-five-year-old who was Mom's executive assistant.

Why would she choose him?

She's a gold digger.

She wants Mom's money.

"Let's get out of here, Charlotte, please. We can go stay with Uncle Jake," Maddi says.

Jake, Mom's brother. He hasn't come to visit since the

funeral. But he's emailed both me and Maddi asking us if we want to stay with him and Aunt Alex. I don't think it's a good idea. I think adding more family to the mix will just add to the drama. Cause problems that we don't need.

But maybe I'm wrong. Maybe a break from Dad, and Amber, and even this house would be good for my brain. It feels so tired and worn. Like it's spinning in circles all day long. Like I'm losing control in all the places I need to get a grip.

"Can we at least call him? Tell him what's happening with his sister's house and belongings? Her wedding ring?" Maddi says.

She stands up and paces. She does that when she's worried about something. She looks thin and frail in her sweater. I wonder if she's stopped eating.

This was Mom's house. She inherited it when our grandmother died, before she met Dad. Together they remodeled it and made it beautiful. They changed it from an old sea house to a modern home with granite counters and stainless steel. It's what inspired Mom to start a real estate investment business.

"Isn't there another way?" I say. I hear the heat click on, and I'm grateful. I'm chilled to the bone. I glance at Maddi's door— it's open a crack.

I hear someone walking down the hall and before I can shut the door, Amber sticks her head in.

"I know you girls are mad at me, but this isn't about you. Do you understand that?" She stands there and stares at us. I glance at Maddi. Her mouth has dropped open. I'm too shocked to say anything. Can't bring myself to speak.

Maddi clears her throat. "We know you don't love him. You

probably didn't even love our mother. You only stayed around for this, didn't you?" I can tell by the look on Maddi's face that she's holding back a scream. Holding back anger that I can feel boiling out of my body.

Amber laughs and then opens the door a little wider. She's changed into silk pj's and has her hair pulled up into a bun. She's holding another glass of wine.

"You two are spoiled little brats," she says, looking straight at us. "You had no complaints when I was helping around the house. Managing the stuff your mom couldn't: cleaning, cooking, hanging out. We used to be close. Friends. Now you don't want me around? Now you want me to just fuck off? Well, that's not going to happen."

Before I can respond, Maddi stands up and slams the door shut. I hear Amber shout, "Fuck!" on the other side. Maddi turns the lock before Amber can get back in.

"What the hell, Madison?" Amber says.

We sit in silence until we hear Amber walk down the hall, into Mom and Dad's bedroom. Hear the door slam behind her.

"Wow," I say.

How dare she.

Who does she think she is?

Maddi sits down on her bed and pulls out her phone.

"She's a fucking bitch," Maddi says. When she does, I let out a large breath and then laugh.

"What are we going to do?" I say.

Six months ago I didn't hate my father.

Six months ago I didn't hate Amber.

Six months ago was a different life.

"Just let me think," Maddi says in a harsh tone. She keeps staring at her phone.

What's the harm in a simple message to Uncle Jake?

It'll just cause more problems. More issues. More grief that we don't need.

We don't know that. He could help.

When I was young, I was afraid of my uncle. Sometimes he would bring over creepy books like *Helter Skelter, The Shining,* and other books my mother didn't like Maddi and me to read. Dad said he was harmless, but they were never close. Uncle Jake only came for a handful of visits, but for some reason he always creeped me out. Though maybe Maddi's right and we need him right now.

I grab my phone and see that I have a new message. The contact name is a flower and heart emoji.

Charlie?

I stare at the message.

My whole heart wishes this message was from Stephen, but I've had his number memorized for years, and he stopped sending me messages a few weeks after I stopped returning his calls. I guess it was only fair, even if it didn't feel fair. I wish every day that he had tried a little harder. Or that I had.

It's the weird girl from school.

Of course it is.

"If you do decide to call Uncle Jake, come in and tell me," I say, and stand up. Maddi's still staring at her phone. She's not usually like our zombie classmates, who are addicted to their phones. But right now, she looks like one. Only she isn't typing away or laughing.

Just staring.

I glance out the window. The sky is getting darker by the minute. Gray clouds billow in the distance.

I go into my bedroom and crawl under my blanket. I pull it up to my chin. It's soft and cozy. Mom bought it for me when I was little, and I haven't had the heart to get a new one.

I pull out my phone and look at the message again.

Lana, right? I type.

It has to be. Who else would it be?

Even with the blanket wrapped around me, I'm still cold. It's almost like Dad's trying to freeze us out.

Before I have time to look away from the screen, I get another message.

Should we get together? What are your plans for this weekend? What about today?

What's wrong with her?

She's nice.

She's a phony. She just wants to know my secrets.

Or maybe she just wants to help, like she said she did.

I stare at the message. Just like Maddi with her phone about five seconds ago.

I haven't spent time with someone outside of this house in months.

It's a trick.

It's not a trick.

Before I can talk myself out of it, I respond.

Why not come over now? You know where I live. Just call when you get here.

Everyone knows where we live. The haunted house on the

hill. It's one of the biggest houses in the neighborhood. I used to like that about it, but now it's embarrassing. Knowing that people know where I live.

Where we live.

Where Mom died.

If I regret sending the message, then I regret it. But at least I can figure out what Lana might be able to help me with.

I lie down with the blanket still wrapped around me. The light from the window slowly dims. It's almost dark in my room now.

I don't need a friend. I need answers.

I could use a friend.

I need answers. She's just going to make things worse—like Uncle Jake.

I'm lonely.

Who cares.

I care.

And I do.

Maddi

He can't be serious.

He. Can't. Be.

I lie on my bedroom floor and stare up at the ceiling. Listening through the walls and down the hall to hushed voices talking.

Dad and Amber.

That woman.

I want to stand up and scream bloody murder. I want to run into their bedroom and tear every piece of clothing out of Mom's closet and throw it out into the cold.

Does Dad even care that Mom is dead?

That the baby is dead?

That our family is falling apart? That Charlotte isn't sleeping, and I can barely hold down a glass of water without feeling sick to my stomach?

If Mom were here, what would I tell her? What would she think? Would her heart ache as much as mine does now?

Dad and I have never been close, but I didn't expect this from him.

Again, the rage that grows inside me feels hot.

I take a deep breath and try not to feel it. The anger. But with every breath I take, another wave of anger gets sucked in.

"This can't be happening," I say out loud. Like Mom's here somewhere, hiding, listening to me.

Would she want me to call Uncle Jake? Would she want me to involve her brother? She wasn't close with him. Said he was selfish, which is why he wasn't ever around.

I can't do this alone anymore. Can't keep everything together for Charlotte. I want to be strong, but I need help. Dad is only making things worse. And Amber doesn't care about anyone but herself.

I get up off my floor and go to the kitchen. I haven't had an appetite for the last few months, but I've started drinking tea every day. It makes me feel closer to Mom.

I open the cupboard with the coffee maker and tea bags and realize there isn't any tea left. I know Mom had Amber buy her tea in bulk toward the end, when she stopped going out.

"Where did you put it?" I say aloud.

I check a couple of drawers with no luck. All I can find is coffee and sugar. I open the last place Mom may have stored it. The very back of the pantry. The shelves are full of food Mom never ate. Chocolate, cookies, chips, instant rice. All stuff Amber eats. Loaded up on the shelves. There's an empty cardboard box on the floor that the Instant Pot Amber ordered was shipped in. I move it to the side. Behind it is a bottle of what looks like weed killer. Mom never used stuff like this. I take the bottle out of the pantry so it's easier to read the label.

Rodent killer. The active ingredient is zinc phosphide. "What is this?" I say out loud. I do a quick Google search.

Zinc phosphide is highly toxic in acute exposure to humans. It may be consumed accidentally or intentionally as means of suicidal or homicidal acts. Other routes of entry into the body could be via inhalation or through the skin.

I'm hit with a wave of fear, and suddenly I feel sick to my stomach. I stare at the bottle for a few moments until I realize what it means.

What it could mean.

Homicidal acts?

Why is there poison in our pantry? Did Amber buy it?

I take the bottle into my room and shove it in the back of my closet, behind all of my winter coats. I don't know why I don't just throw it away. But something in my gut tells me I need it. Tells me it's evidence of something. Something I really don't want to believe.

Charlotte

What's that thing people always say about love? I guess people say a lot about it. But when I fell in love with Stephen, I wasn't expecting it at all.

He was a loner. I used to see him walk down the halls, reading. It was like he was removed from the world around him. Caught inside a place more exciting, more inviting.

I had a lot of friends back then. And I dated a lot of boys and girls. But none were like Stephen. He was different. He was special. And it's corny as shit to say, but that's what I loved about him.

When I was given an assignment with him I realized that he was a real person. An actual person with real opinions about life and love and politics and movies and everything else. He wasn't constantly hooked to his phone, he didn't care about Instagram followers or TikTok, he was just himself. He taught me things I never knew I needed to know. He helped me find love in the smaller, simpler things in life. Like reading in the halls, or kissing in the back of a theater, or just sitting in the car listening to music.

After our assignment, I couldn't leave his side. I needed him with me. He was my other half.

Maybe I was obsessed with him, or maybe I was just so intrigued because I'd never met anyone like him. But eventually he fell for me.

"How's it feel to be out of the game?" Catherine had asked me a couple of weeks after I started seeing Stephen.

The game. The dating game. The love game.

I was good at playing it. But it wasn't fun anymore.

I'd laughed when Catherine said it.

It felt good to be out of the game. Because I was in a different game, a different world, with someone I loved.

"It feels good to be with him," I said. And it did.

"Well, I can't say I blame you. Eric Rogers sent me an unsolicited dick pic yesterday on Snapchat. I guess this is my future as a single sixteen-year-old," Catherine said. Then she laughed.

She was jealous of my relationship, but I didn't really care. I also didn't blame her, though. It's hard, meeting a nice person. Sometimes it feels like people have ulterior motives for everything they do.

"Did you block him?" I said.

"Cockblock," Catherine said, and then she laughed again.

We were sitting on her bed. It was summer. The air was thick and humid, and I could feel sweat on the back of my legs, even though the air-conditioning was on inside.

"Seriously, I hope you're not going to see him again," I said.

Catherine just shrugged.

"Probably won't, but it's too bad. He was one of the nice ones," she said.

Something about that made my stomach turn, and I wasn't sure why. The thought of losing Stephen or of him not being one of the nice ones crept into my thoughts.

"Sounds like he *wasn't* one of the nice ones," I said. "Maybe I can find you someone."

Catherine laughed. She knew I was too self-absorbed to find her someone.

All I cared about was my someone.

And myself.

Charlotte

I wait on the porch for Lana. She said she only lived a few miles away.

The wind picks up and brings the bitter cold along with it. The wind chimes that Mom hung years ago ring. The sound makes me think of her. Remember her before the baby. Before the sadness and fear crept in and took over her thoughts.

Sometimes I'd get jealous of how close she and Maddi were. Like they were in on their own little secret. Even though Mom and I shared our days together out in the garden and had girls' nights, it didn't always feel the same. I wonder if Maddi ever felt like that, too.

She loved us both.

I fucking miss her.

I watch our neighbor's trees rustle and the last of the leaves drift to the ground.

Goodbye, fall.

I hear Lana's car before she turns the corner. Music blaring, the squeal of tires. She pulls into our driveway right behind Amber's B(itch)MW.

Lana drives an old rusted Subaru hatchback.

A year ago, I would have freaked if a car like that had pulled into our driveway, but now I find it sort of funny.

Why is she here?

What are you thinking?

It's a good question, but maybe she really can help me. Or maybe I do need someone new in my life. Someone to help me get out of this funk that I seem to be sinking further and further into.

"I found you!" Lana shouts as she gets out of her car. She's changed out of the red lace dress and is wearing what looks like blue velvet. When the wind gusts, it looks almost as if she's modeling her clothes for the world. Her hair blows up into the air, her skin almost glows. I walk to the bottom of the driveway to greet her. Though I'm not sure why.

Who is this girl?

Someone new.

Someone weird.

Someone different.

I've never seen someone so confident in my life. Something about Lana makes my heart jump. I used to pretend to be that confident, but I can tell there's no faking with her.

She's amazing.

When she gets to where I'm standing, she puts her arms around me in a hug. She smells like old weed and flowers.

My body goes stiff when she hugs me. I don't know what to do. My arms hang straight at my sides until she lets go. How long do you have to know someone before you can hug them? One day? Two? Apparently just a couple of classes at school and a text message, according to this girl.

"I brought you something," Lana says after the hug finally ends. She reaches into her purse and pulls out a glass bottle. It's small and black, with no label.

"What is it?" I take the bottle from her and stare at it.

Poison.

Perfume?

This isn't real.

Lana follows me to the wicker chairs on the porch. We both take a seat, even though I'm freezing my ass off. Lana's dress is sleeveless, and I wonder if she's freezing too. I'm in an old hoodie and I feel like my insides are turning into a fridge.

"It's oil. For stress and meditation," Lana says. She smiles at me like this makes perfect sense. Like all of this makes perfect sense.

Meditation?

"Do people actually meditate? I just thought that was something they did on TV." After I say it I realize how stupid I sound.

Of course people meditate.

You're an idiot.

"Totally. People love it. I pretend to do it, but mostly I just relax. My mom can get all zen and it's super crazy. I'm not to that point yet. But even if you don't meditate, try the oil for the stress," Lana says.

She must see the stress on my face. How could she not? I'm a mess.

"Thanks," I say. I'm not sure if I'll use the oil, but it's a nice thought.

Is it a nice thought?

"So, thanks for inviting me over," Lana says. "What should we do? I was thinking of skipping the first- and second-period assembly tomorrow. We could go into the city tonight instead." She reaches into her bag and pulls out a rolled cigarette.

Only I can tell that it isn't just a cigarette. She lights it up without even asking if it's okay.

She's kind of a bitch.

Or maybe she's just comfortable.

She's not comfortable around me.

"Hope you don't mind," Lana says. "Keeps me focused. Want a hit?"

Cat and I have smoked a couple of times at parties, but I never liked it much. Made my skin itchy and hot. I almost felt like a stranger in my own body. It was more of Cat's thing than mine.

"I suppose a few puffs couldn't hurt," I say, taking the lit joint from Lana. I breathe in deep and cough. My mouth fills with the taste of ash and burned fruit. The paper she's rolled the joint with is sweet.

You look ridiculous.

She doesn't even notice.

She does.

"So what do you think? Hit the city?" Lana says. Her eyes are glassy and wet-looking. Like she's about to cry, only I know she's not. Do I look like I'm about to cry?

My ears start to rush with the sound of water and everything suddenly seems brighter.

You're high.

No, you're high.

Whatever.

"I'd rather stay here, if that's okay. We could see what Maddi is up to," I say slowly. The feelings of life before all this mess start to creep up on me. Before Mom was dead and before I stayed hidden in my room for days at a time. Maybe I can do normal stuff like I used to. Maybe I'm feeling better?

"That's fine by me," Lana says. She stands up and walks into the house like she knows where she's going.

And maybe she does.

Charlotte

"Amber, Charlie needs you to braid her hair!" Mom shouted from the garden.

She and I sat and watched the sun set. It was something we did every Monday night if I wasn't with Stephen. Maddi had basketball practice that night, and Dad always stayed late at work, so it was just the two of us.

We'd visit in the garden before I went to cheer. Amber was the only other person home, and she stayed out of Mom's and my way.

By that point, Amber was doing more than just assisting Mom at work. And honestly, Mom had sort of given up on her business by then. She'd sold almost all of her properties except a few that Dad managed. For the most part, things were slowing down a lot. Instead of firing Amber, Mom had her move in and help with daily chores, which Mom hated to do.

"I don't have to braid it tonight. Practice is only an hour and I'll just be shouting at everyone anyway," I said.

I didn't like when Amber did little tasks for me. I found it demeaning. Even though she worked for Mom, it made me feel weird. She was supposed to be an executive assistant, not a housekeeper. Amber had moved from Arizona for this job. We were the only family she had in Massachusetts, which is why I felt like she kept up with the little tasks, even though they weren't in her original job description.

Mom loved my hair braided for cheer practice. Said it made me look more confident. But after she lost the baby, she didn't bother with things like that. That's what she had Amber for.

"Nonsense. Amber? Did you hear me?" Mom shouted again. I could tell by her tone that she was in a mood. Mom tried to be kind to Amber most of the time, but some days she came off mean and angry.

I couldn't tell if Amber could hear Mom or not. The windows to the house were open, but that didn't mean Amber was nearby. Sometimes when she wasn't around, Mom would get extra cranky and call her names.

"Give me a moment, Charlotte, and I'll be right out," Amber called. She sounded far away, distracted, not her usual chipper self. It was like no one had fully recovered from the death of the baby. Including Amber.

"Sometimes I think that girl has the sense of a peanut," Mom said. I could tell Amber was getting under Mom's skin. Little things. I thought it was because Mom was sick, and sad. She'd get over it eventually. She was still grieving and she took her sadness out on everyone around her.

"She's doing fine. Everyone's allowed a bad day," I said. Though I wasn't even sure what Amber had done that day. I just didn't want to push the topic.

Mom laughed. "Not at what I'm paying, she isn't."

Sometimes I thought it was always about money with Mom and Dad. Usually Dad. But Mom would make remarks like that from time to time and it made me realize she was the same as he was.

I didn't want that type of stuff to matter to her. But of course it did. When you have a lot of money, you have to care about it.

"All right, how would you like it braided?" Amber walked over to us. She was holding hair ties and a brush. I felt sorry for her, standing there. She looked lost and sad. Exhaustion was all over her. There were dark circles under her eyes, and her hair wasn't neat and tidy like it usually was. Overall, she looked unhappy.

"Just give her a regular french braid," Mom said. Her tone was harsh and she sounded annoyed.

Amber smiled at Mom, but I could tell it was a fake smile. Amber had hate in her eyes. Hate for Mom? For me? Maybe for herself. Maybe for our entire family.

The sun made the yard glow with yellows and oranges. The flowers were blooming strong, and if I breathed deep enough, I could smell them.

"French it is," Amber said. She pulled a chair up next to mine and started brushing my hair.

I felt like a four-year-old.

I thought about how Amber felt. Did she want to do this her whole life? Take care of a family that wasn't her own? Did she even want a family? Were we enough for her?

The sadder Mom got, the more work Amber had to do. By the end, she was doing everything.

The sadder Mom got, the meaner she got, too. She also always seemed to be aching somewhere. Her back, her head, or someplace else. But the worst was her moods and attitude.

Demanding.

Bossy.

Angry.

Mom wasn't herself by the end. And I knew without having to ask that Amber was relieved when she finally died.

Maddi

I sit on my bed, trying to calm down.

That bottle of poison. What I read online made me sick to my stomach.

I pick up my phone and call Uncle Jake.

"We need your help," I say when he finally answers. I had to call him twice before he picked up. Maybe he really doesn't want to help us. Maybe he just said that because that's what you're supposed to say when someone in your family dies.

"I'm glad you called. Alex and I were thinking of heading out that way soon. What's going on?" Jake says.

I don't know how much to tell him. Or how much he'd even believe. But something is shifting in our family, and I'm starting to worry that Amber wanted Mom gone. Maybe even Dad did too. He's tried to erase the memory of her. And I'm not sure what to do. Or if there is anything I *can* do. I'm starting to feel like a crappy older sister who failed. And the daughter who didn't pay enough attention.

"My father is acting strange, something doesn't seem right. He's engaged to Mom's old assistant and I'm also worried about Charlotte. Maybe having visitors will help."

Does any of this matter to Jake? Am I making a mistake?

I don't tell him about the poison. I think that's a conversation we need to have in person. I don't want him to think I'm paranoid and not come.

"The young one from the funeral? Amber? Somehow that doesn't surprise me. I'll talk to Alex. We'd love to see you girls. Just try to take it easy. It's been a tough couple of months. God knows it's been hard on your aunt."

Alex and Mom were best friends as children. They grew apart after Jake started dating Alex, but that doesn't change the fact that Aunt Alex also lost someone she loved.

"Just let me know if you can come. The sooner the better," I say. He must know I wouldn't call unless I absolutely needed his help.

"We'll make it happen. I'm sure everything is okay. But it would be nice to visit," Jake says.

"Maybe things are okay. But I don't trust Amber. I don't like her living in the house with us. And it's like my dad doesn't even care that Mom is gone. It's too much," I say. I don't tell him about the rage. The anger. Everything that's going on inside me. Would he even care?

"I'll book a flight for next Sunday," he says.

After he hangs up, I feel a little uneasy.

Dad's behavior can't be normal, can it? Has he always been this way, and I never saw it? How long has Amber been in the picture? The more I think about it, the more questions I have.

Charlotte

Lana and I sit on my bedroom floor. Lana rolls a joint while I look through my Spotify for something to listen to. The silence is uncomfortable, and I don't like it. It reminds me of this old EP Stephen and I used to listen to. *The Silence Is Deafening.*

I quickly scroll down to one of the playlists Stephen made for me and click play.

Why is she here? To make us feel weird?

No.

Yes.

"So are you and Stephen Echols still seeing each other? That kid is such a doll," Lana says. She licks the edges of her rolling paper like she knows what she's doing. Probably because she does know what she's doing.

Stephen.

Hearing his name said aloud makes my heart tighten.

"How do you know Stephen?" I watch her roll two more joints.

I notice a stain on the carpet a few feet from where we sit. Mac and cheese. There are other stains, but I pretend I don't notice them. If I don't, maybe Lana won't either.

How many joints does this girl need?

Maybe she's saving some for later.

Or maybe she's a couch potato in a dress.

The stoners at school sit huddled by the vending machines. My friends and I used to make fun of them behind their backs. I'd call them lowlifes, which now that I think about it is super hypocritical since they were the ones who helped Catherine find pot or Molly before a big party or dance.

Lana doesn't seem like she'd fit in with that group either.

Even though weed is technically legal in this state, there does seem to be a vibe that comes from the kids who are open about smoking it. I guess I prejudged all of them, just like I have Lana.

For good reason. She's weird AF.

"He's in my math class. We've done a few projects together. I asked him about you before you came back to school. He's so quiet, I usually can't get anything out of him," Lana says.

She looks at me and smiles. Her teeth are crooked and white. Everything else about her is perfect. Her hair, her skin, her eyes, everything. A natural beauty.

When was the last time I felt beautiful? Long before Mom died.

Now it doesn't matter. None of that crap matters. Except when I look at Lana, I feel self-conscious.

Why didn't he have much to say?

Probably because he's afraid of you.

Probably because he doesn't love you anymore.

"He and I broke up. I think; I'm not really sure. I had to stop

74

seeing him. I had to stop seeing everyone," I say, though I'm not sure why I'm telling Lana this.

My bedroom suddenly feels stuffy with us both sitting on the floor. Like the heat's on too high and the walls are too thick, even though I'm still cold.

Shut up.

Nancy would be proud of me. For socializing. For having someone over. But that doesn't relax me much. Maybe it'll give us something to talk about next time I go see her, whenever that may be.

Probably never.

I glance at the pile of unwashed laundry stuffed in the corner of my room. Does Lana notice it? Can she smell it? Does she even care?

You shouldn't care, either.

"I heard about the little freak-out at your mom's funeral. That must have been rough. You know my mom was there?" Lana says. She hands me one of the freshly rolled joints, then stands up and goes to my closet. She opens it and starts sifting through the few T-shirts and dresses that are still on hangers. "Save that for a rainy day. Anyway, Mom told me it was the saddest funeral she'd ever been to."

I feel my face grow hot from the memory of the funeral. I pray that Lana doesn't notice or feel the embarrassment that is radiating off me like sunshine.

Why is she talking like this?

Her mom saw me act that way.

She's a bitch. She needs to leave.

"I guess." Not sure what she wants me to say. "I don't want to talk about my mother's funeral." My voice comes out meaner than I intended. I cough, to try to hide it. "It just bums me out is all," I say. I force a nicer tone, though I'm not sure if it works.

The memories of the funeral try to creep into my head, but I push them away. If I had a way to wipe them from my brain, I would.

Lana shrugs and then pulls a T-shirt out of my closet. "Mind if I borrow this?" The T-shirt is black with a print of a girl with purple hair and the word AWAKE on the front. It's one Stephen bought me at a music festival we went to together a while back. I'm hit with a memory from that night, of us dancing together, singing along, kissing. I never wore the shirt, and now I'm not sure why.

"Sure," I say, and immediately regret it.

What if he sees her in it?

He won't even notice.

"Cool! Let's go get some food. I have the munchies like a bitch," Lana says. She takes the shirt off the hanger and stuffs it into her bag.

I stand and follow Lana out of my room. On our way to the front door, she sticks her head into Maddi's room.

"Hey, girl, we're getting grub. Wanna join?"

I peek inside Maddi's room and see she's on her phone.

Uncle Jake?

"Sorry," Lana whispers, and then shuts the door.

Does she just barge in wherever she wants to?

"Milkshakes!" Lana shouts when we get outside. She sways and saunters to her car. I follow, trying not to notice how good her body looks in her dress. How put-together she is, even in wacky-ass clothes.

The cold air hits me hard, and I'm covered in goose bumps, but Lana acts like she's immune to the cold.

Only time will tell, I guess.

Let's just have a friend. Maybe she really can help.

Whatever.

Charlotte

The day they buried my mother was the day everything really changed.

"I can't go alone," I'd said to Stephen. I sat on my bedroom floor, crying into the phone. I begged him to come with me. To just ride in the stupid car with me. But he wouldn't do it.

"Your sister will be there. This is for family only. I'll be there, Charlotte. I promise," he'd said.

But that's not what I wanted. I wanted him to be there with me, at that moment. To support me. But he'd said it wouldn't be respectful to Maddi or Dad. I didn't really give two shits about that, I just wanted him there with me.

In the obit, which we'd shared in the local newsletter, we asked everyone to wear their favorite spring colors to celebrate Mom's life, rather than something sad and dark.

At the cemetery people were wearing bright yellows, pinks, lavenders, all the colors Mom loved. Even the men wore light-colored ties, pastel shirts under their suit jackets. Maddi had worn the brightest sundress in her closet.

I wore the white Easter dress Mom bought me. She'd loved it so much. At the time, I hated that dress. It was itchy under the armpits and the material didn't breathe. That didn't matter, though, because I knew it would have meant a lot to Mom.

I sat next to Mom's casket and looked at the sea of colors.

It was a warm day. Spring had just ended, and it was transitioning to summer. For Massachusetts, it was bright and sunny. The humidity was thick, and it added to the itchiness that I felt under my arms. I could smell the stink of flowers. It made my stomach turn, but I tried my best to ignore it.

Looking at all of Mom's friends, I felt a little bit of comfort. They had all come for her. And they really wanted to make this easier for my family. To comfort us, even in such a small way.

But then I saw Stephen.

Stephen. My person. The only other person who made me happy besides Mom and Maddi.

He was wearing a black tie with a dark gray shirt.

At first I wasn't sure it was him, my eyes were so blurry from tears and smeared mascara. I thought maybe a stranger had shown up. Someone who didn't know Mom at all. But then my eyes cleared, and I realized it was him.

"How could he?" I said to Maddi. The casket was shiny pearl white, with a bouquet of flowers on top. Knowing my mother was trapped inside that box made me want to rescue her.

Maddi gripped my hand tight, like if she let go of me I might end up in the ground next to our mother.

"He's just being him. He always wears black," Maddi said. I could tell she wasn't really listening to me. And why should she? I was talking about my boyfriend at our mother's funeral.

I looked past Stephen. Everyone around him was like a

bright light, a sea of color and happiness, and there he was, a dark cloud that ruins the day at the beach.

Mom didn't need a dark cloud at her funeral.

Dad stood up then and walked to the microphone set up a few feet from the open grave.

A dark cloud and a brewing storm.

Open mic night at Mom's funeral.

Dad talked, but I couldn't listen. My body took over my mind and I stood up.

"What are you doing?" Maddi whispered when I let go of her hand. She tried to pull me back down next to her, but I shook her off.

"How *could* you?" I shouted.

Stephen looked right at me. His eyes were filled with tears.

I walked over to him and pointed to his tie.

"How could you do this? Why would you do this? You know she hated gray. You fucking know she hated it!" I screamed in his face. My blood was boiling, and I could feel heat growing in my belly. Behind me, I heard Maddi say my name.

"Charlotte!" Dad shouted into the microphone. "What are you doing? Sweetie?"

He slurred his words, and the more he talked, the more I could hear the whiskey behind his voice. But I didn't care. Let him drink. If I could have had a drink, I probably would have.

I stepped closer to Stephen and shouted, "Why? Doesn't it matter? Does any of it matter to you?" I was crying hard even though anger was flowing through my whole body.

I know I looked crazy.

I felt crazy.

It was like a new me had taken over this body. A new Charlotte, and I couldn't stop her. I didn't want to stop her.

"Charlotte, don't." This was Cat. Cute little Kitty Cat. Coming to the rescue.

Cat walked up and put her arms around me. Or was that Maddi?

Whoever it was, I shoved them off and continued to scream at Stephen. He'd taken a step back and bumped into another guest. My voice came out like a screech. I didn't recognize it.

"Why would you? How could you? Why would you? How could you? Fuck you. Fuck you!" I shouted in his face.

The more I looked at him, the more I saw fear in his eyes.

I scared him.

I scared him. And I scared myself.

"Why? Why?" I screamed again. It was everything I could do not to hit him. To hurt him. He just stared at me. I didn't recognize the look on his face. It was like he hated me.

"Why?" I said again, only this time much softer. People around me were speaking in whispers.

Before I knew it, Uncle Jake and someone else grabbed me. I felt their grip tight around my arms. I went limp as they pulled me away from Stephen.

"Why? Why?" I said, crying.

Then Dad was there. He picked me up and carried me to the car. The limo that brought Maddi and me to the cemetery. The fancy car for my mother's funeral. He set me on the back seat and closed the door. I screamed and cried. The look on Stephen's face was burned into my eyes.

The fear. The fear he had of me.

Charlotte

When Lana and I get to the diner, I start to regret leaving my cave. There are people here. People from my neighborhood. From my school. And strangers. Lots and lots of strangers.

Lana's a stranger.

Lana and I walk in and I'm hit with the smell of grease and onions. I used to love to come here. Drink milkshakes or have one too many chocolate sundaes. But I haven't been here since before Mom died.

"Let's sit in the back by the window," Lana says.

I follow her into the back corner. There's a small booth by the windows. Just by looking at it I know that it's drafty. But I don't say anything.

Is this a mistake?

Probably.

Let's just find out what she knows.

Lana plops down in the booth and I sit across from her. I realize how unprepared I am for this. She looks like she's ready to go out and talk to people. And I feel like I've just rolled out of bed.

The waitress comes with a small notepad. She takes our

order and walks away. Leaving me alone with Lana. I want the waitress to come back and talk to Lana so I don't have to. But she doesn't.

"So," Lana says. She gives me a big smile. Showing those crooked teeth again.

Now what?

Now? What?

"So what do you know? How can you help?" I say. My voice comes out loud, and I feel my face go hot. I look out the window. Winter always shows up faster than it's supposed to, and by the time it's at our door, there's no way to escape it. Especially in Massachusetts. One day it's warm and the next it's a frozen wonderland.

"Damn, girl, just going right for it, huh?" Lana says. Then she laughs, like maybe this isn't a big deal.

Is she being serious?

Is she joking?

"You told me you could help." I try to add more confidence to my voice. "I'm all for hanging out. But what's most important to me right now is finding what you know about my mom. And if you're willing to help, that's great. If not, tell me now," I say. "I miss her a lot, and when she was alive, I never asked her much about her childhood, and I regret that."

Why do we have to go to strangers to learn more about our mother?

She says she can help. Maybe this is more than learning about Mom.

Our waitress drops off our drinks. I take a huge gulp of my vanilla Coke before I say anything else. The flavor is strong and it reminds me of Stephen. He and I used to come here late at night. We'd talk about movies and things we'd watched on

Netflix. The memory is like a dream, like it never happened. A distant wish that won't ever come true.

"I understand," Lana says. She stirs her shake around with her straw. For a second I think she might be embarrassed.

I've hurt her feelings.

Does this girl even have feelings?

"I'm sorry, I thought you wanted to help," I say. I glance out the window again. I don't know if it's the weed or just the awkward feeling growing inside me, but I don't feel comfortable in my own skin right now. Sitting here, trying to get information about Mom.

You were stupid to do this.

But I need to know. Anything. Anything is better than knowing nothing.

What's there to even find out? She's dead.

"I get it," Lana says. She takes a sip of her milkshake and continues talking.

"It may seem worthless to you. But like I said, my mom used to know your mom. And she actually has some letters your mom sent her a few months before she passed away." Lana says this so nonchalantly that I almost gasp.

Letters?

I can't even find Mom's journals, and Lana has letters?

"What? How?" Suddenly everything around us is loud and bright. I hear a plate shatter in the kitchen. A man a few booths over coughs into his hand. A girl nearby bursts into laughter. It's like a pencil being jammed in my ear, and my head starts throbbing again.

Depression hurts from the inside out.

"What do you mean by letters?" I inch closer to Lana's face. The smell of her perfume hits me. Herbs and weed mixed with something sour. I try to focus on anything but my headache.

Lana takes another sip of her milkshake and then sighs.

"Your mom wrote my mom letters. Before she died. My mom hid them, but I found one in her underwear drawer. I don't know why she never reached out to you. But when I saw that you were back at school, something told me I needed to show you."

Letters?

What could they say?

"Can I read it?" I try to hide the panic in my voice. I try to cover up my excitement and my fear, but I know I can't. Lana has to sense them. Because they're right here, out in the open. All laid out on the table like cards in a poker game.

"I didn't bring it. I didn't want my mom to notice it was gone," Lana says.

I look at her and nod like this makes perfect sense, even though none of it makes perfect sense.

"I'd like to see it. I haven't been able to find her journals. It would just be nice to see her handwriting," I say.

Lana nods and takes another sip of her shake.

"Makes sense. But between you and me, I'm not sure you're going to like what you read. Your mom seemed really . . . stressed," Lana says.

Stressed?

Stressed.

What?

"Oh," I say.

Was it her illness? Was it her anxiety? Her depression? All of them?

"I just want you to know what happened to her," I say quietly. "She was stressed, yes. But it wasn't like that all the time. She cared a lot about the people around her. I bet she cared about your mom."

Lana nods. "I'm sure that she did. My mom loved her. Said she was always sweet. Which is probably why they stayed in contact."

"I miss her," I say. I feel my eyes well up with tears, but I fight them off. Nancy always told me there's no shame in being sad, but I hide it anyway. This girl doesn't need to see me cry. Doesn't need to see my pain.

"I'll work on getting the letter for you. Maybe you and Maddi can stop by sometime and I can show you," Lana says.

Okay.

You can do that.

You've waited this long.

"Okay, yeah. That sounds good." I smile at Lana, hoping to hide the sadness from her.

I take a sip of my Coke and wait for the food. We sit in silence for a few minutes until Lana starts talking again. I'm only half listening to her. Something about a DJ she saw in Boston a few weeks ago. I nod. She keeps chatting away until our food comes. I pick at my fries for a few minutes before I tell her I need to go back.

"Yeah, I guess it's getting late," she says. We get our bill and pay, then walk out to her car and drive home.

"Thanks for coming out with me. Let's do it again soon.

Maybe tomorrow or sometime over the weekend?" she says. We pull up into my driveway. Her car is old so it hasn't even heated up yet.

"Just text me," I say. Then, before Lana can say anything else, I get out of the car and head inside.

A letter.

A letter from *Mom*.

Charlotte

I'm just on the verge of sleep when Maddi knocks on my bedroom door.

"Charlotte. Are you awake?" she whispers through the crack in the door. She sounds more tired than I feel.

Pretend you're asleep.

Answer her.

"Sort of. You can come in." I sit up and flick on my lamp. Next to it is the joint Lana left me for a "rainy day."

Hide it!

It's too late. Maddi's already opened the door and is walking into my room.

She's wearing an old robe that Mom gave her for Christmas. She looks so much like Mom that it's creepy sometimes.

Maddi sits at the foot of my bed and crawls under the blanket, briefly letting the cold air in. My room is an icebox.

With winter coming, it's all the more reason to stay in bed for the rest of the school year.

Maybe the rest of my life.

"What's going on?" I say. Maddi isn't one for waking me up in the middle of the night.

Unless it's to bring awful news.

Is there more awful news?

Who else is dead?

Hopefully Amber.

Don't think like that.

"I talked to Uncle Jake. He's coming to visit," Maddi says. She looks down at my comforter when she says this.

"If you think that's the best idea, then I guess it's a good thing," I say. What Maddi says is a good idea usually is. She's smart. A lot smarter than I am. So I have to trust her. Trust everything she says.

Maddi shrugs and then scoots close to me.

"I'm worried. I don't think he took me very seriously. But something in my gut is telling me we need help. I don't understand why Dad had to give her Mom's ring. Their whole relationship is so messed up."

Maddi sounds scared when she says this. Her voice shakes and her eyes water.

"There's something else," she says. Her voice almost a whisper. Fear shoots through my body, but I try to ignore it.

What could be worse than what's already happened?

What could be worse than losing our mom?

"What?" I say, leaning close to her.

"I found poison. It's, like, for killing gophers and rats and stuff. For outdoor use. But I looked it up, and it's highly toxic for humans. I've never seen it before. And we've never had a rodent problem. And if we did, Mom wouldn't have used poison," she says.

Poison?

Mom felt like something was eating her from the inside out.

Were they poisoning her?

"What does this mean? Would they actually hurt her?" I say.

"I don't want to jump to any conclusions. But something is off. It was in the pantry, hidden," Maddi says.

I take a deep breath and try to focus on that. Nancy wouldn't want me to freak out. She would tell me to think about this logically. Why would they hurt Mom?

She was in the way.

I can't think like that.

"Maddi, can I ask you something?" I hadn't planned to bring it up, but now seems like the time.

Don't tell her.

Don't say anything.

Keep it to yourself.

"You can ask me whatever you want," Maddi says. She scrunches down under the covers, close to me. It reminds me of when we were kids and we'd have sleepovers in each other's rooms after we watched a scary movie, or when Mom and Dad let us stay up late. How I wish I could go back. Live in that comfortable little world forever.

"It's cold as hell in this house," Maddi says.

I imagine an ice storm coming and trapping us here with Amber and Dad. I imagine that there's no food left and we have to eat each other.

Stop thinking like that.

Stop it.

Stop.

"Maddi, do you think they were together before Mom died?

Do you think they wanted Mom out of their lives?" It's the first time I've said it out loud, the thought that won't leave my head. Won't leave my brain.

She was sad.

Overwhelmed.

But that's not a reason to cheat.

Not a reason to break up an entire family.

Maddi looks at me and I can see that she's upset. Upset about all of it. Maybe I shouldn't have brought it up. Despite Dad and Amber's relationship, we know our father.

Don't we?

Do we?

"I don't know. I know that Amber isn't who we thought she was. Her true colors are starting to show. And that poison freaked me out," Maddi says. "But I don't know. I really don't."

How could he do this to her?

To Mom.

She loved him so much.

Charlotte

"Something is eating me from the inside, Charlotte. Something isn't right," Mom said. We sat in our usual spot in the garden. Mom didn't look good. And she actually sounded afraid. Which scared me a little.

Now that the baby was long buried and Mom's physical wounds had healed, I started to think that this was something else. Something more than just a late-term miscarriage and a little postpartum depression.

"Nothing is eating you. You're not eating enough. All you drink is this rose tea. You need more. This isn't healthy." I grabbed her cup and smelled it. It smelled bitter with a hint of roses and something else. Tea was practically all that she consumed anymore.

Normally I pretended not to care when Mom skipped meals, but the last few weeks she hadn't seemed right. It was like she didn't have any energy because she was using it all on her sadness. She was losing weight, and every time I saw her, she looked smaller and weaker.

"I'm trying to kill whatever's inside me, Charlie. There's something crawling around. I can feel it," Mom said.

She'd looked so old that day. She sipped from her cup and I could see the wrinkles on her hands. Her dark hair had strands of gray throughout it. Her skin had gotten saggy and she looked tired.

In fact, she looked worse than she ever had. But I knew if I told her I was scared for her, she'd get more afraid. I wanted her to get help, but I had asked her so many times, it was like beating a dead horse. It was impossible. She was impossible.

"Well, you need real food, Mom." I handed the cup back to her.

Mom shrugged and took another sip.

"Rose tea," she said, and then smiled at me. Her smile didn't look real, and I felt a stab of pain in my heart. Guilt and hurt for her.

It was the perfect day to be out in the garden. We were on the tail end of spring, so the air wasn't too humid. The flowers had really started to bloom, despite Mom not being able to work as often as she had previous years. Everything around us felt alive and happy. Even the sun seemed to shine brighter than normal. We'd made it through another cold winter and rainy spring. For the next four months I was going to be able to relax with my boyfriend and soak up the sunshine.

I'm here, Stephen texted me.

Come on back!

I watched him walk around the house to the garden. His dark hair shone in the sun and his skin looked clear and smooth.

He was so beautiful.

I loved every ounce of him. Every single bit. Seeing him

made me feel better about what was going on with Mom. It calmed me down, and I wasn't sure why.

"Come over here!" I shouted.

He looked at me and grinned. His teeth were so white. How did I have someone so perfect?

"You love him?" Mom whispered, almost as if she'd read my mind.

I smiled at her and then nodded.

"Don't tell him, he doesn't know yet," I said. Stephen and I hadn't used the l-word yet, but I thought it every time I saw him. Every time he spoke.

"He knows. Trust me," Mom said. Then she stood up and greeted Stephen with a hug.

I think that Mom loved Stephen too. I think that she knew how good a person he was.

"Sarah, how are you? Are you feeling any better?" he said. Stephen knew all about Mom's "illness." He seemed to be the only one who took her seriously. Or at least pretended to, anyway.

"Better now that you're here. Charlie has been waiting for you. I've kept her company, but I'll leave you two alone. Here, drink this, she has something to tell you." Mom handed her cup of tea to Stephen and gave him a peck on the cheek. Then she went inside.

"She's a weirdo," I said. Stephen walked over and kissed me hard on the mouth.

He always tasted the same. Smoky and sweet. Like a toasted marshmallow.

"We're all weirdos," he said, then kissed me again.

Even after almost a year, he still gave me butterflies.

"What should we do today?" Stephen took a sip of Mom's tea and then coughed.

"What is this?" he asked, then took another sip.

"Rose tea. Mom's trying to kill whatever's inside her, remember? Apparently this is the new way to do it." I reached over and took a sip from the cup.

It tasted like rose tea and cough syrup. I hadn't realized she was using sweetener. It tasted terrible.

"Well, it's a shitty way to go. Tell your mom to switch to coffee. At least that doesn't taste like poison," Stephen said, then laughed.

The sun shone bright on his face, and it made his freckles stick out. I wanted to kiss them, but held back.

"Shut up," I said, smiling.

Stephen set the cup down and put his arms around me.

"You and your family are so weird, but that's why I like you," he said. I knew he was teasing me. He did it whenever he came over. My family was totally different from his, which I liked.

"I'm not weird, just happy," I said, snuggling close to him. "I love you," I whispered. Then kissed him hard on the mouth again.

Stephen's grip loosened. He pulled back a little.

"What?" he said.

When I looked at him I saw something different in his eyes. I wasn't sure what it was.

Fear?

I shouldn't have said anything.

I let go of him and sat back in my chair. I felt a breeze blow through. It brought the smell of the ocean with it. Salty and sweet. I wondered how many fishermen were out at the docks, catching their dinner for the evening.

"Nothing," I said. I couldn't look at him. Couldn't let him see the shame that I knew had appeared on my face.

"Charlotte," he said. He leaned in close and kissed me lightly on the cheek. "I didn't know you felt that way."

He paused for a moment longer, and I felt the shame on my face darken and panic rise in my stomach. *WhatdoIdowhatdoIsay?*

"You know how I feel about you." I looked up and he grinned again. Showing those pearly white teeth.

At that moment I'd never felt happier. Everything was perfect. My life was perfect.

Maddi

Mom's funeral was one of the hardest days I've ever had.

I remember the drive to the cemetery. Me and Charlotte in the back of the limo. It was a pretty day out, gardening weather. Mom would have spent that whole afternoon outside, had she been alive.

On the drive, I watched as Charlotte twisted and turned in her seat. She was upset because Stephen wasn't there with us, even though she'd asked him to come. It bothered me that he couldn't be there for her, but I didn't have time to worry about it. Everything else going on around us was much worse. And I didn't want to make Charlotte more upset than she already was.

"I just don't understand. I just don't understand, Maddi. Why wouldn't he come? Why wouldn't he come?" Charlotte kept saying. Her voice was panicked, and everything about her gave off the vibe that she hadn't slept in days.

I was numb that whole week. Hadn't cried, or laughed, or shouted. Nothing. I felt nothing. But watching Charlotte, feelings started to grow inside me.

Fear.

"It's okay, just relax. He'll be there," I said.

I didn't want to do any of this.

I missed Mom so much. The thought of putting her in the ground hadn't crossed my mind until just then, and it made me sick. But I pushed all of that aside and tried to comfort my sister.

"No, Maddi, no. You don't get it. He was supposed to come with me, he *promised* he would ride with us. I shouldn't be doing this alone." Her hands shook as she spoke, and her panic was starting to rise. I pulled my Juul out of my purse and handed it to her.

"Take a few puffs of that. You're not alone. I'm here with you. And Dad is in the other car. It's going to be okay," I said. I grabbed her hand, but she pulled it away.

She took a few deep breaths and then puffed on the Juul. It seemed to calm her, but not a lot. She was still shaking as she got out of the car.

When we got to the gravesite, I was almost relieved. There were so many people there. So many people there for us and for Mom. All dressed in beautiful pastel colors, just like Mom would have wanted.

Me and Charlotte took our seats up by the casket and the podium. It's like we were on display. Dad insisted, I'm not sure why. If it had been up to me, I would have sat in the sea of people. Hidden away. But that's not how these types of things work.

"Help me get through this," I said under my breath. Hoping Mom would answer. Knowing she wouldn't.

I looked out into the audience. Everyone stared back at me. The looks on their faces exactly what you'd expect.

Pity.

Sadness.

Heartbreak.

Then something caught my eye, and that's when Charlotte grabbed me by the wrist, hard.

"How could he?" She was talking about Stephen. I knew without having to ask.

"He's just being him. He always wears black." I said.

Stephen was wearing a black button-up, a gray tie, and black slacks. He was the only person in the crowd in those colors. A wave of annoyance came over me, but I pushed it away. It didn't matter what he wore. My mom was dead. I shouldn't care about what someone was wearing at her funeral.

"That fucking asshole, I can't believe it," Charlotte said. I could feel the heat of her anger growing next to me, and I reached over and grabbed her hand again. Right as I did, Dad walked up to the microphone.

He looked strung out. Hungover and drunk at the same time. He cleared his throat, getting ready to say who knows what. As Dad started to speak, I glanced over at Charlotte. Before I could stop her, she was up and walking toward Stephen. He was a few rows back from the front. She grabbed his tie and started screaming.

"Honey," Dad said into the microphone. But it was like Charlotte couldn't hear him. While she screamed, I sat there, stunned. Not sure what to do or how to stop it. My sister looked like a different person at that moment. Like someone I didn't know.

"Fuck you! Fuck you!" she kept screaming. I stood up, but my legs wouldn't move.

"Charlotte," I said, though I was sure she couldn't hear me.

Cat appeared and grabbed Charlotte by the arm, but Charlotte immediately pushed her away.

More screaming. More shouting.

Eventually Dad ditched the microphone and grabbed Charlotte. Uncle Jake helped him.

As they carried her out to the limo, my sister cried and screamed the same thing over and over.

"How could you! How could you! Fuck you. Fuck you! How could you!" Her shouts still ring in the back of my head.

She was screaming at Stephen, but the more I think about it, I wonder if she was talking to someone else altogether.

Charlotte

When I get out of bed, I peek out my bedroom window. What do I find?

Snow.

And a lot of it.

Shit.

Double shit.

I used to look forward to the first snow. I'd run outside with Maddi and we'd build a snowman, make angels, have snowball fights. I'd soak up the holiday season that came along with winter. I loved everything about that. It reminded me of being a kid.

Not anymore.

I walk past Maddi's room and hear her on the phone. I stop in and sit on her bed next to her. She's still wearing her pj's even though it's nearly eleven a.m. She must have slept in, too.

I didn't think she was going to skip school, but I'm happy that she followed through with it. Maybe skipping today will make her realize how stupid school is and that we should never go back. We don't need it. We don't need any of those people. We could do online studies. We could teach ourselves. We did it during the pandemic, why can't we do it now? It's completely possible.

Mom wouldn't like that.

She's not here anymore.

Remember what Nancy said about going out? Making friends again? Being normal? Skipping school is the opposite of those things.

Maybe.

Maddi hangs up and smiles at me.

"That was Uncle Jake. He and Alex will be here on Sunday," she says. She walks over to the window and opens the blinds.

"Great, snow," she says.

You're telling me.

"Have you told Dad yet? You know he's not gonna be happy about this," I say. Dad and Uncle Jake have never gotten along. It wasn't that they hated each other, it was more that both Dad and Uncle Jake are control freaks. They both want things done their way. Mom told me when she first started her business, it was hard sometimes because of how controlling Dad could get. Dad said something similar about Jake when he and Mom decided to remodel the house. Even though the house was Mom's, Jake tried to get involved. After that, Jake didn't come to visit anymore.

Bringing him here makes me uneasy. What if he makes things worse? Makes things harder for us? But at the same time, I want to believe he can help us. Maybe he can talk some sense into our father. Tell him that the way he's treating us, treating the memory of Mom, is wrong.

"No, I was hoping we could both talk to him today." Maddi gets off her bed and pulls a bright yellow summer dress out of her closet and then a pair of red rain boots.

"You'll freeze if you wear that today." I point to her dress.

She shrugs. "I'll wear a coat."

Charlotte

I hear Dad's car pull up in the driveway. I walk outside to meet him. I know he's not going to like me springing something like this on him, but I might as well get it over with. The air outside is crisp and still, like it always is after a snowstorm. The yard is pure white, and the snow sparkles when the light hits it just right. Out on the road, there's a big pile of gray slush. I imagine driving my car into it and sliding on some ice. I've never been the best at driving when the weather's like this, but Stephen had his jeep, so he'd pick me up for school every morning. And if he couldn't, Maddi would drive me to school with her. Dad had bought us the car to share, but usually I don't drive myself unless I have to.

Dad parks his Porsche in the driveway and gets out. He's holding a Taco Bell bag. I'm surprised he even went into work at all. But I figured he'd be home for lunch. This is the only shot I have at talking to him without Amber around. Every day he looks different. Almost like someone I don't know anymore. His beard has gray in it, and his hair looks even thinner than it did at Mom's funeral. Has he lost more of it already?

"Dad," I say.

He doesn't smile or wave.

"I need to talk to you," I say, watching him trudge up the driveway through the snow in his big duck boots. There's at least three inches of snow, and none of it has been shoveled.

Before, we would have hired someone to do that. Now, I wonder if the snow will sit there until spring.

Maybe they want to trap us inside the house.

Make us suffer through this winter.

Dad usually skips work on days we get a lot of snow. He has the ability to come and go as he pleases. Today, I sort of wish he wasn't home. That way I wouldn't have to talk to him about Uncle Jake coming to visit.

Dad gets to the bottom step of the porch and crosses his arms. I'm sure he's still mad about what happened the other night with Amber. Guilt rumbles in my belly, but I push it away. I shouldn't care. He should be the one who feels guilty. He's the one who should care.

For betraying Mom.

We don't even know that he did.

For forgetting about Mom.

"What, Charlotte? What do you need?" He sounds tired and irritated, and doesn't even bother to ask me why I'm not going to school today. I guess he's used to me skipping now.

Should I care? Even though I know he doesn't love me anymore, it still hurts when he talks to me like that. Like I don't matter. Sometimes I wish he'd at least pretend that I did.

"Maddi and I invited Uncle Jake and Aunt Alex for a visit. They'll be here on Sunday. They're staying in the guesthouse. They said they plan to stick around for a few days. I told Jake he could look through some of Mom's things. He wants to see if there's anything of Grandma's that Mom may have saved for him," I say. The lie is a good one. Why hadn't I thought of it before? Maddi put together a box full of old photos and home videos for Uncle Jake a few weeks after Mom died.

Dad's face changes, and he looks even madder than before. Like I've disgusted him, like just looking at me makes him ill.

"Are you crazy? You can't just invite someone to stay in our home without discussing it with me first," he says. Then he walks past me and through the front door.

His words hurt. Whenever he and Mom fought, he would ask Mom if she had lost her mind, or tell her that her head wasn't screwed on right. They didn't fight all that much until after the baby. But I remember him saying the same thing to her when I was little. I could tell by Mom's face it hurt her.

Thinks he can say and do whatever he wants.

Has he always been like this?

Has he always been mean?

I follow him into the kitchen. He goes to the fridge and pulls out a beer and then walks into the living room and turns on the TV. It blares and I imagine the noise busting the windows in half.

I knew he'd be a jerk about it.

I don't care. They have to come now.

No, they don't.

"Dad, I'm talking to you." I walk over to the TV and flick it off.

Dad does a heavy sigh and takes a sip of beer.

"I'm done talking, Charlotte. Those people are nothing but

moneygrubbing users. They just want to take advantage of a situation and I won't allow it. End of discussion."

Whenever Dad said *end of discussion* to Mom, she would stop talking.

I guess I'm not Mom.

Money?

Is it always about money?

"Take advantage? How about what Amber's doing? *That* isn't taking advantage?" The words slip out, and I know I shouldn't have brought Amber up. But how is it fair for him to pick and choose who stays and who goes?

"That isn't the same, and you know it. She's family. She's been here the whole time. Your uncle never came when your mother needed him, so why should he come now?" Dad's words are mean, and partially true. But I don't care. Because Jake is coming now, and maybe Maddi is right. Maybe he *will* help us.

"Fine. Don't talk to them. But they are coming to visit me and Maddi regardless. If you really care, leave. Go somewhere else for a while. Take Amber. But they're coming, and I don't care what you say. They're family." I walk away.

I hear Dad shout something at me, but I slam my door.

Shout all you want. I don't care.

Yes, you do.

No.

Maddi walks into my room and sits on my bed.

"So you told him," she says. She looks relieved, like a weight has been lifted. But I'm not sure I feel relieved.

"Maddi, what if this isn't a good idea? He's so angry. What if bringing them here just makes things worse?" I've never feared my father. But now I think I may not know him at all. I can't get that bottle of poison out of my head.

Why would he have it?

What would he need it for?

Why would Amber need poison?

Maddi shrugs. "Who else can we call? They're family. I really hope Uncle Jake will help with Dad. He *has* to. Besides, what could be worse than what's already happened?" She echoes my thoughts. Only she doesn't sound that convinced.

Plenty.

It can always get worse.

And I don't trust our father anymore.

What if he's the reason Mom was so sad toward the end of her life?

What if she knew he didn't want to be with her?

She was upset because of the baby.

Would Amber try to get rid of her?

"I guess we'll find out when Uncle Jake gets here," I say.

"Why don't you call your friend Lana? I'm curious about that letter she found, the one from Mom. We also need to find Mom's last journal," Maddi says.

I'd almost forgotten about the letter.

And the journals.

Maybe Mom mentioned something about Dad in the letter. About going off the deep end.

Or maybe there's nothing. Either way, we deserve to know what she wrote. What she was thinking.

Charlotte

When can we come over to read the letter?

I send the text to Lana.

I have to see the letter.

None of it makes sense.

If her mother was really friends with Mom, then maybe it makes sense.

"Did she tell you what type of letter it was? Is she sure it's from *our* mom and not someone else?" Maddi says. We're bundled up and sitting outside our favorite coffee shop. The snow has stopped falling, but now that the sun is going down, it's getting colder and colder.

My ass feels frozen through my leggings on the metal chair I sit on. I regret what I'm wearing, but I haven't washed a pair of jeans in months.

I take a sip of my coffee. The girl at the register recognized me and Maddi, so we both got free shots of espresso in our drinks. It's nice being here, but it's not nice being recognized.

"I heard about what happened to your family. It's on the

house," the girl said when we tried to pay. I felt my face blossom into what I imagine wasn't an attractive hue of red. I'm getting a little tired of feeling self-conscious and uncomfortable.

"I don't know, Maddi. But what's the harm in looking?" I say. Maybe the letter will help answer some questions. Anything would be better than what we have right now.

There's always harm when someone has an ulterior motive.

She's going to help us.

No one can help us but us. We need to take matters into our own hands.

"I can't stop thinking about how angry I am at Dad," I say.

I've been angry at him since the funeral, but Amber and the engagement? Now I don't know how I feel. I didn't think he would go to these lengths to try to get us to forget about Mom like this.

"Hush, we shouldn't even be talking about it," Maddi says. She's probably right, but how can she expect me to ignore it?

"Maybe Mom mentions him in the letter," I say.

I don't understand how she has a letter from Mom and we don't.

At least we're getting it now.

"Let's just try and not worry about anything until Jake gets here. He'll know what to do," Maddi says. Although every time she mentions Jake, she sounds unsure about the whole thing.

My phone buzzes.

When are you free? Missed you at school btw.

"Lana wants to meet up." I hold out my phone for Maddi to see. "Should we invite her here?"

Maddi stands up and grabs her coffee and car keys. I still

can't believe she skipped school with me. It's been nice spending the day with her.

"Let's just go to her. Do you know where she lives?"

I don't even know Lana's last name. Maybe I'm making a mistake trying to get information from her.

You are *making a mistake.*

You have to at least take some chances.

What would Nancy say?

It's been months since we had a session.

Could Maddi and I come over? What's your address? I type.

5544 Cherry Lane. I'll see you in a few.

I hold my phone out for Maddi to see again.

"Let's go," she says, and stands up.

You're being stupid.

I have to know what she knows.

She doesn't know shit.

I guess we'll find out.

Charlotte

"So? How can you help?" Maddi says when Lana opens the front door.

Lana stands there in a dark gray floor-length chiffon dress. Her hair is done up in a huge bun with flowers in it. She wears a purple faux fur coat that's probably three sizes too big. I almost burst out laughing when I see her.

She looks like Marge Simpson.

I'm not sure what she looks like, but I'm digging the faux fur.

Don't even start.

"Settle down, settle down," Lana says. "Come inside. I'll make us a drink, we can talk." She steps away from the door and lets Maddi and me into the house.

Her home looks exactly like I imagined it would. Old-fashioned, but there's also something welcoming about it. Abstract art hangs on the walls, plants everywhere, and an old blood-red velvet couch in the living room with a loveseat to match. Mom would have said it was tacky, but I can't help but like it.

Lana takes us to the kitchen, where she pours both Maddi and me a glass of juice.

"I'm so glad you girls came over," Lana says. "Maddi, I've been wanting to hang out with you since Charlie and I started chatting."

I feel a pang of jealousy when she says this, and I don't know why.

Don't be a freak. Who cares if she wants to hang out with Maddi. It'll get her off our back.

"That's nice," Maddi says, "but listen, we aren't here to hang out. We're here to read the letter." I can hear in her voice that Lana bugs her. That she's annoyed.

Why is she annoyed? What did Lana do? Does she hate Lana? Am *I* bugging her?

Of course she hates her. She knows Lana's probably full of shit.

"Yeah, yeah, I get that. But I was hoping the three of us could be great friends," Lana says. She walks to the freezer and pulls out a bottle of vodka and pours a little bit into her cup of juice.

"Want some?" she says to me.

I shrug.

"She doesn't. And we do want to be friends, but right now Charlotte and I are really busy. So let's get on with it." I can tell by Maddi's tone that she's mad at me. She thinks this is stupid.

She probably thinks you're stupid, too.

What did Nancy say about mind reading?

"Come on, Lana. Just tell us what you know," I say. My voice comes out desperate. I don't want Maddi to hate Lana. But more than that I want to find out what's going on with my family. What was going on with Mom before she died.

Your heart doesn't just stop.

I have to see the letter. Just to see her handwriting. And if the only way I'm going to get that is by having a couple of drinks with this girl, then so be it.

And maybe I can make a friend in the meantime.

"Let's go into my room, my mom will be home from work in an hour," Lana says. "You guys, this might be painful, and it might be worthless, but whatever I tell you, I don't want you to blame me."

Blame her?

Maddi and I follow Lana down the hall and into her bedroom. The house smells so strongly of incense that my eyes water. It's a rich smell, like pine and smoke. Something about it reminds me of a witch.

A bitch witch.

"Before we moved here, my mom told me that she grew up just a few blocks up the road from this house. And that her best friend was just a few miles past that," Lana says.

She sits down on her bed and opens the drawer to her bedside table. She pulls out a small joint and lights it up.

Maddi and I sit down on the floor below her window on two fluffy pillows.

Lana's room is covered in pictures of landscapes and paintings of all kinds. She has crystals and rocks all over her desk. Between the incense and the weed, the air is thick and sweet.

"Right, right, *and?*" Maddi says, urging Lana along. I haven't seen her this impolite in years. At this point I'm surprised she's not tapping her foot. Usually she's the nice one and I'm the impolite one. But she wants to get the hell out of here. Run for the hills. And I want nothing more than to stay here as long as I can. It's warm and comfortable. And Lana isn't like anyone I've ever met before.

"Well, it turned out her old best friend was your mom," Lana says.

Does she have to be so dramatic about it?

I'm reminded again, talking to Lana, that I didn't ask my mom much about her childhood. A stab of guilt hits me hard in the heart. Mom rarely talked about her high school years or her friends growing up. She told us how she met Dad, and always about how much she had loved to garden her whole life. She said that she and our grandmother would do that every Saturday. Why didn't I care to ask more?

I should have asked more.

"What did she say about our mom?" I ask. Trying to push the guilt out, though I can't.

"I guess they always stayed in touch. Wrote letters to each other every few months. Talked about their lives. My mom even told me that one day we would come and see you. Then all that shit happened with my mom's boyfriend and here we are," Lana says. She doesn't sound too thrilled about the last part.

Big-city girl stuck in this small town.

She's probably bored. That's probably why she wants to "help" us.

Or maybe she just wants to help us because she cares.

You know that's not true.

"Our mom stayed in touch the whole time?" Maddi says. "What did the letter say? Have you read it?"

Lana takes a drag off her joint and then sets it down in a glass on her bedside table.

"That's what I'm getting at, Maddi. My mom said that the last letter your mom sent was pretty . . . disturbing."

Disturbing?

What could her mother know?

What could Mom have said?

Mom wasn't like that.

"What do you mean by 'disturbing'?" Maddi asks. She stands up and sits at the foot of Lana's bed and stares at her. She sounds scared.

She sounds exactly how I feel.

"My mom didn't say, but you can judge for yourself. I've never met your mom, so I don't know what she was like," Lana says. She gets off the bed and walks out of the room and closes the door behind her.

I look up at Maddi. "Do you think this is for real?" I say. "Why would Mom tell this woman anything? And why haven't we ever heard of her before? Do you think Mom kept her a secret on purpose?"

Maddi shakes her head. I get up and sit on the bed next to her. She grabs my hand and I can feel that she's shaking.

Or am I shaking?

"I don't know. But let's not get our hopes up. For all we know this girl is just plying us for information," Maddi says.

See?

She's not. I know it, in my gut.

"I think she's sincere," I say.

But what if my gut is wrong?

What if Lana conned us over here to get information to tell people to make herself seem cool? Would information about

115

my mother's death make her look cool? Cool to who? This is a small town, but is it that small?

Fucked-up people, that's who.

But she's not fucked up.

That we know of.

"I think I trust her, Maddi," I say.

Maddi nods. Does that mean she trusts her, too?

"Let's just see what the letter says."

The door opens and Lana walks back into the room. Hands Maddi an envelope and sits on the bed.

"Just sort of brace yourself, okay? Because it isn't great."

Brace yourself.

Maddi grabs the envelope and pulls out a letter. I sit close to her and see Mom's handwriting. The clunky block letters she used in her journals and her letters to us.

I watch Maddi as she reads. Her face, her eyes, all of her looks sad.

"What does it say, Maddi? Tell me." I know I sound bossy, I know I sound panicked, I know I sound like everything I shouldn't.

Stay calm, it's going to be okay.

It's already not okay.

I know.

I glance at Lana. She's relit her joint and is blowing big O-shaped rings in the air.

Is she bored with us? Or just waiting?

Either way, I don't care by this point. All I care about is what that paper says.

"Maddi?" I say again. This time she hands me the letter and stands up.

"Now I'm worried," she says.

STEPHANIE,

I CAN'T WAIT TO SEE YOU AND FINALLY MEET YOUR DAUGHTER, LANA. I KNOW HER AND MY GIRL CHARLIE WILL GET ALONG.

I HOPE YOU HAVEN'T CHANGED YOUR MIND ON YOUR OFFER OF LETTING ME STAY WITH YOU FOR A FEW WEEKS. TO BE HONEST, THINGS HAVE GOTTEN HARD OVER HERE.

ANDREW AND I AREN'T TALKING MUCH ANYMORE. I THINK THAT THE MARRIAGE IS ENDING. I CAN FEEL IT IN MY BONES. THOUGH MY HEART IS BRUISED AND HURT ALL OVER, I'M ALMOST RELIEVED.

I SHOULD HAVE NEVER LET AMBER MOVE IN. WHEN I SOLD MY BUSINESS, I SHOULD HAVE LET HER GO. I THOUGHT I NEEDED THE HELP, BUT I SHOULD HAVE BEEN A REAL MOM AND DONE THE COOKING AND CLEANING ON MY OWN. BUT AFTER I LOST THE BABY, IT WAS TOO HARD TO EVEN TRY. I THOUGHT THAT WE WERE A FAMILY. I THOUGHT THAT AMBER LOVED US LIKE HER OWN PARENTS, BUT NOW I KNOW THAT'S NOT THE CASE.

THEN THERE'S THE FEAR. I DON'T KNOW IF IT'S PARANOIA, OR IF IT'S SOMETHING ELSE. BUT IT ALMOST FEELS LIKE ANDREW IS TRYING TO GET RID OF ME. TO HURT ME. I HAVE NO PROOF, BUT THE FEAR IS STILL THERE. IT HANGS OVER ME LIKE A CLOUD.

MY ILLNESS, WHATEVER IT IS, HAS GOTTEN WORSE. MY

LEGS ARE WEAK AND I CAN HARDLY KEEP MY EYES OPEN. I'VE
STOPPED EATING THE FOOD AMBER MAKES, BUT I'M STILL
GETTING WORSE.

PLEASE, COME VISIT SOON.

YOUR FRIEND,
SARAH

"I think I'm going to be sick," I say. I stand up and my head spins.

He was cheating on her.

And Amber? She was trying to *hurt* her.

Amber prepared all her meals.

The poison!

She was hurting her.

Was she the reason Mom was sick all the time?

"Here, let me get you some water," Lana says. She gets off her bed and runs into the kitchen.

"*Did* they have something to do with her death, Maddi? That fucking poison you found, and now this?" I say. I hold out the letter for Maddi to take from me. My hand shakes. Maddi puts her arms around me and tries to calm me down.

"We don't know that. Mom could have been overthinking it. Plus she was really sad at the end," Maddi says. I can hear the tears in her throat. She's trying to hide it from me. Hide her fear from me.

"Mom had problems. She wasn't perfect. Maybe it was something else," she says.

What kind of problems?

That's not why she's dead.

Your heart doesn't just stop.

Why would she go down to the beach that late at night?

Why would she go alone?

Just a few years ago Mom and Dad were friends. They went on dates, flirted in the kitchen, and kissed in the garden.

Now Mom's dead, and Dad's sleeping with her assistant, and I'm lost in confusion as to why he would do it. He's cheating on Mom, and suddenly she *dies*? It all seems like a shitty Lifetime Movie cliché.

Dad wouldn't hurt Mom.

Why would he hurt Mom?

For money.

For love?

Love doesn't come from murder.

Charlotte

"When Uncle Jake gets here I'm showing him the letter, and we're going to figure out what all of this means," Maddi says. We practically had to beg Lana to let us take the letter. I could tell it bothered Maddi. I don't want to get Lana in trouble, but at the same time the letter was from Mom, and it's only fair we take it.

We're both at the house, lying on Maddi's bed.

"Does this look like Mom's handwriting?" Maddi says.

It's exactly the same.

Maybe a little messier, but she was probably in a rush when she wrote it.

"Who else's handwriting could it be? It looks exactly like Mom's," I say.

The window to Maddi's room is open a crack. As the wind blows in, it makes a noise that reminds me of a crying ghost. When I was little, the sound of the wind scared me. I would sneak into my parents' room and make a pallet at the foot of their bed. Just hearing Mom's and Dad's snores would calm me down, and I would forget all about the ghosts outside.

The air is so cold that the windows are already starting to

frost. The outside world looks like total doom and gloom, and it's not much better in here, either.

I've read the letter over and over, and I still don't believe it. But somehow I do.

It's her handwriting. She wrote that letter. She wrote that letter because she was scared.

"What do you think Uncle Jake will do about it, Maddi?"

What can he do?

Call the cops?

Don't be ridiculous.

"More than anything, what can you and I do?" Maddi responds. She's been angry since we got home. Angry because of everything. But mostly because Lana kept this letter from us until now.

"We have the letter, and they just got engaged. The poison, that has to mean something," I say. "Maybe there's more in her journal. We need to find it."

Would anyone take us seriously? The police? We can't even get our father to take us seriously, let alone a stranger who has no idea what's been going on. And you can buy rodent poison anywhere.

Maybe we could tell Nancy.

I don't want to talk to Nancy.

"I just hope he can help us," Maddi says. Then she sighs. "Why do you think Lana kept that letter hidden? I've been at school, why didn't she show *me*? Why did she wait to show you?"

If Lana had showed Maddi, then maybe we could have done something sooner.

I don't trust her.

121

"Do you think her mother went to the police with it?" I ask. What might have happened if she had? Would Mom still be alive?

"I doubt it. A letter like that isn't proof of anything. Especially since Mom wouldn't go to the doctor," Maddi says. She rolls onto her side and faces me.

"No matter what happens, we have to stick together." Maddi's eyes fill with tears again, and I can see the fear, and hurt, and everything else pour out when her tears spill down her face.

"We'll always stick together," I say. And I mean it.

Everything will be better soon. The weekend will fly by, and then Jake will be here to help. We won't have to do this alone anymore.

Just three days, and everything will change.

Please let that be true.

Charlotte

The next morning, I wake up early. Dreams and fear kept me up all night and lying in bed is only making it worse. I know I'm supposed to be relieved about Uncle Jake coming tomorrow, but I can't help but feel anxious about it all. About how Dad is going to react, or if Jake will even care about what's been going on.

My room is pitch black except for the little sliver of light that peeks beneath my door. Not only is it dark in here, it also feels like a freezer. Like someone forgot to turn the heat on. I glance at my phone. It's six-thirty a.m. on a Saturday, so I'm sure Maddi is still asleep.

I try to force myself to fall back asleep, but can't. I roll out of bed and throw on some leggings and a baggy sweatshirt. I glance at myself in the mirror and notice how grubby my hair looks. I haven't brushed it in days.

Who cares what you look like.

I head to the kitchen for a cup of coffee. When I walk into the room I feel like I've been struck with the sadness bat.

Amber. She flinches, just a little, when I appear.

Of course she's up.

She's wearing a thick white bathrobe and standing at the coffee maker with her arms crossed like she's frozen, too. Nothing about her appears out of place. I've seen her make coffee so many times that it's almost normal. Only now my gut wrenches and I know I can't be in the same room with her. Of course she still gets up early for morning coffee. I'm sure she's never stopped doing this, I've just been sleeping. Even on Saturdays, she was the first up in the house.

"What are you doing up so early?" she says.

Her tone is the same as it was so many months ago when she greeted me in the morning. Light and airy.

How could she have been so close to us?

How could she have once been a part of this family?

"What are you doing? You shouldn't be here." I shove past her. She steps to the side of the stove and watches me get a mug out of the cabinet. Then I grab the pot of coffee she's just made and dump the whole thing down the sink.

"Very mature, Charlotte," she says. Her voice changes, but only a little.

I ignore her and start a fresh pot.

Don't want anything that bitch has touched.

Amber and I stand there and avoid eye contact while I wait for my coffee.

The sound of the water bubbling as it drips down into the coffeepot seems extra loud in this silent space.

Amber moves out of my way and walks over to the kitchen window. It looks out onto our backyard. Even in the darkness I can see how sad the garden looks. How much the backyard has changed. The cold weather has killed every last one of Mom's beautiful flowers. That and the renovations Dad's made out there.

I glance at Amber. To think that she and I used to be friends. Almost sisters. And now look at us. It's like hate steams off the walls.

"You know, your mom and dad were over long before I came into the mix," Amber says. "You act like your mom was so fucking perfect, but she wasn't."

My throat closes up and tears shoot to my eyes. I didn't think she'd dare talk to me. I try my best not to let the shock show on my face.

"What did you say?" My voice cracks a little when I speak.

She couldn't have meant to say it aloud, could she? She couldn't have really just said that to my face.

"Your mom and dad, they were through a long time ago. You do realize that, don't you?" Amber says again. This time she says it louder, with more confidence.

She's trying to get under my skin.

She's trying to make me lose my shit.

I could throw that whole pot of coffee on her and not feel a thing.

Don't think like that.

I could do it.

"No one gives a fuck what you think," I say. I pour a large cup of coffee, then I dump the rest down the drain.

"Be a bitch to me all you want, Charlotte, but your father won't allow you to behave like this much longer. The grieving daughter act will only get you so far," Amber says. Being mean like this doesn't suit her. It's not like her to talk like that. To swear and try to hurt me. But, of course, maybe it is and I just never saw it.

"This whole act you're putting on won't get you very far," she says.

It takes everything I have not to turn around and scratch her eyes out.

Hit her.

I could do it, and not think twice about it.

I stare at her. Her little body wrapped tightly in her bathrobe. Without all that makeup she usually wears, she looks younger, weaker.

"I'll remember that," I say.

Then I turn and walk away.

I will remember that.

I'll remember all of it.

Maddi

I sit in bed and wait for Dad and Amber to leave. Usually on Saturdays they spend the day together away from the house, and today is the same. Around eight-thirty, I finally hear the garage door close. I get out of bed and go into Mom's room.

The curtains are drawn and it's dark. Nothing like how it used to be. When Mom was alive, this room was bright and homey. Now, it's almost like a hotel.

Could Dad really be hiding something like this from us? Something about Mom? I know he and Amber are keeping secrets, but why? Are they really capable of hurting someone? Hurting Mom?

I walk into the master bathroom and start to open all of the drawers.

Amber has shelf after shelf of expensive makeup and lotions. I guess she always has put in an effort to look nice, even when she was just cleaning the house or cooking. It has always been obvious she likes fancy things. Which is totally different from how Mom was. She didn't care about makeup and designer clothes. The only thing like that that Mom ever purchased was perfume. But Amber is the opposite of my mother. And I guess she always has been.

I open the medicine cabinet. Inside is a bottle of aspirin, a box of tampons, and a few other basics. I start to think this is a waste of time, that I'm not even sure what I'm looking for, but then I see it. On the very bottom shelf. A prescription pill bottle. The bottle is half full of little white pills. Most of the label has been torn off, but the date is still visible. It's from last spring. I grab the bottle and go back to my bedroom and close the door. Even though Dad's gone, I still feel exposed, like I could get caught.

"This couldn't have been yours," I say under my breath to Mom.

She never took pills.

Even though the name of the medication has been peeled off, it's easy to find out what it is by Googling the numbers on the pill.

Oxycodone.

I sit on my bed for what feels like hours, just staring at the little bottle. I feel sick trying to figure out why Amber has these. What would she need pain medicine for? She hasn't had surgery, so why would she have oxycodone?

I've heard about how bad oxycodone is—how addictive—but not much more about it. I Google the effects of the medication with alcohol or other prescription drugs, and realize how dangerous it can be.

When I hear Charlotte get up and use the bathroom, I go wait for her on her bed.

I know what this is going to do to her. But she deserves to know.

"Hey," she says, standing in the doorway. She looks alert, like she's been awake for hours.

"Look at this," I say. I toss the bottle of pills to her.

Charlotte

Pills?

"What are these?" I say. "Where did you find them?"

"The medicine cabinet in Mom's bathroom. Well, Amber's bathroom. With all of her stuff," Maddi says.

"Why is the label peeled off?" I say.

She's a drug addict.

No, she's not . . .

Maddi sighs. "It's oxycodone. And I have no idea how she got a prescription. The wrong amount can be deadly. Look at the date on the bottle."

I look at what's left of the label and my body goes cold.

Thirty-milligram pills. And the date is from when Mom was still alive.

Why would Amber need these?

She doesn't.

Right?

I think about Mom. She didn't believe in doctors or painkillers. Rose tea and herbs. That's all she took.

Is this why Amber is with Dad?

To feed an addiction?

That doesn't make sense.

Did she slip these in Mom's coffee? Did she put them in Mom's food? Blend them into Mom's morning smoothie? They wouldn't be as obvious as poison. She could probably easily hide the taste.

"Are you sure you found these with Amber's stuff?" I say. Though I already know the answer.

Maddi nods.

Half the pills in the bottle are gone. I wonder how many Amber started with. How many it takes to kill a person.

You can't think like that.

Why not? What was that this morning? All that shit she was talking on Mom?

Cheating with Dad? Moving in? Wearing her jewelry? Poison? Pills? Engaged?

None of this is normal.

"I fucking knew it. I fucking knew it!" I say, my voice rising. Though I'm not sure what it is I thought I knew. Did I really believe they would hurt Mom?

I do now.

At least Amber.

She wanted Mom's life, didn't she?

"Hush, you have to be quiet," Maddi says. She grabs me by the arms and tries to calm me down. It's everything I can do not to burst into a million pieces.

"Did they do it, Maddi? Did they kill our mother?" I say.

Maddi sits next to me and puts her arms around me.

"I don't know. But we'll figure it out," Maddi says. "We're going to find out what happened."

Your heart doesn't just stop.

She did it.

She did it.

Even though I knew, I *knew,* I still wasn't expecting it.

I wasn't expecting this.

Maddi

Sunday night I lie in bed trying to sleep. I can hear Charlotte in her room, next to mine.

She cries in her sleep.

Today was hard. Trying not to overreact about the letter Lana gave us on Friday. Trying to avoid the tension building between us and Dad, pretending like nothing is wrong. Trying to keep Charlotte calm after finding those pills on top of everything else. Waiting for Uncle Jake to arrive, but he never does, even though he promised he'd be here Sunday.

I'm stressed out, but more than that, I'm exhausted. And tonight, I can't sleep. And Charlotte's crying doesn't help.

I don't think she realizes that she does this. But every night since Mom died, she's cried.

Sometimes it's quiet, but tonight it's not. It's loud, and I'm kind of surprised she hasn't woken herself up yet.

The clock on my bedside table says 2:03 a.m. I lean over and flick on my lamp. It takes a moment, but my eyes adjust to the light. I roll out of bed and walk toward Charlotte's room. Before I open her door, I notice a light on in the living room. I tiptoe to the end of the hallway and peek in. Dad's sitting on the couch.

He's holding a glass of whiskey and staring at the TV. A show is on, but no sound is coming out of the TV, and he's staring at it like he's actually interested in what's going on.

"Dad?" I say, walking into the room. I sit down next to him before he can respond. "What are you doing awake?"

The glass he's holding is almost empty. I wonder how many drinks he's had tonight. If he's been drinking since this afternoon. He doesn't work on Sundays, so he's "relaxing" more than usual.

Dad has been upset since he found out about Uncle Jake and Aunt Alex coming. I've been trying with him still. Trying to be nice. Because I want this visit to go smoothly, and having Dad angry at me won't help.

Dad and I aren't friends. I would like to say we were close when I was little, but even as a kid, I always gravitated toward Mom. She was the nurturing, caring one. Dad got along better with Charlotte.

After Mom died, I knew I had to change something between him and me. But living with someone you don't like is hard, and it's even harder now that I think he may have hurt Mom. I know I have to act like he's still my dad.

"Stressed," he says, holding up his glass. The ice jingles.

I sigh and pretend like the booze doesn't bother me. Like I don't know he'd rather be somewhere else, even mentally, than here with us. I wonder if that's how Mom felt.

"What am I supposed to do about her?" Dad says.

For a second I think he's talking about Mom. But only for a second.

He means Charlotte.

Sometimes when he talks about her, I can see the embarrassment on his face. Like he's more ashamed than worried, and that makes me want to scream. Makes me want to shout. Makes me want to rip down all the artwork and everything breakable he cares about and just shatter it.

But I don't. Of course. That's not me. And also because Dad is the only dad I'm gonna get. And despite him being embarrassed about Charlotte, she's right that Dad knows something about Mom. I hope to God he didn't have anything to do with her death, but I'll never find out the truth acting like I hate him. Acting like Charlotte does when she's around him.

"She's stressed out, Dad. Can you blame her? Things in this place have been flipped upside down since Mom died and you can't deny that," I say. Then I point at his drink. "At least you can drink your stress away." I realize how rude I sound, so I push out a fake laugh.

Lucky for me, Dad can't tell when I'm telling the truth or faking it. He sighs when I laugh, and I know I've probably said the wrong thing.

"I get it, Maddi. I'm a terrible father who doesn't love his children."

When Dad says this, I actually *do* want to laugh. Because he's not far from the truth. But of course, he's the one being sarcastic now.

"Just ease up on her. She's coping in her own way. Parading Amber around like she's our new mom certainly isn't helping, though," I say carefully. I scoot a little closer to Dad on the couch and try to soften my tone. "I get it, you're in love. But just try and see this from our perspective. It hasn't even been six months since Mom died."

Dad doesn't say anything for a moment. Just stares at the TV. An old episode of *The Office* is on. It would be nice if him and I were actually watching it together. Doing something normal. Laughing, talking about school, whatever.

"Between the renovations in the garden and Amber acting as if she owns the house and wearing Mom's jewelry and sleeping in Mom's bed, don't you see how messed up that seems?" I want to mention the poison and the pills, but I don't. Because he could be responsible for all of that.

"You understand I deserve happiness, too. Don't you, Maddi? This is how it works. I've moved on. I want to live my life, too." When he says this he stares at me. He looks sad. It's no secret that Mom's death has taken a toll on everyone, but I hadn't realized Dad felt any sadness about it. He's never acted as if he had. And maybe he doesn't. But he looks as unhappy on the outside as I feel on the inside.

I take a deep breath and try to figure out what the right answer is. What Dad wants to hear.

I want him to talk to me. Maybe if I understood him better, it would help me see the whole situation clearer. But I just don't get him. Don't get why he acts as if Mom's death is no big deal. Why he loves Amber.

"Do you miss her?" I say.

They did love each other once. When we were little, we'd go on family vacations. We'd spend time together. That had to have meant *something*.

Dad clears his throat and then finishes his drink.

"I don't want to get into it right now, Maddi. It's late. You should be in bed. We can talk another time."

When he says this, a shiver of anger runs through my body. I take a deep breath and try not to show it on my face.

He doesn't care at all. He doesn't miss Mom. My mom. The woman he spent all those years with. He doesn't care that she's gone. And now it all makes sense.

He's glad she's dead.

I walk back to my room and get into bed. I fall asleep listening to my little sister cry in her room.

Charlotte

"Charlotte! You have grown," Uncle Jake says, with a hug and a grin. We're standing in the living room of the guesthouse.

He hasn't changed much since I last saw him.

I seriously didn't expect him to show up. Sunday, Maddi and I sat around waiting for him all day, and he didn't even bother to call. And now here he is, Monday morning, arriving like he's just on time.

His dark hair is slicked back and his skin is saggy, even though he's only about eight years older than Mom.

Now that he's here, I regret not getting to know my uncle better. He invited me and Maddi to visit every summer before Mom died. We never went, even though Mom encouraged it in the beginning. She and Uncle Jake weren't very close, but she wanted us to have a relationship with him and Aunt Alex.

Alex looks a lot younger than Jake, with long hair and skinny legs. Her head looks too big for her body. She's so small she could have bird bones. Hollow and easily damaged. She used to be Mom's best friend when they were kids. Mom would talk about her sometimes. But after they grew up, and Alex married

Jake, Mom told me they grew apart. I think that's one of the reasons she wanted us to visit. She knew how great Alex was.

Strangers.

Family that we never bothered to get to know.

"You remember Alex, right?" Jake grabs his wife and pulls her toward me. He holds her wrist tightly, and I wonder if he could snap it. He probably could if he wanted to.

But why would he want to?

Alex smiles at me and gives a small wave. There's something about her eyes that worries me. I haven't seen her in so long that I'd almost forgotten about her. I don't even remember seeing her at Mom's funeral, though I know she was there. She's a very forgettable person. I bet when she and Mom were kids, Mom was the loud one and she was the quiet one. The one that people forgot about.

She looks scared.

Everyone is scared.

"You guys wanna sit?" Maddi appears in the doorway and walks into the living room. I follow her and sit on the couch next to her. The vintage couch Mom adored but Dad couldn't stand, so he moved it out here to the guesthouse, where it could be forgotten. Just like her velvet chaise longue and everything else she picked out.

The guesthouse is filled with things that Mom loved. Every corner reminds me of her. Old paintings hang on the walls, mostly landscapes of the desert. She used to travel and collect art when she was younger. There's an antique piano jammed in the corner by the front door, and bookshelves filled with novels, mysteries, and picture books on every wall.

Uncle Jake looks at us and smiles. His teeth yellow and crooked.

I still can't believe this is my mother's brother.

Jake and Alex sit on the couch across from Maddi and me. Alex scoots to one end, by the armrest.

Maybe I'm imagining it, but it looks like she's trying not to touch him.

She hates him. He gives her the creeps, I bet.

Is that it?

They're both strange.

"All right, ladies. Please tell me why you've dragged us all the way out here. What kind of information have you found out about my poor deceased sister?" Jake says.

Does he even care that she's dead? If this is such a hassle to him, why did he bother to come? Money? Everything that wasn't left to our father was left to Jake.

Everything but the house. That's Maddi's as soon as Dad moves or Maddi gets married.

Maddi looks at me and gives me "the look." The look that says, "Maybe This Was a Mistake." She's full of those types of looks. Secret messages told with her eyes. Secrets that only I can decipher.

"Well, Uncle Jake. Before I tell you anything about what's been going on, I want to know how you can help us," Maddi says.

Maybe she should have figured that out before she called him.

Give her a minute. She has a plan. She must have a plan.

"Well, if it's lawyers you want, I have the best in my pocket. If it's cash you need, I have that, too. But I would like to know why I'm here," Jake says. His tone is annoyed and harsh.

Alex looks at him and then at us. Did she pick up on his tone, too?

"Jake, please. This is important to them," she says. I start to relax a little bit. I'm grateful she's here. Maybe she can be the voice of reason. Calm everyone down.

"She's right. I don't know why you're acting like all of this is such a pain in the ass," I say. I can feel my bitch look spread across my face, and I know they can see it. Maddi reaches over and squeezes my hand. I know that means she wants me to shut up. To calm down and act like none of this is a big deal.

I hate him.

You don't even know him. Maybe he really will help.

I hope so.

I stare at the rug a few feet from me. It's old with red and white spots on it. Mom bought it at an estate sale. For a few months she actually kept it in the house, but eventually it was moved out here.

"Jake, we think that Mom was murdered." When Maddi says this I watch the look on Jake's face change from boredom to shock.

Alex gives a little gasp, like in a movie.

"By whom?" Jake says. Now I can see that we have his attention. His voice has changed, it sounds weaker, like maybe he doesn't fully trust it anymore.

Good. Maybe he'll take us seriously now.

"By Amber. Maybe even by our dad," I say. Maddi gives me another look. This one says *Shut up.*

"What?" Jake says, and then stands. "What the hell are you

girls talking about? Your mother's heart stopped. She died of natural causes."

Says who?

Your heart doesn't just stop!

"Calm down, honey," Alex says. She grabs Jake by the arm and he sits back down next to her.

"Shh," Maddi says. "If our father hears us, we're all in trouble. We don't know for sure, but it's weird. Mom never had heart problems, did she? Plus we think we might have some evidence."

The engagement.

The poison.

The letter.

The pills.

Jake taps his foot on the floor fast and loud, like being here with us is making his blood pressure go up. He puts his face in his hands, just for a moment, and takes a deep breath.

It's a relief seeing him act like this, like a human.

"Is that possible?" Alex says. "The thought of someone trying to hurt your mom makes me sick." Her voice rises a little bit, but then she stops talking, and I can tell she's about to cry.

My mom.

Her friend.

Killed.

And by who? The man she loved?

But was she really? Did he really do it?

Your heart doesn't just stop.

"Your father and I have always had our differences, but this is far-fetched," Jake says. "Everyone knows he's never been faithful, but a murderer? I doubt that very much."

Does he even care that she was our mother? That she loved Dad? That she trusted him? Does any of that matter to him?

Where's the sympathy?

"But none of us really know Amber," Maddi says. "She could be anyone. And who would gain the most from Mom's death?" Maddi knows exactly how to stay calm. I don't know where she learned it, because no one else in our family has ever been able to do that. Not even Mom.

Why can't you be like that?

"Could you tell us what evidence you've found?" Alex says. Her voice is quiet and shaky. I can hear the tears in it. Her face has lost all color, and she reminds me of a ghost. I feel sorry for her. She has sadness in her eyes.

"Yes, let's talk about evidence. Tell me what you know," Jake says. He starts to pace from one side of the room to the other. I can smell his cologne and it's sharp and bitter. His clothes hang off him like they're slightly too big. He's not well put together. He almost looks like how Mom looked toward the end. Frazzled.

"Well, for starters, Mom had been telling me for months how much pain she was in," I say. "She said it felt like something was eating her from the inside out, and then a few months later Maddi finds *poison* in the house." When I say this I suddenly want to burst into tears. She said that to me for months. Why didn't I see the signs? Why didn't I take her seriously? Why didn't I listen to her?

I hope Mom wasn't scared.

I hope she didn't feel pain when she died.

I hope she isn't in pain now.

"Poison? What are you talking about? What type of poison?" Jake says. The annoyance in his voice is getting under my skin and I want to shout everything in his face.

Maddie looks at me like she wants me to shut up, then says, "Charlotte's right. I found zinc phosphide in the pantry, which is highly toxic. It's for killing rodents. Honestly, I get that it doesn't seem like a big deal, but Mom *never* used poison like that. And why would Amber or our dad need it? They cut down most of the garden." She's trying to sound calm, and I can tell she's bothered that I brought up the poison. But I don't really care. We were going to tell him anyway.

"Okay. But that isn't really evidence, Maddi. If you were to take that to the police, all they'd think is your dad had a problem with gophers or rats," Jake says. "Do you girls have actual physical evidence?"

He's right.

No, he isn't. That is *physical evidence.*

"Did you know that he and Amber got engaged? Just a few nights ago. He gave her Mom's wedding ring," Maddi says. "She's taken over Mom's room. She wears her jewelry. They both act as if Mom never existed. Like they wanted her gone or something."

Jake nods like this makes sense. "I had a feeling something was going on between them when I came for your mom's funeral. But people get engaged every day."

I want to stand up and shout that this isn't normal.

This isn't *normal. None of it is.*

143

Why did he come here?

"It's more than that," Maddi says. "Like Charlotte said, Mom said she wasn't feeling well toward the end. We found the poison, which clearly you don't think is a big deal. But I also found this in the medicine cabinet with all of Amber's stuff. And we have a letter Mom wrote." She hands the pills and the letter to Jake. "Why would Amber have these pills? What would she need them for? And the letter proves that Mom was afraid."

It proves that Dad didn't want her around anymore. That he wanted her gone.

Is that really proof?

Uncle Jake scoots closer to Alex and I watch them both read the letter. Alex looks surprised and then looks at me and Maddi.

"I'm sorry you girls have had to go through all this. We should have been here after she passed."

Jake nods and then clears his throat. "Okay. This does seem pretty serious. I'll look into it and find out about the autopsy." Jake looks at Alex and she gives him a little nod.

The tightness in my chest loosens and a bubble of hope grows inside me. He's going to help us. Maddi was right to call him. We do have some family on our side.

Maybe he's strange, but why would he come all this way if he didn't want to help?

He loved Mom. I can see that now.

He's actually going to help. We won't have to do this alone.

Maddi

Suddenly I don't feel so worried. Even though I'm not sure how convinced Uncle Jake is about everything that's going on, I'm glad to know that someone is here to help. Maybe even on our side. We won't have to deal with Dad and Amber by ourselves.

Charlotte and I leave Jake and Alex to get settled in the guesthouse, and head inside to get ready for school. Jake said we can get together later and discuss what we're going to do.

Charlotte and I are already late. We'll miss our first few classes, but I want to get out of the house as soon as possible. After talking to Dad last night, I'm not sure I'll be able to keep a straight face around him. I'm still so angry.

"I'm glad you called him," Charlotte says. We're in the bathroom, doing our hair. Well, *I'm* doing my hair, she's just sitting next to me.

I haven't seen my sister attempt to get ready for the day since Mom's funeral. The most she'll do is shower and brush her teeth. It's so far from how she was, it's another thing that nags at me during the day.

How much and how fast she's changed.

"We'll see what happens," I say. It was hard to read Jake. He seemed annoyed with everything, but from what I understand, he's sort of always been like that. Probably why Mom didn't get along with him as they got older.

"I still can't figure out why Lana kept that note from me, though. Why she waited for you to come back to school to show you," I say. I apply mascara and then finish my hair. Even when she's not trying, Charlotte is beautiful. I've always had to try harder than her. And that's okay. She's never been very confident, though, and now it really shows.

Today Charlotte lets me wear her white dress to school. I don't know why, but for some reason it makes me feel closer to Mom. She gave Charlotte and me dresses every Easter, and Charlotte's white dress is my favorite out of all the ones Mom got us. Charlotte hasn't worn it since the funeral, and I hate seeing it just sit in her closet.

"I told you, you guys don't share any classes," Charlotte says. She sounds annoyed, irritable. I can't remember the last time she wasn't annoyed.

"Right. Whatever. Let's get going," I say.

We walk into the kitchen and Amber is there with Dad. They're both sitting at the table eating. I'd hoped they'd be gone by now. At this point, I'm not even sure what Amber does all day. I thought she was working at one of the properties, but since the engagement, she's been hanging around the house more.

"Hey, girls," Dad says. He looks at me and slaps a fake smile on his face, which fades a little when he sees Charlotte. "You look lovely this morning, Maddi," he says. Amber sits close to him, sipping coffee from a mug. She looks too comfortable, and the good mood I was attempting to have today starts to go out the window. Charlotte told me what happened with Amber this weekend. I wish Amber would just leave. Leave us alone. Let us be. It's hard enough to get up and go to school, but having her around makes it that much harder.

"Morning," I say quietly. Charlotte doesn't say a word.

"Do you ladies want to join us?" Dad says. He pulls the chair on the other side of him out, as if me or Charlotte would consider sitting there. He doesn't even look hungover. Maybe he's used to drinking until all hours of the morning and then getting up and going to work. My body aches from exhaustion, but he seems fine.

Before I can say anything, Charlotte laughs. It's loud and fake, and I can tell that it bugs Amber.

"You don't have to have that attitude," Amber says.

She's getting braver around us. And it makes me want to pull her hair out.

"What?" Charlotte says. She takes a step closer to Amber. *Please, God, don't let there be another fight. I don't have the energy.*

"I said you don't have to have that attitude with your father, he's just asking a simple question." Amber's tone is bitchy and she has an entitled look on her face.

I have to swallow my rage. I grab Charlotte by the wrist. "Let's go," I say under my breath. But Charlotte jerks away from me.

"I'm not sure who the fuck you think you are, but you're not allowed to speak to me like that," Charlotte says.

Before Amber can respond, Dad shouts, "Language!" as if he cares about how we talk all of a sudden.

"Calm down," Amber says to Charlotte.

"You're not our mother, you don't have any right to tell us what to do," I say. Charlotte takes another step toward Amber and grabs the cup of coffee out of her hands. Before I can stop her she throws it down on the table, splashing hot liquid all over the kitchen.

"Charlotte, what the hell are you doing?" Dad stands and grabs her by the arms. "I'm not sure where you get off acting like this, but you need to leave."

My sister jerks away from Dad and storms toward the front door. I follow her outside. As she walks to the car, she slips on some ice and falls.

"Charlotte," I say. I walk up to her. She's sitting on the cold cement, crying.

Seeing her like this makes my heart ache. The sadness that I know she's feeling seeps into me and tears spring to my eyes. I take a deep breath and do my best to hold them in.

"How could he do this. How *could* he!" she says. She pounds the ground with her fists.

She looks like a child, and I try to picture how our life was before, but at this moment I can't. All I can see is how heartbroken she is. And how little I can do to help her.

"It's messed up. It's all messed up. But it won't be like this forever," I say. I hold my hand out to her, but she ignores it.

"It'll never get better. It'll only get worse. I just know it," she says. I haven't seen her cry like this in a long time. Normally she's just angry, but today is different.

"You can't think like that. This isn't forever," I say.

My little sister. Before, I was able to help her when she was having a hard day. But now I know there isn't anything I can do.

"Whatever," she says.

She pulls her knees close to her chest and holds herself and continues to cry. I watch her like this for a long time, then sit down next to her. The cold, melted ice immediately soaks into my coat. I put my arms around Charlotte and hold her for what feels like hours.

"I know you miss her," I say.

"I would do anything to bring her back," she says.

If there was a way, I would do anything too.

Charlotte

I don't know how, but I go to school with Maddi.

The second time I've gone since Mom died. Only this time around I'm glad to get out of the house. Seeing Dad and Amber just made all the sadness I've been carrying around turn into a ball of anger. The house also feels different. Even though Jake is here now, and he says he'll help us, fear sits at the bottom of my belly. Fear that Dad is sort of done with me. The look on his face when he saw me this morning scared me.

Nancy would say I'm being paranoid. She'd want me to write a thought record about this whole thing. To calm myself down. But I know what I know.

This isn't just paranoia. This isn't just anxiety. Something about Jake reading that letter and taking us seriously shows that we were right to worry. To be afraid.

We walk down the halls, and that same silence follows us.

Small towns.

No one knows anything.

Yes, they do.

The first few weeks after Mom died and I missed classes, Dad got letters from the principal and half of my teachers.

Phone calls every day. Threats that they were going to kick me out if I missed any more classes. Eventually Dad got sick of the calls and was able to get my homework sent home for me to pretend to do. It worked out perfectly for me. But now I can't stay home. Not with her there.

At our lockers I see Cat just a few lockers away. She spots me and walks toward us. Her hair is pulled into a high pony. The highlighter she has on her cheekbones is bright and shimmers with every step she takes.

"Charlotte. When are we gonna get together and catch up?" Her voice has that same piercing tone it had before. For a moment I miss her. Miss being like her.

Happy.

This was my best friend. The girl I spent countless hours with. Hundreds of sleepovers. We were almost as close as me and Maddi.

Has she always been like this?

Has she always had that tone?

Have I never cared or even noticed?

I look at Cat and shrug. The thought of having a normal conversation with her, of going out and drinking coffee with her, all of it sounds like something I can't do anymore. That I'm not allowed to do anymore. Even if I wanted to.

"I've been a lot busier than I thought," I say. It's an excuse, but not one good enough to use on your used-to-be best friend.

Cat smiles at me, showing her shiny white teeth. She's trying. I can tell.

Guilt hits me hard in the heart. She and I were so close. We were inseparable. We'd stay up late and watch Netflix and

YouTube. We'd drink so much coffee our teeth would chatter, just so we could stay awake and talk.

"What if you, me, and Stephen all went out for a drink, like old times? I've been dating Cassi, I could bring her along too."

Old times. Cat always had a date, and I always had Stephen. Now I'm not sure who or what I have. Maddi.

And Uncle Jake.

Maybe Uncle Jake.

I take my math book out of my locker and read the cover. I don't want to look at Cat. I don't like making excuses. I just wish she'd realize that I'm not the same girl I was six months ago. I don't want to drink beer in her mom's basement and talk shit on girls in our cheer squad. I want to figure out why Mom is dead and if Dad had something to do with it.

"I haven't talked to Stephen in a while," I say. And it's true, I haven't. The painful truth.

I glance back up at Cat. Her smile has faded a little. Like she feels sorry for me. Or maybe she really does want to spend time with me.

Has he been seeing someone else?

Who cares, you can't ask her that.

But I care.

I care a lot. Even though I was the one who left Stephen doesn't mean I've forgotten about him. Forgotten about us.

"I know. He told me. He's sad about it. But I've been there to keep him company. We knew you'd come back. He would love to see you," Cat says.

I just shrug again. Because I don't know if any of it is true.

"We'll plan something soon. Sound good, Charlotte?" Maddi

says. She knows I don't want to talk about Stephen. Knows I don't want to be doing *any* of this.

I nod.

I miss him so much.

"Just text me or something," Cat says. Then puts her arms around me and gives me a tight hug. The smell of tanning lotion and coconut fills my nose, and I am hit with all the memories of before. Of my life before. I want to hang on to her, to tell her I miss her, but she pulls away from me and walks down the hall.

The guilt comes back. Harder this time. Not only because of what's happened with Stephen but also because of what's happened with Cat. My best friend isn't even a part of my life anymore. And it's all my fault.

Charlotte

When I walk into math class, Stephen is already there. He looks up at me and smiles.

The classroom feels gray and lonely. And somehow the only place in the room where the sun shines is over by Stephen.

Your eyes are playing tricks.

Maybe.

Miss Brush sits at her desk and stares at me as I stand in the front of the room, like she can't start class until I sit, even though we have a few minutes before the bell rings.

The desk next to Stephen's is empty.

The desk where Lana sits is empty, but I know she'll be here soon enough.

I should go to him.

Better than sitting next to phony princess Lana.

I take a deep breath and walk over to the desk next to Stephen's. He follows me with his eyes. When I sit down, he mouths *Hi* at me.

Just like he did a few years ago, when we first met.

Before I can stop myself I smile. I can't help it. He brings me joy and despair all at the same time. And I don't know how or why.

Don't be so dramatic.

His hair is longer. And his skin is darker, like he's been out in the sun, even though it's been cold and gloomy for weeks.

Maybe I've just missed the warmth and glow he has. Just missed the calmness he brings with him everywhere he goes.

Before I can say anything, he speaks, and my heart pounds loud in my ears.

"I've missed you," he says to me.

And my heart breaks in three.

For my mother. For myself. For Stephen.

I turn away from him and look ahead, at Miss Brush. She wipes down the whiteboard.

Say something.

Say something to him.

I glance back at Stephen. He's still staring at me. He doesn't smile, just looks. Can he tell I'm not the girl he cared about all those months ago? Can he see that I'm someone else now? That I've changed, and I don't know how to find my way back?

Do I want to find my way back?

"I'm sorry," I whisper. I don't know if he hears me or not.

But I mean it.

I am sorry.

Charlotte

"So are we ever going to get together again?" Lana follows me out of class.

My mind isn't here. Isn't in this hallway. It's somewhere else. Wandering off to a world before this moment.

Stephen.

Mom.

Uncle Jake.

Dad and Amber.

"I haven't heard from you since you came over. You doing okay?" Lana says. Today she's wearing a jumpsuit. It's black from top to bottom, with bright purple trim. I don't even have to ask to know she made it.

"Sorry, my uncle just got into town. Let's just say he's not the easiest person to entertain," I say.

Why are you telling her this?

Why not?

You don't trust her.

"Ugh, I hate when family visits. Maybe you could come by sometime tonight or tomorrow. I found another letter and I want you to see it. Your mom wrote it a while back," Lana says.

Another letter? Why didn't she mention it earlier? Did Mom leave me or Maddi any letters? Maybe in her journals?

I need to find the journals.

"What?" I say, then, "I could probably skip next period. Want to go now?" I try to hide the desperation that must be seeping from my pores. Can Lana sense it?

You skip class you know they'll call home and tell Dad.

Who cares?

Just more shit to deal with . . .

"Yeah, let's do it. Do you think Maddi will mind?" Lana says.

Maddi needs to be there.

I don't have time to try to find Maddi.

You can't go without her.

"She won't mind," I say, even though it's a lie. I need to know what the letter says, and I need to know now.

Listen to your gut. What would Nancy say?

"Great! I'll drive," Lana says.

We trudge out in the cold toward Lana's old beat-up Subaru hatchback. It's actually brighter today than it has been the last few weeks. The sun is up there somewhere, hiding behind the clouds.

I zip my coat tight and try to avoid puddles of gray slush as we walk through the school parking lot.

When I get inside Lana's car, I notice how dirty it is. It smells like old pot.

"Sorry, I practically live here during the weekends," she says, knocking old Coke bottles off the passenger seat. I get inside and try to convince myself that this isn't a bad idea. Isn't a bad move. That it's only going to help.

The drive to her house is a quick one, and when we get there, the driveway is empty. None of the snow has been shoveled. It sits in small mounds, slowly melting. It looks the same way the day after Christmas feels. That's how the winter always is. The first couple of snowfalls are exciting, but after a while it just gets old, dark, and dirty.

Lana's house is small and brown with a sad-looking Welcome sign on the door. I didn't notice when I came here before with Maddi, but the whole place looks a little run-down.

I follow Lana inside, and she says, "Go ahead to my room. I'll run back and grab the letter."

The house has the same smoky smell it did before. Thick and sweet with incense. The type of place that would have given Mom a migraine. Last time it felt cozy, now I'm not sure what I'm feeling.

I walk back to Lana's room and sit on one of the dark pillows on the floor. Lana has a lot of stuff. So many different knickknacks scattered about, I wonder how she keeps everything organized. My room is twice the size of hers, and I can barely keep track of my socks.

I'm only there for a few moments before Lana comes in. She's holding a folded piece of paper that looks like it's been handled a lot—it's crumpled in places.

"Is that it?" I stand up fast and take the letter out of her hands before she can stop me. She makes a funny face, but then smiles.

"Sorry," I say. I feel the blood rush to my face.

Why are you sorry?

It's our mother.

"No worries. It's a short one. But better than nothing," Lana says. She plops down on her bed and pulls out her phone. Of course this isn't fun for her, and what did I expect, for her to hold my hand? To comfort me?

"Where was it? Are there more?" I ask. Why didn't she give this to Maddi and me last week when we were over? How many did Mom write?

"I found it packed in an old craft box. I was looking for ribbon and stumbled on that. I asked my mom how often she and your mom talked. She said they were pen pals. So I bet there are more," Lana says. She actually sounds excited when she tells me this. Like maybe she knows she's helping or something. I take a deep breath. If there are more letters, then that could be more info for Uncle Jake.

"Can I take this one home, then? Since it was packed away?"

Lana pauses for a minute and then nods. "Sure! I bet Mom has totally forgotten about it." I picture Lana somewhere in this house, looking for crafty things to glue onto her weird clothing.

Guilt rushes over me. I know I should wait for Maddi, but I can't help myself. I unfold the paper and right away I recognize the handwriting. Slanted block letters. Only this letter is written in marker instead of pen. I try to picture Mom writing a note like this with a permanent marker. It's dated a little over a year from today.

Where was she when she wrote it?

Where was I?

Oh, Mom. How I miss you.

STEPHANIE,

HOW IS EVERYTHING? HOW'S YOUR LANA? WHAT ABOUT YOUR EX? DID YOU END UP PRESSING CHARGES FOR THE DOMESTIC SITUATION? I SURE HOPE THAT WAS TAKEN CARE OF. THAT TYPE OF THING CAN BE VERY DANGEROUS AND FRIGHTENING.

THINGS HAVEN'T GOTTEN MUCH BETTER OVER HERE. STILL TRYING TO MAKE THINGS WORK WITH ANDREW, BUT EVERY TIME I DO, IT'S LIKE WE TAKE THREE STEPS BACKWARD.

MY GIRLS LOVE HIM, BUT I CAN SEE OUR RELATIONSHIP CHANGING. ENDING. AND TO MAKE EVERYTHING WORSE, I CAN SEE THE GIRLS PULLING AWAY FROM HIM, TOO. I HOPE SO MUCH THAT ISN'T MY FAULT.

GIVE ME A CALL AS SOON AS YOU SELL YOUR HOUSE, AND I'LL ASK AROUND FOR SOME RENTALS IN THE NEIGHBORHOOD.

THANK YOU FOR ALWAYS BEING THERE FOR ME.

MUCH LOVE,
SARAH

Maddi

Dad is right about one thing.

Charlotte is struggling. The weeks before she started coming back to school were scary. She wasn't eating, she wasn't sleeping, she was just . . . there. She had been going to therapy for a few months but stopped after something happened with the therapist.

"Aren't you heading to therapy this afternoon?" I'd said one day.

Charlotte was in the kitchen drinking a cup of tea and staring at the garden. The plants were all dead, and Dad was in the process of having the hot tub installed. The large white pine tree that we sat under with Mom had just been chopped down. A small ax sat a few yards from the stump of the tree. Dad had tried to cut it down himself, but quickly gave up and hired someone. I loved that tree, and now it was gone, too. Just like the garden.

I knew it bothered Charlotte. It bothered me too, but I pretended it didn't.

"No," she said, then took a sip of her tea. I could tell it was hot, because she grimaced when she drank it.

I sat at the table next to her and grabbed her hand. We used to be so close, but just touching her hand felt different now. Like we'd turned into strangers.

I missed her. Missed how she used to be. How our *lives* used to be. Charlotte's bubbly personality that she brought to everything. How she lightened a room. All the confidence in the world. She was so fun, and so happy. Now she's someone else entirely. And it hurts my heart to watch her change.

"How come? I thought the sessions were helping," I said. I wasn't even sure if they were helping or not, but I'd noticed her eating more. Which I thought was progress.

"Because it's a fucking waste of time. She keeps telling me I should forgive Dad and Amber, and I'm sorry, but that's never going to happen," Charlotte said. I could hear real anger in her voice. I couldn't blame her, because I didn't forgive Dad for being with Amber, either. I would hate to be told I *should*.

"When did she say that? Did you tell her what was going on?"

It had only been a few days before this that we'd caught Dad and Amber in the kitchen kissing. Their hands all over each other. In Mom's house. No shame. Like they didn't care if we saw them or not.

"I told her that last week. It's not worth it. Waste of time, waste of money," Charlotte said.

I sighed. I couldn't blame her. But I wanted her to be better, too. With everything going on around here, she needed a few glimmers of hope.

"I'm sorry. I hope you know you can always talk to me," I said. I looked at Charlotte, and she stared down at her cup of steaming tea. She looked as if she might cry. I felt tears well up, and I quickly wiped them away.

"I know I can. But I'm so angry. And you're not," Charlotte said. Then she picked up the steaming mug of tea and chugged it. I saw pain spread across her face.

"Charlotte!" I said.

She stood and left her mug on the table. A few moments later, I heard her bedroom door slam.

I sat at the table staring at the mug.

She's confused and doesn't understand. But I *am* angry. Angrier than she will ever know.

Charlotte

"I should probably call my sister," I say.

"Do you want to stick around for food or something? We could order a pizza? Or maybe we could hang at your place? I know my house is kinda boring," Lana says. She sounds disappointed, but honestly I don't really care.

Why did you do this?

Why did you come here?

"I don't know," I say.

We sit in silence for a few minutes. I stare at the shiny stones and rocks on her desk and wonder what someone would need them for.

"I'm sorry that letter wasn't much help," Lana says. Almost embarrassed. She gets off her bed.

I call Maddi and she agrees to come pick me up. Lana and I head into the kitchen to wait for her.

"Thanks for letting me come over. I'm sorry to leave so early. Maddi is sort of pissed I ditched school without telling her," I say. Lana opens the fridge and looks inside. She grabs a soda and sets it on the counter, then walks over and gives me a hug. My body stiffens, and I wish she wouldn't touch me. I feel sick, and I'm not sure why.

"It's okay. I'll keep looking. If there are more letters, I'll tell you," she says.

I nod, then head outside and wait on the porch for Maddi to pick me up. The smell of the house was making my stomach turn, and the fresh air is a relief. The cold calms me down. It's stopped raining, and the sun is setting. I knew it was hiding up there somewhere.

Maddi turns onto the street and I watch her drive up the road. She pulls into the driveway and parks. She looks pissed. When I get in the car, I'm relieved by the heat.

"I can't believe you went without me," she says. "Not only that, you skipped school? I was freaking out when you didn't meet me at the lockers." Her voice is raised, but she isn't yelling. I've only seen Maddi lose her cool a handful of times.

"I'm sorry, I just needed to get out of there. Lana had another letter." I hold out the note. Maddi looks at it and then sighs.

"I'm driving, Charlotte. Should I pull over?"

This is important. Of course she wants to pull over and read it. *I* couldn't wait. But I want to get home. My brain needs to rest.

"Just drive fast and we can read it together at home," I say.

Maddi does a heavy sigh and then takes a puff off her Juul. She only smokes when she's really stressed, and I know this is my fault.

The rest of the drive home is silent, and when we pull into the driveway my stomach drops.

"Shit," I say.

Dad and Uncle Jake are out on the front porch. Practically blocking the front door.

The setting sun makes the snow almost pretty. Maybe, at the right angle, it's beautiful.

"What are they doing back? I thought we weren't meeting him until later," Maddi says. She's talking about Uncle Jake. We'd planned on getting dinner. I wasn't expecting to see him until then, and especially not with Dad.

Maybe he's been talking to Dad to get info.

Maybe this is a good thing.

Dad's bundled up in a huge parka, and Uncle Jake wears a large black trench. They both hold glasses filled with dark liquid.

Maddi turns the car off and we get out.

Are they fighting?

It looks like they're playing nice.

Maybe Jake is faking.

Hopefully, Jake is faking.

"Maddi, Charlotte, come over here." Dad waves us over.

Maddi looks at me and shakes her head.

"What is this?" I whisper. Maddi will know. Maddi always knows.

"Let's find out," she says. "But I have a bad feeling."

The fact that Dad has called us over to talk to us worries me. Just this morning he and I were fighting. Maybe he's already too drunk to remember that.

Doubt it.

Maddi walks toward the porch and I follow. We're careful not to step on the hunks of ice scattered on the porch steps.

"Hello, where's Alex?" Maddi says. She sounds calm and relaxed. As always.

How is she so calm?

Why is Dad?

She's still good at talking to Dad.

At least, better than me.

Maddi sits down in the chair next to Jake. I stand on the step closest to Maddi and stare at the three of them. They almost look like a happy family.

How long has Dad been drinking? His cheeks are flushed and his eyes are glassy.

"Your uncle here just had some interesting things to share with me. Do you girls care to hear?" Dad says. He's slurring. Which means I was right. He's drunk.

My heart jumps and I know we're in trouble.

Uncle Jake betrayed us!

I knew it. I fucking knew he would.

But why?

"Of course, we'd love to hear," Maddi says. I can see the panic start up in her face. No one else would notice but me, though. I can see it in her eyes.

I walk over and sit next to her. The chair is cold and damp against my legs.

The wind picks up and carries a breeze that's frigid and smells like sadness. I look over at the flowers Mom planted this spring. She lined them up all along the driveway. Every last one is dead. Mom had a green thumb, but I'm not sure even she would be able to bring these flowers back.

"Well, ladies, I was just telling your father how interested I am in buying the place when he and Amber get married," Jake says.

Relief floods through me like running water.

He's kept the secrets. He hasn't told Dad.

But what is he doing?

"You're selling the house?" Maddi says to Dad. He takes another sip out of his glass and smiles at her, showing his teeth. I can smell the alcohol on him, even though he's several feet away. The smell is sour and sharp and it makes my stomach hurt.

"Amber and I were thinking about it. You girls are almost out of high school. We don't need a place this big," Dad says.

"But this was Mom's house," I say. "She left it to Maddi." I try not to lose my temper. "She was raised in this house, and so were Maddi and I."

Dad just smiles and drinks.

He's trying to push our buttons.

Trying to get under our skin.

"I was also raised in this house," Uncle Jake says. "I grew up here with my mom and dad. The house would still be in the family. You'd be welcome to visit any time you'd like."

He can't mean it.

They can't mean it.

"How does Alex feel about moving?" Maddi says. "Doesn't she teach at an elementary school in Baltimore?"

Jake just shrugs. "Alex will do what I ask."

When Jake says this, a spark of horror hits me.

168

We can't trust this man.

We can't trust anyone.

"Where is Alex?" I ask, not looking at Jake. He's a phony. He's a fake. He's playing us.

Isn't he?

"She's out with that lovely girl Amber," Jake says. He tips back his whiskey and finishes it. Then he winks at me.

A fucking wink.

They're both drunk.

I look at Maddi. She must know Jake's full of shit, too. And that we're both in trouble. That we made a huge mistake inviting him here. We made a huge mistake asking for his help. He's going to make everything worse.

"Well, that's not going to happen," Maddi says. "Mom left the house to me and I have no intention of selling it to you when I turn eighteen." She stands up and walks inside. I follow her, still trying to understand what's going on. And what we're going to do now.

What would it be like? To fix all of this? To end all the pain that my sister and I have?

What would happen if I just ended it?

Everything would start over.

Everything could begin again, and we'd be happy and free.

Charlotte

Maddi and I sit in the living room with the TV on. An old episode of *Bob's Burgers* is playing, but I hardly pay attention to it. I'm trying not to worry, trying not to be angry, trying to pretend that Uncle Jake isn't a huge liar, that Dad isn't trying to ruin our lives.

We're on the couch under a fleece blanket Mom bought several years ago.

"Do you remember when we'd have movie nights with Mom? Do you remember how much we loved watching all those corny old movies together?" Maddi says. I can tell she's trying not to focus on her anger, but under her fake smile and calm attitude, she's just as heated as I am.

"I loved movie nights," I say.

Every month Mom, Maddi, and I would all have a movie night together. Mom would choose all kinds of weird flicks. Her favorite was one called *Throw Momma from the Train*. It was about an aspiring author. Whenever Mom watched it, she'd laugh so hard tears would roll down her face.

"What was that last movie we watched together? Do you remember? It had the really hot old dude in it," Maddi says.

The last time we had a movie night was over a year ago. We stopped doing them as much after Mom lost the baby. But I still remember that last film.

"*Dead Man* with Johnny Depp!" I say, louder than I intended. Maddi laughs. Which calms me down a little.

It's going to be okay.

We're going to figure this out.

"That movie was so weird. But Mom loved it." It was true, Mom did love it. She told us she'd watched it when she was little, too. She knew everything that happened and kept spoiling it for us as we watched. Telling us what was going to happen and when.

"I miss movie nights," I say.

How good those nights together were. Eating junk food, laughing, and just being together.

And now she's gone. Just a memory. Almost like she wasn't really here at all.

"I miss her a lot," Maddi says. She scoots in close to me and rests her head on my shoulder. She smells just like Mom, and for a second it's like Mom is here. In the room with us. I close my eyes and try to picture her on the couch. She'd be wearing light pink joggers and a sweater. Or old leggings with a hoodie. She loved lounge clothes. If we were watching a movie with someone cute or young, she'd be the first to point it out. Maybe she would crack a joke, or cry when something got sad. Whatever it was, she was the best person to watch movies with. She responded in all the right ways.

While Maddi and I are watching TV, Alex and Amber come home. They're both holding large shopping bags.

So now they're besties.

Of course they are. I bet Amber paid for it all. With Dad's money.

Mom's money.

Our money.

I see Amber glance into the living room. She smirks at me, or at least I think she does, and it makes my blood boil. Alex walks by and waves. I say nothing as they make their way to the kitchen.

Why did they have to come home now?

Not right now.

Maddi looks at me and gives me a half smile. "Don't worry about them. Let's just have a good night," she says. But the anger is creeping up on her again, too.

She's right. She's totally right. But sometimes it's hard to let the little things go.

I look back at the TV. Bob from *Bob's Burgers* is trapped inside the walls of his burger joint. He speaks to one of his kids through the walls. Maddi laughs at all the right places, but I still can't get stupid Amber's face out of my head.

Let it go.

Let it go.

After a few minutes, I hear Alex and Amber go back outside where Dad and Jake are. Dad's car starts up, and a few moments later it's silent outside. Even though I'm scared Jake is going to tell Dad what we told him this morning, I'm happy they're gone. I don't want them in the house with us right now.

Maddi and I watch three or four episodes before I'm so tired I can hardly keep my eyes open.

"I need to go to sleep," I say. I hand Maddi the letter Lana found and then hug her tight. What would I do without my sister? Would I be able to get through this?

"Everything is going to be okay," she says. She doesn't sound convinced, but it still calms me down a little bit.

I go to my room and crawl into bed. I stare up at the dark ceiling, just hoping, praying, that Jake kept our secret. That he's still here to help.

Go to bed.

I need to sleep.

Go to bed.

Maddi

I realize now that inviting Uncle Jake here was a mistake.

He doesn't want to help us. He came here for selfish reasons, and he brought Alex with him to act as if he cared.

I sit on the living room couch and try to watch TV. The volume is so low I almost can't hear it. But I stare at the screen anyway. Charlotte's gone to bed, but I can't bring myself to yet. So much has happened today, I'm not sure I'll be able to relax even if I try.

The new letter Lana found. Despite how I feel about Lana, at least Charlotte has a friend.

Reading the letter from Mom made me really sad. She sounded more heartbroken than ever. And even though I know that the letter doesn't prove anything, it does show me how alone Mom felt. How much Dad really did stop caring about her.

I've never felt this type of anger toward someone. Especially not my father. How could he have put Mom through so much? Put *us* through so much?

I stare at the TV for a few more minutes until I hear Dad's car pull up in the driveway. I grab the remote and shut the TV off. I pull a blanket off the back of the couch and crawl under it and close my eyes. I don't want to have to fake small talk, and if I'm asleep, maybe they won't bother me.

Dad, Alex, Amber, and Jake all come back to the house. I hear the garage door open, and the connecting door from the garage to the kitchen. Dad is talking in a loud voice as he comes in.

"Let's finish this evening with a glass of wine," he says. After a couple of moments, I hear glasses clinking and Amber's obnoxious laugh.

I don't want to hate her as much as I do, but I can't help it.

Her voice. Her laughter. It's all like a hot poker to my heart, and the anger sears throughout my body. I hate feeling like this.

"Charlotte is so much like her mother," Alex says. Her tone is kind enough, but a stab of guilt pierces me. Charlotte would hate it if she knew they were talking about her like this.

"She's out of control," Amber says.

I get off the loveseat and move to the end of the couch that's closer to the door of the living room so I can hear better.

"She's probably still sad. Her mother just died," Alex says. She sounds defensive. So maybe Jake isn't here for us, but Alex is? She loved Mom growing up. They were best friends.

"I'm so tired of giving bad behavior an excuse," Amber says, her voice raised.

It's everything I can do not to get up and defend my sister. But I don't. I stay where I am.

"We're going to encourage her to go back to therapy. Maybe medication. It could help a lot," Dad says.

I thought therapy had been helping Charlotte, but she hated

it. I don't know what the right move is for her. But I don't want to encourage her to do something she hates. Alex seems to be the only one who gets it. Charlotte is still grieving. We're *both* still grieving. And Dad hasn't given us any time. He's changing everything.

"Just send her away. Get her out of the house," Jake says. "Neither of your girls should be living in the home their mom died in anyway. Alex and I will take over the utilities. Alex has a sister out in Pennsylvania who would take the girls for a few months. Just until Maddi is eighteen."

Dad says something I can't hear. Then Amber chimes in, loudly, "That's such a good idea, Jake. Charlotte really isn't who she used to be. It's probably not healthy for her to be here anyway."

"Have you actually tried to talk to her? To see what you could do to help with whatever it is she's going through?" Alex says. "When my grandma died, I went to grief therapy. It helped a lot." Her tone reminds me of Mom's. Kind and loving. It's no wonder Mom and her were so close.

"It's fucking pointless," Amber says.

Who is she trying to impress?

It's obvious she's already convinced Jake to send us away.

Of course—he wants our home. Our *mom's* home. Everyone will benefit if we're out of the picture. Everyone but us.

I sit for a few more minutes but can't make out what anyone is saying. I take a deep breath and then stand up. My car keys hang on a hook by the door to the kitchen. I grab them and my gloves and coat and head out the front door, slamming it behind me.

I hope they're embarrassed. Hope Dad is ashamed. That he would even consider sending us away.

I pull my coat and gloves on, shaking from anger and probably from the cold too.

On my way to my car, I grab the door handle of Dad's Porsche, checking if it's unlocked. Maybe there's something in here that he doesn't want us to find. Mom's last journal, or a letter she wrote us. A sign. But the car is locked.

"Fuck," I say, hitting the window. Guilt rushes up on me, and I know Mom would hate me talking like that. "Sorry," I say to Mom, even though I know she can't hear me.

I walk over to the rental Jake and Alex have. I go to the rear door, try it.

Surprisingly, it's unlocked. The back seat is clean. I look in the front and notice a purse on the passenger seat. Before I think twice, I grab it and dig through it.

Wallet. Sunglasses. Compact. Lipstick. At the bottom of the bag is a necklace with a small pendant. I grab it and stuff it in my coat pocket, then put the purse back and head to my car.

When I get inside, I sit there for a second with the heat going. It blows out cold air, but I don't care.

I look at the necklace again. The rose pendant reminds me of something, but I can't place what. My heart is racing. I still can't believe Dad. Still can't believe *any* of them.

"I shouldn't have trusted them," I say aloud.

Why would I think that Dad cared? Why would I think that *Uncle Jake*, who Mom never trusted, would want to help us?

A feeling of helplessness rushes over me and I want to

scream. This is *our* house. This is *our* family. Mom is gone, and now they want to send us away, too?

We were right. They did want Mom to die. She was a burden. She kept them from being together. What else did she keep Dad from? Money? Freedom?

Whatever it was, they are getting everything they want, and getting rid of Charlotte and me in the process.

I back out of the driveway and head toward the cemetery.

It's not very often that I do this, mostly because I hate leaving Charlotte behind, especially at night. But those first two months after Mom died, I went all the time. Mom didn't have a headstone—she still doesn't—so I just sat on the dirt above where she's buried. You couldn't miss it, because everywhere else had grass or plants growing.

Tonight, I go because I can't sit in that house with them. I take a couple of deep breaths as I drive, trying to calm myself down.

The streets are empty and my car's still cold, and while I drive, I can see my breath. The cemetery's not far from the house, so the car likely won't warm up before I get there.

Everything around me feels dark. The streetlights give off an eerie glow. The town really is small. Less of a coastal town in the winter and more like a place people come to grow old and die.

I pass the McDonald's, my favorite coffee shop, and a few auto shops. I keep driving until I get into another neighborhood. It's not as nice as the one we live in, but it's not run-down either. At the end of the road, I see the gates to the cemetery.

The snow on the ground is ugly and sad, and it feels colder than the worst blizzard. I puff on my Juul a few times before I park and get out of the car.

As I walk through the gates, the grass cracks under my feet like crispy potato chips. There are only a few streetlights to light my way, but I'm not worried about that. I know where I'm going.

When I die, I'd like to be cremated. Save my loved ones the trip to a depressing place like this.

Mom is buried toward the back, under a large red oak tree. The leaves on the tree have all fallen off, but in the summer and fall, that thing is bright red and fiery. Before, it gave me a little comfort knowing she was under something so beautiful. But right now, it looks dead and sad.

It's going to be a long winter.

I plop down on the cold frosted grass and stare at the mound of dirt Mom is buried under. Dad says her headstone should be here any day, but because we chose something that's a special color, who knows how long it'll take.

The whole thing is stupid.

Does it really matter if there's a headstone or not? It's just a reminder that she really is never coming back.

"Everything is so messed up," I say. As if Mom can hear me. I know that she can't, but it's nice to pretend sometimes.

She and I used to talk about everything. It didn't matter what the topic was. She'd listen to me, or I'd listen to her. I miss that so much it hurts.

"I'm so tired of all this chaos, and I don't know what the

right answer is," I say. I look up at the sky. It's cloudy and dark, but the moon's peeking out behind the fog.

I think about the last night I spent with Mom.

She was in her bathroom, washing her face. I sat on the toilet, just hanging out. Charlotte was out with Stephen, and Dad was who knows where. It was just the two of us.

"You know what we need tonight? Champagne." Mom grabbed her bathrobe off the back of the door and threw it on.

I followed her into the kitchen, where she opened the liquor cabinet and grabbed a bottle of champagne.

I'd seen her drink the stuff, but only a few times. Usually during celebrations or when she was really happy. That night she looked happy. Happier than I'd seen her in months.

"Don't tell your father. This is a two-hundred-dollar bottle." She peeled the foil off the top and popped the cork. It flew into the fridge. I screamed when it did and Mom laughed.

"Let's drink out of the crystal glasses, shall we?" she said.

"That sounds great," I said.

I never drank, but this felt different, so I decided I would. Just me and Mom.

Mom grabbed the crystal champagne glasses and handed me one. She filled the glass, and the champagne bubbled and spilled over the top.

"Sip it!" she said, laughing.

The bubbles stung my nose, but other than that, the drink was good.

We both sat down at the kitchen table and then clinked glasses.

"I love champagne," Mom said, smiling.

"Me too. At least, now I do," I said.

"This is a good day, Maddi. It really is," she said.

I didn't know why it was such a good day for her, but I nodded like I understood. And we drank our champagne like we were celebrating something.

Now, I just stare at that mound of dirt and wish so hard that I could crawl into that memory and hug her. Hug Mom and tell her that I love her.

"I wish you'd come back," I say.

God, I wish so much she would come back.

I pull the necklace out of my pocket and realize why it looks familiar. It's almost exactly like the one Mom had. The one Amber was wearing the day Dad told us she and him were engaged. The small rose-shaped pendant. The only difference is that Mom's had rubies, and this one looks like it has sapphires. It makes me sick to my stomach knowing Amber could wear Mom's stuff, jewelry that was special to her, and not even care how that might make us feel.

Maybe Alex really did love Mom. But if she loved her so much, why would she let our uncle do this to us? Pretend he was going to help, and then turn around and stab us in the back? Try to take our home. Side with Dad.

"I can't trust anyone anymore," I say. And I know it's true.

Charlotte

I wake up the next day and I feel like I actually slept. I grab my cell phone and check the time.

12:37.

Maddi didn't wake me up for school, and I'm relieved. I probably wouldn't have made it anyway. I get out of bed and go to Maddi's bedroom door. When I peek into her room, I see that she's still asleep.

Thank God.

I go back to my room and get back into bed and start scrolling through my phone. It's been a long time since I used any sort of social media.

On Instagram, Cat has shared several new photos. Her most recent post is a photo of the two of us from a few months before Mom died. We're dressed in matching outfits with shiny makeup on and our hair colored pink. We both grin at the camera, and I wonder how I was someone else such a short time ago. Cat's current photos are still gorgeous as ever. One post is a clip of her dancing, another of her with her mom and grandma. Everything about her life appears so normal, and for a second I feel jealous.

That could have been my life.

That was my life.

I scroll up to the search bar and enter Lana's phone number. An account pops up with only a few hundred followers. I click on the third photo. It was posted the day before yesterday. It shows Lana standing with a large group of people outside of a restaurant. She's wearing the T-shirt she borrowed from me last week. She looks better in it than I do, but it still sort of bugs me seeing her in it.

I recognize a few of the people in the photo from school. But that's not what catches my eye. In the far right corner of the photo is Stephen. He smiles at the camera. He fits right in with the little group.

She did say that he was a doll.

I didn't realize they were friends.

Of course he caught her eye.

It's probably not like that. . . .

It doesn't matter that Lana knows Stephen. But maybe that's why she wanted to help me. Maybe he told her about me. Told her about my family. That makes more sense. But it doesn't mean I like seeing her in a photo with him. Even if they are standing five people apart.

Don't be jealous. You don't even want Stephen.

I plug my phone into the charger and lie back under my covers. If Maddi can sleep all day, then I will too.

I shut my eyes and fall back asleep, trying not to think about all the shit that's flooding through my head.

Charlotte

When I was seven, we went to Disneyland.

We were such a happy family then.

Mom.

Dad.

Maddi.

We were whole. Everything felt so shiny and alive. The love we had for each other was so real it was like another person in the room.

Sometimes I think about that trip, and I think and think about all the things that happened, things that I probably looked past. That I missed.

The way Dad spoke to Mom.

The way Mom looked at Dad.

Were they happy? *Were* they normal? Did *they* feel the love that I felt?

Did he hate her then? Did he hate her enough to kill her?

Maddi and I rode Space Mountain over and over. Mom and Dad wouldn't get on it with us till the last day, when we finally convinced them to.

"We'll go, but just this once," Dad said. We stood in line and waited our turn. It was summer, and the California air was dry and sweet. Nothing like Massachusetts.

The sun beat down on our heads, and I was glad that Dad had gotten us all matching Disneyland baseball hats. Mine was pink, and Maddi's was light blue.

When we got on the ride, Mom sat by Dad and Maddi sat by me. We were in rows of two.

The roller coaster zipped up and down in the dark. The turns were sharp and my belly was filled with butterflies. I could hear Maddi laughing next to me at every turn.

When we came around the last corner, I saw a flash of light, and I knew it was a picture being taken of us.

A picture of our happy family.

Together.

Enjoying our vacation. Filling up our lives with memories.

When we got off the ride, all of us were laughing and smiling.

All of us but Mom. She was just standing there, sort of like a zombie. Like she wasn't all there or something. I'd seen that look on her face before, but not very often. I hoped she wasn't sick from the ride.

"I'll buy us one of the pictures," Dad said. We went over and he paid for a little framed photo of our family.

I stared at our picture and saw how happy all of us looked.

All of us except Mom.

Mom looked frightened.

Mom looked alone.

Charlotte

The buzzing of my phone wakes me up. I slept hard, and when I sit up, I feel dizzy and regret falling back asleep. My cell buzzes again. I grab it and see I have two unread texts from Lana. It's 3:04 and I'm sure Maddi is probably up and about. I'm surprised she let me sleep this long.

Before I get up, I open the first message from Lana.

Hey girl! You coming to school today?

And then the other one, sent a few hours later.

I found another letter. Do you guys want to come over?

How can there be another one?

What could it say?

Really? I write back.

She told me she'd tell me if she found more.

Where was this letter?

Does it matter?

I found it in Mom's medicine cabinet. Come over!

I walk into Maddi's room. She's sitting at her desk, painting her nails. For a minute, everything looks and feels normal. My sister just doing what she would have done on a Tuesday afternoon.

"You slept in," I say. Maddi smiles at me, but I can tell she's upset. I plop down on her bed. The room is chilly and I notice the window opened a crack. Maddi probably opened it because of the smell of the nail polish, but the cold breeze that comes in doesn't get rid of the strong scent of chemicals. It just makes the room more uncomfortable.

"What's wrong?" I say.

Maddi twists the nail polish shut and puts the bottle in the drawer. Her nails are painted dark blue. The color looks nice on her. I glance down at my fingernails. Chewed-up and dry. I don't remember when I picked up the habit, but I haven't been able to stop biting them in a long time.

"Dad. After you went to bed last night I heard him talking to Uncle Jake. He's planning something. I'm not sure what, but I think he wants to get rid of us just as much as Uncle Jake wants to take the house," she says. Her voice is angry, and the fake smile she wore a few moments ago is gone.

He wants us gone.

Of course he wants us gone.

"What did he say? What happened?"

Maddi sits next to me on the bed. "I didn't hear all of it. He said being here isn't healthy for us. That we need to go somewhere else. I don't know. I wish I could have caught more. I want to find out more about how Mom died. It all just works out too perfectly for them. None of this seems right anymore," she says.

I haven't seen Maddi like this in a long time. She's usually good at keeping her cool, but she's right. This isn't normal. This shouldn't be happening.

"They had something to do with it. I just fucking hate them so much," I say.

The letter.

Tell her about the other letter.

"Lana says she found another letter," I say. Although it doesn't seem as big of a deal now, knowing how worried Maddi is. Maybe these letters aren't helping.

"Seriously? When did she find it?" Maddi gets off the bed and goes to her closet and slips on a pair of rain boots. She looks almost silly. Dressed in a slinky T-shirt dress and her boots. Her legs are thin, and I wonder how much weight she's lost. I can't remember the last time she ate a real meal.

"She just texted me. She said we could come over and check it out," I say, holding out my phone for Maddi to see. She does a heavy sigh and then grabs her coat and zips it up.

"It's supposed to snow. Go get your coat and we'll head over."

In the car, I can tell that Maddi doesn't want to do it—to go to Lana's. And I don't either. This isn't fair, or fun, for anyone. She's stressed about yesterday and the whole house thing, and now this.

Why couldn't Mom have sent the letters to us?

Why didn't she tell us what was going on?

"I don't get this girl, Charlotte. You were just there yesterday. How did she not have the note then?" Maddi speeds down the road. It's started to snow again. Little flakes hit the windshield. She turns on the wipers and the flakes disappear.

Outside it's cold and gray. A little sad, too. Cars that pass us run through slush and ice and I watch it splash up on their tires.

We pass the old smoke shop, and as always I think of Mom. It makes my heart ache. I miss her so much. Sometimes it's hard to talk about it out loud. Especially when Maddi is upset. But I can't help but think about Mom. Think about her last few months. How hard things must have been for her. Knowing that Dad was cheating on her. That no one was there to support her after the baby died. I should have done more.

Why didn't I do more?

Did she know he wanted her gone?

Did she know they wanted her dead?

We pull up to Lana's house, and there's an old van parked in the driveway. It makes me realize how little her house is compared to ours.

Maddi and I get out and head to the front door. When we get there, Lana's mom opens the door as if she was waiting for us.

"Girls. Oh my God, you both look so much like her," she says. Before I know what's happening she reaches over and hugs me, then hugs Maddi.

No one has ever said that I look like my mother.

I don't look like my mother.

She's full of shit too. What is it with these people?

I try to ignore the feeling in my gut when she talks, but it's hard.

"I'm Stephanie. I went to the same school as your mom. I didn't spend much time with her, but you two are bringing flashbacks of my high school years," she says. I glance at Maddi. If they didn't hang out much, why would Mom write to her?

"Come inside, Lana's told me all about you two," Stephanie says.

Did they connect later in life? I fight the urge to ask Stephanie about the letters. But I know if I do, Lana might not give the new one to me.

How do you know that?

Lana's had to be so secretive with them. There's probably a reason.

Maddi and I follow Stephanie into the house. That same smell of incense hits me.

I know I told Lana to tell me if she found more letters. I know she's trying to help. But why does it have to be a secret? Is it because she's been snooping through her mom's stuff? Is there something else? Is there a letter we *aren't* supposed to see?

Before, I liked it here. The smell, the style, the warmth. Not today. Today the peppery smell of incense bothers me even more than it did last time. Gets under my skin and makes me want to scratch my arms. Makes my eyes water.

I glance over at Maddi. She looks stressed, and even more annoyed than I feel. At least I'm not the only one.

Something isn't right.

"Lana, your ladies are here!" Lana's mom shouts, then turns to us and asks, "Can I get you anything? It's almost dinnertime. Would you like me to whip you up a snack?"

Stephanie looks just like an aged version of Lana. She even has on a long bright yellow dress. Her hair is in a beehive and her eyes are bright blue. Crystal blue. Ice blue.

"I think we're okay," Maddi says. When she glances at me I know she's worried.

About Jake?

About this freak of a mother and her freak of a daughter.

"Mom, are you being weird?" Lana comes out of her bedroom. She has her hair in the same beehive. The two of them look like cartoon characters.

"Nice hair," I say before I can stop myself.

Maddi tries not to laugh, and I'm glad I said it. Her smile calms me down a little.

"Very funny. Mom and I were practicing something new." Lana touches her hair. Her nails are blood red.

Bitch.

Stop.

"Darling, I'm just getting to know them. It was such a pity when I found out what happened to your mom," Stephanie says. Only when she says this, it feels forced. Not sincere.

I want to tell her I've never heard of her, that Mom never mentioned her, but I don't. I just bite my tongue and nod.

"It is," Maddi says. Her smile is gone and I can hear the anger in her voice.

She doesn't trust them.

That's because there's something wrong with them.

"Well, I'll let you be. Let me know if you need anything," Stephanie says. Then she walks out.

"Come to my room. We can smoke and have some tea, how does that sound?" Lana says. She disappears into the kitchen and reappears with a jug of iced tea and glasses. What is it with this girl and beverages? And smoking? Doesn't she need a clear head from time to time?

By the end, Mom didn't have a clear head.

It's not the same, Mom was in pain. She was hurting.

Maddi and I follow Lana into her bedroom and sit on the floor.

On her bed, I see it.

The letter.

I see Maddi see it. She reaches over and squeezes my hand.

Knowing that Mom wrote that letter makes me feel closer to her. Like she's nearby. Like she's with us.

Lana closes the door behind her and hands us each a glass.

"It's a cocktail," she says, and then laughs. Her laugh is so pleasant. So pretty, but somehow it's almost painful too.

Painfully annoying.

Maybe she is a real friend.

Stop trying to convince yourself.

Maddi takes a sip of the tea and then sets the glass on Lana's nightstand.

"I'm driving. I won't be drinking any cocktails or smoking any weed," she says. "Could we just read the letter already?"

There's that tone again.

"All right, all right," Lana says. She hands the letter to Maddi. "I thought you'd want to hang out for a little bit, but I understand."

When she says this I wonder if she's lonely. If she has any real friends.

She must.

But who?

Maddi grabs the letter out of Lana's hand. I watch her face as she reads, and by the end of it, she's crying.

She hands the letter to me.

"Is it bad?" I ask.

Maddi shakes her head. "No, it's amazing. I just miss her so much."

Me too.

So much.

Charlotte

DEAR STEPHANIE,

SORRY I HAVEN'T WRITTEN IN A WHILE. THINGS ARE CRAZY AT MY HOUSE RIGHT NOW. CHARLIE HAS BEEN MADE CHEER CAPTAIN. I'M SO PROUD OF HER I CAN HARDLY STAND IT. MY OLDEST, MADDI, IS STILL WINNING GAME AFTER GAME OF BASKETBALL. THAT GIRL HAS SO MUCH TALENT.

HOW ARE YOU AND LANA DOING? HAVE YOU FOUND A HOUSE DOWN THIS WAY YET? IS LANA HANDLING THE NEWS ABOUT MOVING OKAY? IT MUST BE HARD FOR HER.

HOME LIFE HAS GOTTEN WORSE. I KNOW THE AFFAIR IS STILL HAPPENING, EVEN AFTER ANDREW AND I TALKED ABOUT IT. FOR A WHILE I REALLY BELIEVED THAT HE HAD STOPPED. BUT I WAS WRONG.

MY HEART IS BROKEN IN THIS HOUSE. BUT I'M SO GLAD TO HAVE MY DAUGHTERS. AND I'M SO GLAD TO HAVE A FRIEND LIKE YOU.

HOPE TO SEE YOU SOON.

WITH MUCH LOVE,
SARAH

She knew about the affair.

"I need fresh air." I stand up and shove past Maddi and head for the door. The house is cramped and there isn't enough room for me and my thoughts and everyone else. Lana and Maddi follow me.

Of course she knew.

"Why didn't she ever talk to us about it?" I say to Maddi when we're on the back porch. It's a covered porch with three small space heaters and a table with chairs. I sit down and try to feel the tiny bit of heat coming off the heaters. Maddi and Lana sit next to me. Maddi scoots close to me.

It's bitterly cold out here, but at least I can breathe. At least I can *think*.

Most of the backyard is dirt, with small patches of grass scattered about. Frost hangs on the bits of grass, making them shiny like crystals. The yard is a little trashy, Mom would have hated it. I wonder if Lana even notices how it looks.

Two large icicles hang from the roof a few feet from us.

You could stab someone with those.

Stop.

"Because she didn't want us to hate Dad," Maddi says.

Is that why?

"I hate to think that she was so sad before she died," I say.

Mom struggled with a lot of things, but thinking about her feeling alone or sad makes my skin crawl and my heart ache.

Lana gives me a frowny face and then reaches over and squeezes my hand. Maddi sees it and gives me "the look." The look that says "Why Are We Here?"

She officially hates Lana.

I think that's true.

"We should probably just go home now," Maddi says.

She looks at her feet. The old worn-out rain boots Mom gave her a few years back. Her feet are probably warm. I regret wearing my Vans. My toes feel like little ice cubes and my socks are wet from the snow.

"So soon? Don't you ladies want another drink? I bet Mom is almost done with dinner," Lana says. She doesn't sound like she cares if we go or stay, but I still feel guilty leaving. I didn't stick around yesterday, either. And the last thing I want is for her to think we're using her for the letters.

We are.

It isn't fair she gets those letters and we don't.

How many more are there?

"I think we're okay. I've got to get up early," Maddi says. She stands up and dusts the back of her pants off. "Are there any more, Lana? Any more letters?" She folds her arms across her chest, and I can tell she's ready to bolt. Ready to get out of here forever.

"I don't know. After I found that one I searched all of Mom's drawers again and didn't find anything else. I bet that's all," Lana says. She smiles when she says this, but I see something else hidden behind her smile. Is she annoyed? Does she even care?

This is a joke to her.

At least she told us. She didn't have to.

"We really do appreciate you doing this. Finding these and telling us. I hope you don't get in trouble for taking them," Maddi says.

"My mom might be pissed if she found out, but she's so

197

busy right now. I doubt she'll ever notice," Lana says, looking at her nails.

"I'm going to go start the car. Charlotte, want to meet me out front?"

I nod. Maddi walks around the side of the house like she's in a rush to get away from Lana.

She probably is.

She's mad at me.

"She doesn't like me," Lana whispers.

I look at her and shrug.

Lana's right. But that's not something I want to get into.

"Maddi likes everyone," I say.

Maddi does like everyone.

Everyone who deserves to be liked.

"Well, just as long as *you* like me," Lana says. Then she smiles.
I feel my stomach clench again, like I might be sick.

Why?

Why am I feeling this?

Gut feelings are usually true.

Charlotte

"I think there's something wrong with her," Maddi says as we're driving home.

I knew it was coming.

Just a matter of time.

Maddi drives slow, with her window down. She puffs on her Juul every few seconds. The whole car feels like a big ball of stress.

"She's been nothing but nice to me," I say.

Lana's been the only person to really talk to me since I've gone back to school.

Cat has, but she's just doing it because she feels obligated. Right?

Right?

"Doesn't it seem odd that she would keep those letters from me?" Maddi says. She turns the car down our street and pulls up in front of the house.

Jake's rental car is in the driveway. So is Amber's BMW.

"I keep telling you, it was probably because you guys don't have any classes together. You're older."

That isn't really an excuse. But I say it anyway. For some

reason, I don't want there to be a reason Lana's my friend. I just want her to like me.

"It all seems very fishy," Maddi says. She looks over at me and I know she can see the little bit of hurt on my face.

And I am a little bit hurt. Why can't I have a friend?

"That doesn't mean I hate her, Charlotte. It just means I'm going to keep her at arm's length. So should you."

I nod as Maddi gets out of the car.

She's right.

But maybe she's wrong.

But maybe she's right.

Sometimes when I dream, I imagine bodies.

Blood. Skin. Bones.

Bodies everywhere.

I stare at them, the people who are dead, the souls that once lived inside these bodies, but I'm not afraid. I know that they're in a better place.

All it took was a little bit of courage and a knife, a hammer, an ax.

They're in a much better place.

Charlotte

After everyone goes to bed, I drive to Stephen's house. I don't know why, but I have to see him.

It's been a while since I've driven, so I cruise down the streets slowly. Like the neighborhood creep.

He's going to think you're crazy.

I don't care anymore.

The streets are dark and empty. The snow falls, but it's light and fluffy. Reminds me of the type of snow I used to love.

Before.

Before all of this started.

Before all of this happened, and I was in love, and happy, and things were easy.

But were they easy?

I pull up in front of Stephen's and see that all the lights are off except for a very dim one in one of the windows.

Stephen's window.

What do I do now? Knock on the window?

Yeah, that's normal.

I pull out my cell phone and send him a text.

Are you awake?

It's the first time I've contacted him since the funeral. My heart starts to race as I wait for his response.

He doesn't want to see me. He wants to move on with his life.

But I can't move on.

I am. What's up?

My heart jumps.

I'm outside. Wanna go for a drive?

I sit for what feels like an hour waiting for him to respond. He doesn't want to see me. He doesn't want anything to do with me. Not after all the shit I've put him through. Not after all the awful things I've done to him.

But then the front door opens and there he is.

He's like a dream as he walks toward my car. A dream I wish I would never wake up from.

He gets in the car and I swear I can't breathe.

Is he real? Is it really him?

"Charlotte," he says. I look at him and see he has tears in his eyes. I'm already crying.

"I've missed you so much," I say.

He reaches over and hugs me. I breathe him in and realize I've missed everything. His smell, his skin, the way he rests his forehead against mine.

He pulls away after a minute and stares at me.

What's he looking at?

Probably trying to find out which part of me has lost it and which part hasn't.

"What happened?" he says. His eyes are locked on mine. His are so brown they're almost black.

What *did* happen?

Why did I do what I did?

Why did seeing him make me lose it so much that day?

We both know it wasn't anything he did.

I don't answer him. Just look at the floor of the car. It needs to be vacuumed, but other than that it's spotless.

"Charlotte? Look at me. One day we're together and the next we're not. Why?" Stephen says. I can hear he's frustrated with me in his voice. And he has a right to be. I've been silent for months.

Didn't I come over here to talk to him?

To tell him how much I still love him?

To tell him the truth about everything?

"I'm sorry," I say.

Sorry. Sorry. Sorry.

"You don't need to apologize. You just need to tell me what happened," Stephen says. He reaches over and grabs my hand.

Just like the old days. When we'd drive and hold hands. When we'd turn on old songs and belt them out the windows. When we'd play Never Have I Ever on the way to school. When we just were.

Together.

"I don't know what happened," I finally say. And it's the truth.

You snapped.

You went nuts.

You pushed everyone who loves you away.

"Why haven't you spoken to me? Why did you dump me? Why did you put me through all this?" Stephen says. His voice cracks and I wonder if he wants to yell at me. I wouldn't blame him if he did.

Just tell him the truth.

But what is the truth?

"Stephen, I couldn't see anyone. Not you, not my friends, not anyone. I don't know what got into me at the funeral, and I regret it. I don't know what happened." I take another deep breath. "I need to tell you something serious about my mom."

He's going to think you're nuts.

He's going to listen to you because he loves you.

How do you know he still loves you?

I guess I don't.

"What is it?" he says. "Tell me. I've needed to know for months what's been going on. I've been left in the dark, left alone."

I *have* left him in the dark. I haven't explained anything to him. And maybe that's because I haven't known what to say.

You can say it now. You can fix this.

"I don't know why I'm here tonight. But listen, I need you to promise me you won't think I'm crazy," I say.

How can he promise that?

Stephen just nods.

"Promise me, Stephen."

"I promise. Tell me what's going on." He pulls his hand away from me. His voice has a harsh edge now. We didn't fight very often, but when we did, his voice always had that edge.

I've dragged this out way too long.

Why am I doing this to him? To myself?

"I think she was murdered," I say. That's when I start really crying. Because saying it out loud, I know it must be true. That it has to be true.

That my father murdered my mother.

And if he didn't do it, then Amber must have. People don't just die. People don't just drop dead.

Your heart doesn't just stop.

"What?" Stephen says.

Does he believe me?

How could he?

"I think my mom was murdered. I've thought it for a while, and we're starting to find proof."

There's so much proof. It's undeniable.

Isn't it?

Is it?

"Your mom? Who would murder your mother?" Stephen says.

I still can't tell if he believes me or not. But I don't care. He needs to know. Everyone needs to know. My father isn't who he says he is. His fiancée isn't who she's pretending to be.

They aren't who everyone thinks they are.

They're phony.

They're murderers.

"My father. Amber. I think it was them. They were having an affair, and Maddi and I think they killed her," I say. The more I talk, the more it has to be true. It's true. It has to be. "He's marrying her, too. They got engaged. He's moving and selling the house to my uncle. My dad is erasing everything about Mom. As if she never existed."

But why?

For money?

For what?

For love?

"Shit, Charlotte. I'm so sorry," Stephen says. Then he pulls me into a hug and kisses me. It's like a spark on my mouth and it reminds me how much I've missed him. Missed being touched and held and loved.

How much I love him.

Maddi

I call Charlotte's phone three times before I give up. I know that she's fine, but I need to show her what I've found.

One of Mom's journals. Packed away in a box of cookbooks. It's almost as if she *told* me to look in there. I've had it hidden for a couple of days. But tonight, I decide to read it.

I sit on my bedroom floor. It's dark, but I have my bedside lamp on. I don't want to wake Dad. Anger runs through my body like hot lava. I'm so tired of feeling this rage, and I almost regret opening the journal. Reading Mom's private thoughts. I'm on a page dated several months before Mom lost the baby. She was still pregnant, and I try to picture where I might have been when she was writing this.

HE'S BEEN SLEEPING WITH HER. I THOUGHT THAT HAVING THE BABY WOULD FIX ALL OF THIS. THE AFFAIRS ALWAYS STOPPED WHEN I WAS PREGNANT, SO I REALLY HOPED IT WOULD BE THE SAME WITH THIS BABY. BUT IT WASN'T. I JUST WASN'T EXPECTING HIM TO BE CHEATING WITH HER. SHE'S SO YOUNG AND NAIVE. I HIRED HER, AND HE TOOK HER AS HIS . . . WHAT, MISTRESS? I DON'T EVEN KNOW WHAT TO CALL HER.

I slam the book shut. Try my hardest not to scream.

"Was he always a cheater? Even in the beginning?" I say aloud. I don't like to cry. I *hate* to cry. But there's nothing left inside me but screams and tears.

Everything was a lie. Everything between them was a *lie*.

"Why didn't you tell me? Why? We were so close," I say.

HE'S ALWAYS MADE EXCUSES WHEN I'VE CAUGHT HIM BEFORE. I WAS TOO MUCH FOR HIM, OR WORK GOT OVERWHELMING. BUT THIS TIME AROUND I DON'T THINK HE CARES. I THINK HE WANTS ME OUT OF HIS LIFE. TO LEAVE ME AND THE GIRLS. MY HEART IS SHATTERED, EVEN THOUGH I KNOW I SHOULD HAVE SEEN THIS COMING.

How could he hurt her like this? How could he do this to her? To our family?

"He's always been a liar. Since day one," I say to Mom.

He blamed everything on *her*. When he was the problem.

I pick up my phone and call Charlotte again. Knowing that this news is going to break her.

Charlotte

When I get back from seeing Stephen, Maddi is in my room, waiting for me.

"Where have you been?" she says. She's sitting on the floor with a book in her hands. It must be four in the morning—I'm surprised she's even awake.

"I went to see Stephen. To apologize for everything that happened," I say. I know why she sounds mad. I didn't respond to her texts or answer her calls.

"Well, I wish you hadn't ignored me, because I have some news," Maddi says. She hands me the book.

One of Mom's journals!

"How did you get this?" I open the book and see Mom's handwriting. Her block letters. The *i*'s and *l*'s that look that same.

We've needed this for months, and yet now that I have it, I feel weird looking at it. Like it's wrong. Invasive.

Mom's personal journal.

Her secrets.

Her hopes and dreams.

"I sort of lied to you. I found this a few days ago," Maddi says. When she says this, it's like a gut punch.

"What? You lied? Why?" I say. Before I even realize it, I'm shaking.

Calm down.

She fucking lied!

"Before you get upset just wait a minute. You have to hear me out. I found this one and I was worried about how you'd react. But I didn't read it until tonight. I just couldn't do it. It felt wrong. I'm sorry. You've been so stressed," Maddi says. "I figured I could go through it first so you didn't have to. But Jesus, Charlotte, you're not going to believe this."

I stand there and stare at Maddi, trying to figure out why. Why she would lie to me.

I have been stressed.

Who hasn't?

"I don't understand. What else are you keeping from me? What else is there? Are you on *their* side now?" I say. I try my hardest to keep my voice low. Maddi stands up and grabs my hands.

"Of course not. I know it doesn't make sense to you. I'm sorry I lied, I'm sorry I kept this from you. I had to read it first, and I'm glad I did. Because what Mom wrote is so upsetting, Charlotte." Maddi talks fast, and I can hear in her voice that she's sincere. But it doesn't change the way I feel. The sick feeling that's growing inside me. I sit down on my bed and put my face in my hands and take a deep breath.

Maybe she is trying to protect us.

It doesn't make it hurt less.

"Charlotte, he'd been cheating on her the whole time. Almost their entire marriage. He painted Mom as some sort of nutjob, when the whole time he was the problem," Maddi says.

What is she talking about?

She's been lying to me.

It wasn't just Amber he was cheating with?

What?

I grab the journal and flip through the pages until I find an entry dated a year and a half back.

HE HASN'T SPOKEN TO ME IN DAYS. I KNOW WHAT'S GOING ON, BUT I JUST DON'T HAVE THE HEART TO TELL THE GIRLS. I LOVE HIM, I REALLY DO, BUT I'VE FALLEN OUT OF LOVE. THE LIES, THE DRINKING. I DON'T THINK I CAN TAKE IT MUCH LONGER. AMBER WAS A PART OF THE FAMILY, AND NOW I'M NOT SURE WHO SHE IS.

I slam the book shut and toss it next to me on the floor. Suddenly my eyes are burning from tears and exhaustion.

"I don't even know him anymore," I say. My heart aching for Mom. Aching for our family.

"I know. I can't believe it," Maddi says.

The feeling of helplessness washes over me, and I realize that it really is just me and Maddi. Jake isn't here to help, and Dad wants to get rid of us. Get us out of his life so he can move on with his new wife.

Stop mind reading.

It's true.

"I know this is hard," Maddi says. "And it just makes everything worse. But what we really need to focus on is what we're going to do about Jake. What his plan is." It's as if she read my mind.

Uncle Jake has only been here a couple of days, and our hopes of getting him to help have gone to shit. He's not supposed to stay much longer, but I'm starting to worry he'll never leave. That he'll stay until he gets what he wants.

He's going to screw us over, that's what he's going to do.

Maybe he was just pretending. Maybe he does want to help.

And maybe we're surrounded by liars.

Surrounded by liars, cheaters, and fakes.

Maddi

I sit on the floor of my room and go through Mom's journal. I read her words over and over to make sure there isn't something I've missed.

"I wish you'd told me what was going on," I say out loud. I would do anything for her to respond. For her to tell me it's okay, that she forgives me.

After a few minutes, I close Mom's journal and stand up. It's early, probably close to sunrise. I can't sleep. I go to the living room, and I'm surprised to see Amber on the couch, reading.

"What are you doing?" she says when she sees me. I glance at the clock above the TV. It's 4:38. Before, when Amber worked for Mom, she'd wake up around five to get breakfast and coffee started. I guess she never stopped doing that.

She looks much younger. Without the makeup, or the wine, or the dirty side glances me and Charlotte are always getting from her. Right now, Amber just looks like a girl. Sometimes I forget that she's only a few years older than me.

"I was going to watch TV, but never mind," I say. I turn to go back to my room. To get away from her.

"Maddi, wait a minute. Sit down for a second, I want to talk to you," she says.

I've never been close with Amber. Never had much of a relationship with her. I sort of saw her the same way Mom did. As someone who was here to help. Charlotte considered Amber family, but I've never felt that way.

"What?" I say. I fold my arms across my chest and stare at her. She has an old blanket that Mom made on her lap and light pink slippers on. She looks comfortable, *too* comfortable. I can't imagine how Mom would feel, seeing Amber like this. The home-wrecker that she is.

"Despite how you may feel about me, I am really worried about your baby sister. She's not herself anymore, and it's pretty concerning. Your dad and I think she needs to go back to therapy. At least."

As she speaks, I feel my jaw drop, and it's everything I can do not to rip Mom's blanket off her lap, ask her who in God's name does she think she is.

After what she did to Mom.

I take a deep breath and try to calm myself down. Anger coursing through my entire body.

"I don't care about your *concerns*," I say, using air quotes. "You're not a part of this family. You can pretend like you are all you want, but you never will be."

Amber smiles and then stands up. Mom's blanket falls to the ground, and Amber steps on it as she walks closer to me.

"You act like you love your sister, but it's pretty obvious you don't give a fuck about what she's struggling with. At least I'm trying to help. You're just watching her turn into a basket case, just like your mom. You're *letting* it happen."

When Amber says this, something takes over and I shove her, hard. She stumbles to the floor.

"Stay out of my life, and leave my sister alone," I say.

Amber quickly gets back up and grabs my arm tight. I try to jerk away from her, but her grip is too strong. I can feel her nails digging into my skin. She's about four inches taller than me, and weighs more than I do.

"I'm not kidding, Maddi. There's something going on. And if she doesn't get help, we *will* send her away."

She holds on to my arm for a moment longer and then lets go.

"*We?* You don't make decisions for this family," I say, stepping closer to her. So close I can smell the ChapStick on her lips.

"Your mom is gone," Amber says. "Let her go. Let your dad live his life." She has that fake smile on her lips. Like she knows I can't do anything about it. About *any* of it.

"You're a horrible person," I say. I turn away from her and go back to my room. Shocked that that actually just happened. That she would say those things about Charlotte.

"She's the one who needs to go," I say out loud. "She's the one who needs to be sent away."

Charlotte

When I get to school the next day, Stephen is waiting for me by my locker. I'm almost surprised when I see him. Like maybe last night was just a dream and I imagined the whole thing. He's wearing a green sweater and his hair is messy. But he still looks cuter than ever.

Did he sleep last night?

Did he think of me?

"Charlotte," he says with a smile. That smile I've missed so hard these last few months. Maddi had to convince me to go to school this morning, and seeing Stephen now makes me happy that I did.

Does he love me again?

Has he forgiven me?

"Hi," I say. My voice comes out quiet and I remind myself of a child. Afraid of the future, afraid of what could happen.

He grabs my hand. It sends a shock wave through my body.

We haven't touched in public since the funeral.

Since I screamed at him at the funeral.

"I've missed you," he whispers. Then he squeezes my hand and walks away.

Where is he going?

Where is he going!

I watch him walk all the way down the hall. I stand there and stare. I just stare and stare. The first bell rings. Then the second.

I sit down on the floor and stare down the hall where Stephen went.

The grime and dust cover my leggings, but I don't care. I stay where I am.

He is gone.

He's gone from me.

I've lost him.

Charlotte

"Charlotte. Charlotte! Snap out of it."

When I open my eyes, Cat is bending over in front of me. Her face close to mine. I can smell the bronzer she's used on her skin and see the shine of her highlighter on the apples of her cheeks.

"Oh my God! Are you okay? I just walked out to use the bathroom and saw you. Did you hit your head?"

Did I?

Did I faint?

What happened?

"I'm not sure."

I look up at Cat.

My closest friend.

My best friend.

The person I used to go everywhere with. And now she's like a stranger to me. Someone I know nothing about.

Cat pulls a bottle of water from her bag and hands it to me.

"Drink some water. Maybe you're dehydrated."

I take the bottle and sip from it. The water is lukewarm and makes my stomach turn.

Cat sits down next to me on the floor and leans back against the lockers.

Back in middle school, we always ate our lunch in the hallway. We'd watch people walk by and talk about who would make the best date for a dance, or who was the worst at cheer, or whatever else. We haven't had lunch together in a long time, and we haven't been this close in months.

"What's going on with you?" Cat says. She's using a soft voice, which is something I've only heard her do a handful of times. Mostly when she's upset or embarrassed.

"I miss my best friend. I miss the old Charlotte. I miss laughing and gossiping and going to parties. I miss how we were before everything happened with your mom," she says.

I miss her too.

So much has happened. She wouldn't understand.

"Do you hate me? Are we just done?" Cat says. The hurt in her voice shines through like the sun. "I don't know how to make you feel better, but I want to help, Charlotte."

I want to tell her everything that's happened. Not just with Dad, but with Lana and Stephen and even Maddi. I want to tell her that I'm afraid of my home life and that Uncle Jake was supposed to help, but he's making it worse.

"No. I don't hate you. I just, I'm not feeling like myself right now," I say.

At least that's the truth. At least that's something I can admit to.

My head pounds so hard I can hear it. I take another sip of

water, even though I can't tell if it's making me feel worse or better.

"Because of Stephen?" Cat says. Like somehow she knows about last night.

Would he tell her?

Why would he tell her?

"What do you mean?" I say.

I still feel Stephen's lips on mine, still smell him in my hair. We were together just a few hours ago. Would he have had time to talk to Cat? To tell her my secrets?

"You seem so lonely. I don't know. I'm worried about you," Cat says. Then she stands up and holds her hand out to me.

"Let me take you home. You need rest."

I stare at her for a long time. But then I shake my head.

"I'm going to stay here awhile. I'll get back to class soon," I say.

The pounding in my ears grows louder, and my body starts to shake. I wonder if this is what a migraine feels like. Mom complained about getting them a lot toward the end.

Depression hurts from the inside out.

I fold my arms across my chest so Cat doesn't notice me shaking.

Just go with her.

Go with her.

Go.

Cat stands there, disappointment and pain spread across her face. She must know that our friendship won't ever be the same. Won't ever go back to the way it was. That it might even be over.

I lean my head against the lockers and shut my eyes. I don't want to look at her. It makes me feel too bad. Makes me hurt for her.

I wait until I hear Cat walk away before I crawl back into my mind and drift off again.

I could do it.

    End all of this. Make the pain stop.

    It wouldn't take much.

    It wouldn't take much, and you could do it.

    End all the pain for good.

Charlotte

"Charlotte? Charlotte!" Maddi says.

What's wrong with me?

I open my eyes again, only this time it's not Cat who is standing in front of me, it's my sister. The salt from my tears makes my eyes sting. Sleeping in the halls isn't allowed, crying in the halls is even worse.

But was I asleep?

Cat was just here. I was just talking to her.

But then she left. You made her leave you alone.

That was only a few seconds ago.

Wasn't it?

"Are you all right? Cat told me she thought you fainted or something. I almost called nine-one-one," Maddi says. I can hear the panic in her voice. I look up at her. She has the same dark circles under her eyes that I do. Her arms have gotten thinner, and her skin looks dry. Probably from the cold. There's a small stain on the front of her dress. It's orange. I reach out and touch it.

Maddi stands above me, the look of fear spread across her face. Behind her are the school nurse and Lana.

"I think we need to take you to the hospital," Nurse Carmen says.

I'm not going to a doctor.

You sound like Mom.

It was just a nap.

Was that all it was?

"She must have fallen asleep. We had family come in from out of town late last night," Maddi lies. My legs feel weak and cold. The ringing from the headache has gotten worse.

The hallway stinks and the fluorescent lights make everything look yellow. I can hear them humming above my head, and I wonder how I never noticed it before.

"It looks like she passed out," Lana says. "I was at my locker and she was just sitting there all starry-eyed."

She wasn't here when I fell asleep.

I never saw her.

How does she know if I fainted or not?

Maddi glances at Lana and then back at me.

The stink of the hallway is overpowering now, and the smell hits my nose like a fist. I feel like I'm going to throw up. I look around for the bottle of water that Cat gave me. It's spilled on the floor next to where I'm sitting.

"Just be quiet for a second," Maddi says to Lana. Then she leans in close to my face. I can smell her breath. Cinnamon gum. I grab her hand, and she helps me to my feet.

"What's the last thing you remember?" Maddi says. We slowly walk toward the door of the school, just trying to get away. But Nurse Carmen and Lana follow us. My knees shake with every step, and I wish my pants were baggier to hide it. I know it's noticeable.

"I was talking to Cat. She was just here," I say. Though I'm not sure if I imagined it or not. I'm starting to second-guess myself.

I can hear Nurse Carmen still talking about how I need to see a doctor, but Maddi and I ignore her and keep walking.

"I remember Stephen, too," I say. My eyes fill with tears again. I start crying right there. He walked away from me. He ran away from me. He left me.

You left him first.

I had to.

"What about him?" Lana says. She jogs up next to me and Maddi. She sounds defensive, like she knows he's done something to me.

Why does she need to be around?

Because we're friends.

You're not friends.

"Let's just go home," Maddi says, ignoring Lana. "You need to rest, Charlotte. You had a long night,"

"Did Stephen talk to you? What did he say?" Lana asks. She reaches over and stops me. Her hand cold on my arm.

"Lana, leave her alone. What does it matter?" Maddi pulls me closer.

They both grab at me and I feel like I'm being torn in two directions.

My sister and my friend.

My only friend.

Only sister.

Family.

"I'm just curious is all. Relax, Miss Maddi," Lana says. Her voice comes out condescending and mean, and I know Maddi notices.

Maddi stops and stares at Lana. I can see the anger in her eyes and I know she's about to go bitch mode. We're standing in front of the glass entryway. Cold air blows through the cracks and makes a high humming noise. It's always reminded me of a ghost screaming. I look outside and watch the trees move. Like they're trying to get away from the winter air, too.

"Look, I understand you're trying to be friends with Charlotte, but right now I need you to back off," Maddi says. She takes a step closer to Lana.

Lana crosses her arms and looks at me.

"Do you want me to back off, Charlie?" She stands there and stares at me. Today she wears skintight pants and a crop top. The top is pleather and shiny. No one in their right mind would wear something like that to school, let alone in the winter.

She's not in her right mind.

Maybe she's the only one here who is.

"I think I gotta go home. I'll talk to you tomorrow," I say. I need to be asleep in my bed. In my house. With a warm blanket and dim lights. I need to rest.

I haven't rested in so long.

All you've done is rest. It's time to wake the fuck up.

"Whatever," Lana says, and then turns and walks away.

She's crazy.

She's just angry.

She's not right.

I follow Maddi out to the car, slipping on slush and ice.

"We're done with her. We got the letters. We got what we needed. I'll say this again, I do not trust her," Maddi says. I feel sick to my stomach, but the headache has started to go away.

Maddi gets in the car and slams the door shut. I get in the passenger seat and before I can buckle up, Maddi speeds out of the school parking lot. She puffs on her Juul as she drives. "I don't trust her," she says again. She takes a sharp turn and my body moves with the car.

Don't puke.

Can't puke.

Don't puke.

I don't know what I want to do about Lana, but maybe Maddi is wrong about her. Or maybe I'm wrong about her.

"I don't think she meant any harm, Maddi. I think she's just trying to help," I say.

You don't believe that.

I don't believe that.

If you can't stay Cat's friend, why stay Lana's?

"I don't understand. Who is she? How does she have all this information? And where the hell did she come from when you passed out?"

Passed out?

Fell asleep?

It's a good question, but it's one I can't answer. Maybe Lana was following Stephen. Maybe she followed Cat, too.

"I don't know, Maddi. I'm tired of this day already," I say.

Maddi pulls into our driveway, and this time no one's car is there. Not Dad's, not Amber's, no one's.

"Where have they gone this early in the day?" Maddi says.

I just shrug.

Nothing is right anymore. Nothing is normal anymore.

The driveway is slick with ice, and I slip getting out of the car.

Fainting at school?

Blacking out?

What's wrong with me?

"Charlotte," Maddi says. She walks up next to me and grabs my shoulders. "I'm worried about you. I know you and Lana are friends, but I have a bad feeling about her. She isn't normal. Everything that's going on, it isn't normal."

I wasn't upset until Maddi says this. I wasn't angry until I hear her words. Even though I know she's right, something in me screams.

She's being a bitch.

She's not a bitch, she's right. Lana isn't normal.

You're not normal.

She's trying to control us. To control me.

"Whatever, Maddi. At least Lana didn't keep the letters from me." I pull away from her and walk inside.

The house feels lonely, and for a second I smell Mom's perfume. It reminds me of when I used to come home from school at the end of the day. She'd be waiting for me. Sometimes we'd take "sick" days together and go out and shop or get manicures. All before she got ill. All before the baby died. Before that, she was normal.

Or was she always paranoid?

Was she always just a little bit different?

Maddi walks past me and I watch her go into her room. She looks just like Mom.

"Why did she have to die?" I say. I don't even realize I've said it out loud until Maddi stops walking.

She looks at me and then shakes her head.

"She didn't have to die. None of this had to happen."

They killed her.

They killed our mom.

They killed our mom and left us to suffer.

Maddi goes into her room and shuts the door. I hear music turn on and I know she wants me to leave her alone. That she's probably overwhelmed, and I'm not helping any.

Because you're not being you.

No.

Yes.

I walk down the hall to the doorway of Mom's bedroom.

Of Dad and Amber's room.

The smell of Mom's perfume so strong it makes my eyes water.

I haven't smelled her perfume in so long.

Has Maddi been wearing it?

I walk into the room and look around. It's all so different.

Mom's comforter is gone, replaced with a dark duvet and black silk sheets. The walls have been painted dark blue. I remember Dad repainting the room, but I never really noticed how much he changed it until now. Whose idea was this?

Mom hated dark colors.

I walk over to Mom's vanity and sit down. The smell of her perfume is strongest here. And that's when I notice it.

The bottles.

The near-empty bottles.

She's been using them.

She's been wearing my mother's perfume.

How could she?

How could she?

Why would she?

I pick up one of the bottles and spray it on myself. Instead of Mom, I see Amber.

I see Amber when she was a part of the family. When she and Mom were friends. When she was like a sister. I see her, and then I picture her dead.

Chopped up on the bathroom floor. Strangled in the hallway. Beaten and bruised out in the garden.

If I could I would make her drink this bottle of perfume.

See how she likes it then.

I could kill her.

I could kill her. For what she did to Mom.

I look at myself in the mirror. Only it's not me. There's a stranger staring back.

"Why?" I say out loud. The stranger in the mirror starts to cry.

"Why?"

Because life isn't fair.

Because that's life.

Charlotte

"Tell me you love me," I said.

Me and Stephen sat out by the shore and watched the fishing boats pull in large nets of crab and shrimp.

I wondered what the fishermen's lives were like. Spending all day at sea, all day on the water.

The smell of salt was strong in the air, and a breeze brought the scent of fish.

Stephen wore a baggy sweater and had his arms around me. He was so warm. I snuggled in close to him and looked up at his eyes.

"Tell me you can't live without me," I said. Trying to sound dramatic.

Stephen laughed and I felt his chest move up and down.

"You know I love you, Charlotte. You're my life," he said.

His life.

Even at such a young age, I had found someone. I thought about how lucky I was. Lucky I didn't have to go searching for my person, because he'd found me, and he loved me.

Sometimes when I watched Mom and Dad, I wondered how

they were ever a match. If they ever shared moments with each other that made them believe true love was forever.

"I think we should run away together, when we turn eighteen," I said. The thought had never crossed my mind until that moment. But once it was there, I couldn't think of anything I wanted more. Being alone with Stephen. Maybe in a tropical place. With no winter, no drama, just each other.

"Don't be weird, Charlotte. I love it here. So do you. Why would we leave?" Stephen said.

I could really only think of a couple of reasons for running away, mostly because of Mom.

She was so sad. She wasn't herself anymore. Losing the baby had changed her, and sometimes I thought it might be easier not being around her for a while.

"I know I do. It's just a romantic thought is all," I said.

Stephen nodded.

I watched a boat in the distance sail toward the ocean.

I wondered where it was headed. If it was off to find a new life, new dreams, maybe start a new family.

I snuggled in close to Stephen.

"I'll be happy wherever you are," I said.

And I meant it.

Charlotte

I hear the front door and I know they're home.

All of them.

They're all enemies now. Uncle Jake, Amber, Dad. Even Alex. Pretending like she loved Mom. Like they were old friends. All of it bullshit.

Jake hasn't come to help his sister. He hasn't come to help us. He's come to take it all. To get rid of us. To send us away.

You have to do something.

But how?

I don't know. But something has to be done.

As I lie in bed I hear Dad laughing. They're in the kitchen. I can tell by the way their voices bounce off the walls.

"So that's why they called me," I hear Uncle Jake say, and I hear Dad laugh again. It's not a pleasant laugh, it's almost as if he's laughing at someone.

Laughing at me and Maddi.

They're laughing at us. I know they're laughing at us.

You don't know that.

Yes, I do.

"They've always had wild imaginations. Just like their mother.

You remember how Sarah was," Dad says, "always assuming the worst." His tone is friendly enough, but when he talks about Mom like that I cringe. Like she was just some nutty lady who came and went in the blink of an eye.

I hate them.

I hate him.

"They think you killed her," Jake says. "I guess they found rat poison in the house." When Jake says this, the room goes quiet. I hear someone move a chair.

Silence.

Silence, and then Amber. I hear her tone, but I can't hear what she says.

I get out of bed and open my bedroom door wider. I peek into the hall to make sure they can't see me and then I walk down the hall a few feet.

"Charlotte's had problems since before her mother died. Sarah and I used to talk about it all the time," Amber says.

Mom would never have talked to Amber about us. In the end, Mom wouldn't even look at Amber.

She's a liar.

"After Sarah died, it got worse. And now Charlotte's trying to pull Maddi into this mess," Dad says.

"That's heartbreaking," Alex says. I can tell by her tone that she's sincere. But it doesn't change the fact that she's in the room with them. Listening to them. Listening to their lies.

Maybe she's not like them. Maybe she and Mom really were friends.

No, they hate us.

They all hate you.

You.

You.

Me.

"She was seeing a therapist for a while, after Sarah passed away. But Charlotte said therapy made her feel worse," Dad says. He almost sounds sad. Maybe deep down he regrets what's happened with our family. What's happened between us.

Maybe I regret it too. But it's too late. It's all different now.

"Charlotte hasn't been the same since her mother died," Amber says, "and her sister isn't helping the situation. She's violent."

Maddi isn't violent.

How can they sit there and listen to this? How can Dad believe anything Amber says?

I want to run into the kitchen and scream in Amber's face.

Tell her that none of this is my fault. That all of this is *her* fault. That I'm the only sane one in this house. I'm the only one with my head screwed on.

This is all because of Amber. All of this is her fault.

But maybe it's not. Maybe it is *your fault.*

No.

Yes.

Maybe it's both our faults.

In my dreams it's all over.

Do dreams ever come true?

The pain is gone, and everything is sunshine again.

The garden is back to the way it was.

Everyone is happy and free.

No more stress. No more sadness. No more worries.

How do you make dreams come true?

Charlotte

I lie in bed for hours and think about what they said.

My blood boils, and it takes everything in my power not to go into the kitchen and have a meltdown in front of them. I try to focus on my breathing, something I learned from Nancy back when I was in therapy.

I want to go in and wake up Maddi. Tell her everything I heard. But I'm too angry to move. Too angry to speak even.

How could *I* be the crazy one? They're the ones who killed her. They're the ones who murdered Mom. He's the one who stopped loving Mom. Who blamed Mom for the baby dying. Who treated Mom like she didn't matter. Who treats *all of us* like we don't matter.

But we don't know that.

Yes, we do.

You don't really know anything.

They're just saying I'm crazy because of what happened at the funeral. But that doesn't make me crazy, does it?

Yes.

No.

Yes.

I pull out my cell phone and send a message to Lana.

Does a crazy person know they're crazy?

Why are you asking her?

Who else do I have?

She's only going to make things worse.

It's late, so I don't think she'll respond. But it's an honest question, isn't it?

How can you tell the difference between a crazy person and a sane person?

Isn't everyone a little crazy?

Doesn't everyone act a little strange from time to time?

Crazy is the new normal.

I lie in bed staring at my phone and decide to call Nancy.

Even though I don't see her anymore, she gave me her personal number in case I ever need to call her.

I dial the number and wait for her to pick up. Our last session didn't end well, but maybe she can help. Calm me down.

"Hello?" Her voice sounds the same.

"Nancy? I'm sorry to call so late. It's Charlotte. Do you have a minute?" My room starts to feel hot, and suddenly I'm second-guessing my decision to call her.

"Charlotte, of course. How are you? What's going on?" she says. I remember sitting in her office all those weeks ago. Right after Mom died. She let me cry for an hour straight. She listened to me. Maybe I was wrong to take my anger about Dad and Amber's relationship out on her.

"It's my dad. Or I guess my family. Everything I was worried about before is starting to happen. My dad and Amber are engaged. He's giving her everything of my mom's. Her jewelry from when she was a kid, her engagement ring, everything. And now he's trying to give my mom's house to my uncle. It's all so fucked up, and I'm starting to feel like I'm losing my mind," I say.

She's going to think I'm overreacting.

She's not going to get it.

"What else is going on? Why do you feel like you're losing your mind? This sounds like a lot to handle, Charlotte," Nancy says. Her voice is calm and understanding.

"You're not going to believe me. But I think he hurt my mom. That *they* hurt my mom. I've found evidence: pills, letters, *poison.* Your heart doesn't just stop, but that's all my dad ever says about how my mom died, that her heart stopped. What if he hurt her?" I lower my voice when I say this, even though I'm sure no one can hear me.

"What type of poison? Where did you find it? What letters? Slow down a little and tell me what's going on," Nancy says.

I could show her the letters.

Show her the pills. The poison.

Tell her the things Amber has said about Mom.

"Before Mom died, she complained about stomach pains. Maddi found rodent killer in the pantry, but Mom would have never used that. And our dad has never helped with the gardening and neither has Amber. They actually killed the garden. And we found drugs, too. Prescription drugs that can be deadly. And now it's like my dad is trying to replace Mom, like he *wanted* her dead or something."

Nancy is quiet for a moment. And then I hear her take a deep breath.

"Okay, the poison, or whatever. Can you think of any reason that would be in the house? Didn't you say your dad was remodeling the garden? Chopping down trees? Maybe he realized there was a problem with racoons or something," Nancy says.

She's trying to convince me that I'm wrong.

Or maybe she's trying to help me see things more clearly.

"He *was* chopping down trees. They've been remodeling on and off for months. Why would they have the poison inside, though? And what about the drugs? The lies? The *cheating?* None of it makes sense," I say, trying to keep my voice low.

"Charlotte, I'm sorry you have to go through this. Have you tried to speak to your father? Ask him about this? Maybe there's an explanation for the prescription pills. How is your sister handling this?"

I can't tell by her tone if she believes me, but she hasn't come outright and said she doesn't. Though I'm starting to realize, even if she does believe me, what can she do?

"He hates me now. He refuses to talk to me. It's a fight. I know it sounds far-fetched, but what if he's trying to get rid of me, too? Get me out of the picture because I'm a burden too?"

Being paranoid.

But he does want me gone.

"Charlotte, are you concerned for you and your sister's safety? All of this sounds really stressful. Maybe you and I should meet up. I'm free whenever you're ready. I can't tell you what you're feeling isn't valid, but if you are worried your dad is capable of something like that, maybe you need to get out of the house," Nancy says.

Does she believe me?

Does she think I'm lying?

I lie there in silence for what feels like an eternity. Not knowing what to say. Not knowing what the right move is.

"Charlotte, are you there? I really want to help you," Nancy says. She sounds kind, but tired now.

"Let me talk to Maddi," I say. "I'll let you go to sleep."

"Charlotte, this is a difficult situation you're in, but if you're scared for your safety, please let me help," she says.

"Let me talk to Maddi," I say again.

Nancy is still speaking on the other end of the line, but I hang up.

Maybe she believes me.

Maybe she doesn't.

But one thing's for sure. She knows something is wrong.

Charlotte

"He dumped me," Amber said. She plopped down on my bed. I'd been asleep, but she always walked in without knocking. She was pretty much family by that point, so I pretended I didn't care.

"Travis?" I said. My throat was dry and rough. I was still half-asleep, but I could tell she was upset.

"Yep. Said I'm too needy, whatever the fuck that means." I could tell she was drunk. Her words slurred and I felt sorry for her. She'd been having trouble with her boyfriend the last few months and couldn't figure out why.

"You want to sleep in here with me?"

My eyes had adjusted to the darkness and I could see her silhouette. Her hair was a little frizzy, and I could smell cigarette smoke on her coat.

Amber was a full-time live-in assistant by then. She'd been living with us for almost six months, so it wasn't unusual for her to be chatting with me like this. Every once in a while after she went out she'd sneak into my room and we'd talk. It was annoying sometimes, but I never told her that.

Amber nodded and then crawled into bed with me.

Maddi thought it was weird how close we were, but I didn't

care. Amber and I weren't as close as Maddi and me, but we were friends. I loved her.

"You'll find someone better, I promise," I said.

I always comforted Amber when she was going through a breakup, which was more often than not.

"I'm almost twenty-three. I should be in a real relationship by now. I can't live with you guys forever. Eventually I want to start my own family," she said.

I'd never thought about her finding a new job or moving out. But of course it made sense. Who would want to stay with us forever?

"You're young, you have years until you need to start a family," I said.

It was true. Mom got married young, yes. But nowadays women wait years before they start families. Being a woman doesn't just mean pushing out baby after baby anymore. It means independence, it means doing whatever the hell you want.

"Do you want to hear something kind of gross?" Amber said.

Amber had basically taught me everything I knew about sex and drugs and politics, everything. So there wasn't a lot she could say that would surprise me. I just wanted her to hurry up and stop talking so I could go back to sleep.

"Sure, what's gross?" I said. My eyes were heavy again and I was only half listening to her.

Amber giggled.

"What is it?" I said. I tried to add some annoyance to my tone. Just because she was a morning person didn't mean I was.

I had to get up for school. She just had to get up to wash some sheets and file some paperwork for Mom.

"Your dad is kinda hot. I'd probably hook up with him. That is, of course, if he wasn't married and stuff," she said.

When she said that, I was suddenly wide awake. I didn't want her near me anymore. I wanted to push her out of my room and slam the door in her face.

But she was only kidding.

Right?

Right?

Right?

So I didn't say a word. Just pretended I was asleep.

Charlotte

"Wake up. Wake up, Charlotte, we need to talk."

When I open my eyes, Dad's standing above me. He shakes my shoulder.

Dad?

Dad?

He hasn't been in my room since before Mom died. He never hung around the house much when Maddi and I were home from school.

"What?" I look him right in the eyes. He looks different, older. The first time in weeks he appears sober. Even alert. But more than that, he looks like he's in pain.

Hurt.

Alone.

"We need to talk. We need to straighten some stuff out."

This is about Jake.

This has to be about Jake.

Maybe it's not. Maybe it's about the fainting at school. Maybe it's about Amber.

No.

Dad sits on the edge of my bed, like he's ready to have a long talk. Like we haven't not spoken in months, except for the few fights. He sits there like we're friends. Like this is a normal thing.

Like he knows me.

Like we're family.

"I'm not sure I want to talk to you," I say quietly. I glance at my clock. It's almost six a.m. What time did I fall asleep?

Has he been up all night?

Talking about me with those people?

Those backstabbers?

"Where's Amber? Why isn't she here trying to make me talk to her, too?" The bitch in me has awoken and I feel the anger start to boil in my belly. The anger toward my father, and his fiancée. The people who took my mother away.

"She's asleep. She doesn't need to be here," Dad says. His tone is the same. Calm and quiet.

"I don't want to talk, Dad." I pull the blankets over my head like I used to when I was little and I didn't want to go to school. It's warm under the blankets. It's safe. Here I can hide from my feelings, hide from my father.

"Please." When he says this, his voice cracks. I hear the tears.

How can he be crying?

Why is he crying?

Because of what he's done.

Because of what I think he's done?

I move the blankets and look at my father. He has his face in his hands. I almost can't hear him. But he gets louder, and I realize he's weeping. I've never seen him cry like this before. Not even when he found out Mom was dead or when she lost the baby.

Seeing him like that makes my insides turn, and the weight of guilt hits me hard.

Is he faking this?

Why is he crying!

Why do I care so much?

"What do you want to talk about?" I say. I try to soften my tone, even though anger still rages in my stomach.

Anger toward him, toward Amber, anger about everything that's happened the last few months. Why is he just now reaching out to me? Why does he suddenly give a shit about how I feel?

I don't even know if he does give a shit.

"I'm worried, Charlotte. I'm worried about you, and I'm worried about your sister."

Since when? Since when does he have the right to worry?

Was he ever worried about Mom?

He never showed it.

"Worried about what? Has something else happened?" What more could he worry about? Is he worried that someone's going to kill us? That Amber is going to kill us, like she did our mother?

Did she kill our mother?

Did he?

Dad wipes his tears and his angry face comes back. Like the tears were fake. Like he was just pretending. Probably because he *was* pretending. No one in this house says or does what they mean. They just try to cover it up with lies and deceit.

"Your uncle told me what you said about the poison. Do you honestly believe I could poison your mom? We bought that because we had a gopher problem. You must see how insane it seems," Dad says.

That doesn't explain anything.

Of course he'd have an explanation.

And the pills? The lies? The cheating?

I sit there and stare at him. Not saying a word as he talks.

"This isn't good, Charlotte. You're acting *delusional.* I'm worried about your physical health. I'm worried about your mental health. You need help."

When Dad says this, I gasp.

Me?

ME?

Has he looked in the mirror lately?

"We need to take you somewhere to get you real help. We need to fix you, before it's too late."

Fix me?

Fix me?

After what he did to Mom?

All the lies, and all the cheating.

None of that matters?

"Get out. Get out!" I don't say it, I scream it. "Get out and never talk to me again. Get out!" I scream so loud my voice cracks and I feel a sharp pain in my throat. I know I've probably woken up everyone in the house.

Dad stands and walks to my door, then turns around and stares at me. He doesn't look fazed by my shouting or by what I've said.

I shake. Like I've been splashed with a bucket of anger. Of cold, hard feelings. And I've been left in the snow to freeze.

"I should have said something to you a long time ago. You have problems. Your mother had the same problems, and I don't want you to end up like she did." Then he walks out of my room and slams the door.

My mind spins in circles. Thoughts rush through me.

I'm sure he wanted to fix Mom, too. Fix all her problems. All the things he didn't like about her and blamed on her mental health.

He's *the one who hurt* her!

He doesn't want me to end up like she did?

Dead?

He's trying to get rid of me.

He's trying to get rid of me.

Just like Mom.

Charlotte

I go into Maddi's room after Dad leaves and get into her bed. Surprisingly she's still asleep. I guess she's been just as tired as I've been, if not more, and was able to sleep through the storm that was the fight between me and our father.

Right now I need my sister, though. I need my best friend.

"Maddi, Maddi, wake up," I say. I shake her shoulder just like Dad did to me a few moments ago.

For some reason the air in Maddi's room isn't as stuffy. She keeps her room tidy, and just being in here makes me feel calmer. Maybe if I took care of my bedroom the way she takes care of hers, I wouldn't worry as much.

"What is it? I'm sleeping." She rolls onto her other side and turns her back to me.

"Maddi, please." I pull the pillow from under her head and swat her with it. I'm hit with a memory of when we were little. Pillow fights in the living room with the couch cushions. Even Mom went along with it. One of the nice cushions tore once and the stuffing popped out. Instead of getting mad, Mom and Dad burst into laughter.

"What the fuck, Charlotte!" Maddi shouts. Her voice is harsh. She sits up and stares at me in the dark. The moonlight from the window shines in on her. The calm feeling her space gave just a few seconds before goes away and the worry sets back in.

"Shhh, you've got to be quiet. Maddi, Dad just came into my room and wanted to talk."

If I was in a different family, a normal family, maybe this wouldn't be as weird.

Does Maddi need to know everything Dad said to me?

What if she decides she agrees with him?

What if he went in and talked to her first?

Maddi flicks on the lamp next to her bed. Her hair is messy and the circles under her eyes are more visible than usual.

"Yeah, I could hear you shouting. What did he say?" she says. She doesn't look or even sound concerned. She must still be groggy. She's not fully getting it.

Give her time to wake up.

"You tell me. Did he come in here first? Maddi, I'm worried. He said some weird shit to me."

Don't tell her. She'll just agree with him.

She won't.

Don't tell her!

Maddi yawns and then looks at me with a grumpy face. "I'm exhausted, Charlotte."

I knew it.

"Maddi. He told me he wants to send me somewhere," I say. When I say it aloud, I start to panic.

He wouldn't really send me away, would he? Maddi would stop him, right?

"I'm not going to let that happen. We're going to fix this, but I can't do it right now. I'm just so tired." She scrunches back down into bed and pulls the blankets up under her chin. Her voice sounds different. Angrier.

Why is she acting like this?

They've gotten to her.

Have they?

She would never side with him.

"He wasn't drunk. He was completely sober. He was crying, Maddi. It really scared me."

This isn't normal.

Something's going on.

Something's going on.

What is going on?

"Charlotte, I just can't right now. I'm starting to feel like if I don't sleep, I'm going to snap or something," Maddi says, and I can tell by the way she says it that this conversation is over. She's done talking to me.

She has been angrier.

Madder.

She's lost more weight.

She does need rest.

She's not herself anymore, either.

I want to stand up and scream in her face. Flick on the lights and tear the blankets off her. I want to beg her to tell me what's going on. To explain to me what I've done.

But I don't do any of that. Because I know there's nothing she can do to help me right now.

Not in this moment.

I have to wait until tomorrow, and even then, what can she do?

What can either of us do?

Charlotte

"So what happened yesterday?" Lana's leaning against my locker, like she's been waiting all day for me to show up.

Being at school sucks, but being at home is even worse now. Before, I could find comfort in my room, safe and alone. Now that's not the case. Not with Dad and Amber making all their plans to send me away.

I stand there and stare at Lana for a moment. The hallway is a rush of noise, and I almost can't hear my own thoughts. A bell rings, and it's louder than normal. My body is exhausted and I have that sick feeling you get after staying up too late. My mind feels drained.

Why is she always waiting?

We're friends.

Not friends.

"I guess I fainted," I say.

Lana stands in front of my locker for a moment more, and then moves so I can get inside. I take out my math book and shove it into my backpack.

Did I faint?

Or did something else happen?

I try to stay cool and pretend like nothing happened, but I'm pretty sure it all shows on my face. It takes everything I have not to tell her about the conversation I had with Dad.

"Why did you send me that strange message?" Lana stands close to me, I can smell the peppery incense coming off her hair. Her lips are painted blood red and her eye makeup is dark.

She looks beautiful.

She's a freak.

Then maybe I'm a freak too.

I forgot I had texted her. I'm not even sure why I did. "Oh, I just had a weird dream," I say. It's a lie and I'm pretty sure she can tell. She folds her arms and steps closer to me.

Someone a few feet away drops a cup of coffee and shouts "Fuck!" I hear Sarah Walters from gym class burst out laughing.

The lights in the hall have that annoying humming noise coming from them. They also flicker. It makes my eyes hurt, and I can feel the lack of sleep throughout my body.

"Why don't you just tell me what's going on? Did something happen with Stephen?" Lana whispers.

Stephen.

He acted as if nothing had happened between us. Like we hadn't kissed in the car.

Did I imagine it? Were we together? Did he let me cry on his shoulder like that?

Why does she always ask about him?

How does she know anything is going on?

How could she possibly know?

Why does she care about me and Stephen?

"I'm stressed out, that's all. I have a lot going on with my uncle in town," I say. That is the truth, but I don't think she really cares.

What she wants is information.

Information about us.

She wants to know our secrets.

My head starts to hurt, and I can tell it's going to be a bad one. The pain comes from my eyes and shoots into my temples. The headaches are becoming more frequent. I never got them before.

"Whatever, Charlie. Just be real with me, I've been real with you," she says.

I stare at her for a moment, not sure what to say.

Is she seriously pissed?

I knew she was a bitch. I knew it.

"I don't know what you want me to be real about, Lana. I told you I've got a lot going on. Is there something you want to know that you're just not asking me?" I say. I fold my arms across my chest and step away from her. That peppery smell coming off her hair, the color of her lips—she's too close.

"I just think you're not being straight with me about some stuff. Like Stephen, and your mom. And Maddi. Like, I thought we were friends, but now I'm not so sure," she says. Then she slams my locker shut and walks away.

What the hell?

Who does she think she is?

As she walks away, I see Stephen down the hall. He watches Lana, he looks her up and down, and then he smiles.

I've seen that look on his face. I've seen that look when he's looked at me.

257

He loves her.

He loves her.

Lana walks past him and I see her lightly touch his arm.

I don't think anyone else would have noticed.

She's sleeping with him.

He's sleeping with her.

She's playing us and fucking him.

She's playing me.

Maddi

Dad calls me during fourth period and tells me I need to come home.

"I'll sign you out for the rest of the day. I'm having one last sit-down with your sister as soon as she gets home. You can join me now so you're aware of what's going on, or you can come home with her. But either way, this is happening. I'm done with the fighting," he says.

I'd hoped he wasn't serious about his plan to send her away. I'd hoped it was a bluff, but now I can see how serious he is.

I text Charlotte and tell her I have to leave school early because of cramps. I'm hit with a stab of guilt about lying to her again, but I have to protect her. I have no idea what Dad's plan is.

When I get home, Dad and Amber are in the living room. They look too comfortable sitting on the couch together, waiting for me.

Amber is wearing a fake smile when I walk into the room, as if she's happy to see me. We both know I don't want any part of this.

Sometimes I wonder if all this is really worth it for her. The drama, the fighting. Is her relationship with my father really worth it? It doesn't seem like it would be.

"Sit down," Dad says.

I stand in the doorway for a moment longer, then sit down on the couch across from him and Amber. It's cold in here, and I wonder if the heat's turned off.

"Where are Jake and Alex?" I say. I half expected the whole family to be in the living room. Ready to pounce on us.

"They're sorting out some stuff at the bank. Finding out about the house," Dad says. I try not to let that get under my skin. But it does. I don't think Jake could legally take the house. But of course, Dad could let him try. Even help him.

"What's going on, Dad? Why are we doing this right now? It's not like anything has changed. You stopped caring about both of us after Mom died, so why do you suddenly care now?" I'm already angry, and I know if I don't calm down, it's just going to make things worse.

Dad sighs, like I'm annoying him. And somehow that makes me even madder.

"I never stopped caring about either of you. But I've asked you before, Maddi, is it so bad that I'm happy? That *we're* happy?" he says, pointing to Amber.

I want to bust out laughing at how easily he was able to ignore what I said and make it about himself. About her.

"So why am I here, then? If you've already made the decision to send Charlotte away, to get rid of your own daughter, why am I even here?" I say, my voice rising.

"Don't talk to your father like that," Amber says. She shifts on the sofa and moves closer to Dad, as if to protect him.

I look at the clock above the TV, trying to will myself not to scream at this woman who is sitting here pretending to be my mother. I try my hardest to distract myself from the anger that's about to boil over any second. It's almost two-thirty, which means Charlotte will be home soon. I only have a little time to figure out Dad's plan and then talk him out of it.

"Look, Dad. I get it, you're with this woman. But does she really need to sit here and run her mouth like this? You asked me to come home so I could be included in what's going on. So tell me. What are you planning to do?"

Amber starts to say something, but Dad cuts her off. And for a moment, I'm relieved. But only for a moment.

"You're right," he says. "Look, your uncle told me what you and Charlotte believe. I know this is all your sister. She's convinced someone intentionally hurt your mother. She's not going to school, she's broken things around the house, she's lashed out at me and Amber, and she's not sleeping. I can tell she's struggling with something, and I'm not able to fix it. I want to help your sister. But I can't do it alone. And neither can you. I found a place up in Boston that specializes in depression and PTSD. They have a bed ready for her, and I want to take her tomorrow morning."

When Dad says this, I feel gut-punched.

He thinks all of this is Charlotte's fault. That the easiest way to fix the family divide is to send her away. And what does he plan to do with me?

He's trying to get rid of us. Just like he did Mom. He wants this life, the money, *everything* that he and Mom built, he wants it all to himself. That's what he's always wanted. I know now that the only way I'm going to get through to him is by playing along. I can't keep fighting with him. He has all the power, and he knows it.

"Why don't you let me talk to her?" I say. "We can call Nancy. Charlotte can start her therapy back up. It will help her, I know it will. Sending her away isn't going to solve anything. Would you let me talk to her about seeing Nancy again? You can't send her away." I start to cry, and I hate it. I don't want Amber to see me like this. But I can't help it. The thought of being here without my sister scares me. I can't do it without her. And she can't do it without me.

Amber looks at Dad, and I know she wants us gone too. She wants to get rid of us even more than he does.

"Fine. Let's talk to her when she gets home and see how she reacts. But if she responds the way I think she's going to, then we are leaving tomorrow. End of story," Dad says.

"Fine," I whisper. Because there's nothing else I can say.

He's made up his mind.

Charlotte

When I get home, they're waiting for me in the living room. Dad, Amber, even Maddi.

"I see we've got the whole family here. Where are Jake and Alex? They didn't want to be here for the ambush?" I ask. I know it's the wrong thing to say, but at this point, I'm so done with all of this.

"They've been sorting stuff out. Not that it matters. This isn't about them," Dad says. Amber is sitting next to him. She's wearing a black dress and black tights. Black, black, black.

Mom would hate it.

I hate it.

She looks like a witch.

She is a witch.

"What is this?" I ask. The room feels hot and clammy. Opposite of how it's been the last few weeks. It's like the heat has been turned up too high. It makes my skin itch, and I feel my feet start to sweat inside my socks.

When I look at Maddi, I can tell that she's been crying. Her face is blotchy and her eyes are all red. There's an empty spot next to her on the couch. It's probably for me.

Is this why she left school early?

Is this why I had to ride the bus home?

"We want to chat with you. We just want to get a grasp on how you've been feeling lately," Dad says. He sounds like a phony.

He is a phony.

They're all phony.

Even Maddi?

"Is this . . . some sort of intervention?" I stand in the doorway of the living room and fold my arms. Anger starts to fill me and I fight to keep it inside. Seeing my father there, pretending like he loves me. Pretending like he's ever cared about me or how I've felt. He doesn't care. He never has.

Maddi pats the seat next to her on the leather couch. I still remember when Dad bought these couches. Moved them in and moved Mom's vintage velvet chaise longue and couch out to the guesthouse. Just thinking about that makes my blood boil.

"Why don't you sit down so we can talk," Maddi says.

She's a traitor.

She's one of them.

"I'm not having a conversation with you guys with *her* here." I glance at Amber.

Amber looks at me and then at Dad.

"She isn't a part of this family and she has no business being here," I say.

I think about how she really used to be a part of the family. And how it was all a lie. How she pretended to be my friend. Pretended to care about Mom.

"Don't be immature, just sit down and hear us out," Dad says. He's using that fake voice again. It makes my skin crawl.

Who is he trying to fool?

Who is he pretending for?

"Charlotte, please. For me?" Maddi says. She sounds desperate, and something in her voice tells me maybe it's better I just go along with all this. Pretend like I give half a shit about what he says.

"This is stupid." As I walk by Amber I step over her shiny black boots. It takes everything in my power not to step on them.

Witch boots.

Bitch boots.

Maddi grabs my hand and squeezes it when I sit down next to her. When she does this, I look at her and she talks to me with her eyes.

This is a trap, her eyes say. *I'm not a part of it,* her eyes tell me.

"The school called. They told us about the fainting incident in the hall yesterday," Dad says. "Why didn't you tell me about it? What happened?"

What is he talking about?

Why would I tell him?

"You could have really hurt yourself," Amber says. She leans in a little bit and gives me a sad face. Like she cares. Like she's concerned.

"Are you serious?" I glance down at my phone. I've been in this room for less than two minutes and already I want to run screaming out into the cold. Tell them all to get fucked and leave me alone.

"Of course we're serious," Dad says. He looks at me and smiles, showing his teeth. Crooked and yellow. He doesn't look like my father anymore. He looks like a stranger. An outsider.

Has he always been an outsider?

Was he a stranger before?

Have I ever known my father?

"Dad, we haven't talked in months. Why would I suddenly tell you anything about my life? And since when did you start giving a fuck?" I want to shout, want to slap him and Amber, want to make Amber cry and make Dad angry.

I hate them both.

I hate them both so much.

"She was fine, Dad. Like I told you, she just got light-headed and fell. She didn't hurt herself or anything," Maddi says.

She is here for me.

She'd never abandon me.

"Don't use that tone with us, Charlotte. I'm doing my best to try and understand what is happening with you. And what you've been going through. But you're not helping."

What's happened to me? How about what's happened to them?

"Stop pretending like you care, Dad, stop!" I shout. My voice cracks and all of a sudden I want to cry. "You haven't been there for either of us. Not since long before Mom died, so don't act like you're going to help now."

That's when I realize it. I've missed him.

I've missed my dad being there.

I've missed him caring.

I look at Dad and see that he's crying, too. For a moment I do see my father. And my heart breaks for him.

Cracks because he wasn't always like this.

Breaks because we used to be a family.

Shatters because I know what he's done. I know now, looking at him, that he killed Mom.

He did.

He killed her.

They both did it.

I don't have a doubt in my mind.

"We think you need help, Charlotte. I see a lot in you that I saw in your mother, and I'm worried about you," Amber says.

When I look at her she has a slight smile on her face. At the edge of her lips. She tries to hide it, but I can see it. I can see the bullshit that spills out of her.

"What did you just say?" She didn't actually just say that. Is she serious?

I glance over at Dad. He's sitting on the other leather couch. Both are stiff and masculine and never seem to get warm when it's cold. The couches clash with the orange rug. Mom bought the rug years ago. I'm surprised Dad hasn't gotten rid of it yet. I try to focus on the good in the room. Like the rug Mom picked out years ago. And Maddi. I try to keep the anger inside.

Maddi squeezes my hand again. She's the best part of the room. My only friend. The only person who still wants me around.

"I said I think you need help. I think you need to go to a hospital. I'm worried about you. You're going down the same path as your mother," Amber says.

Mom. The same path as my mom.

Mom was always there for me. Mom always did what she

was supposed to. It wasn't until Amber got involved that Mom really started to change.

And the baby.

No! This is Amber's fault.

Is that true?

"You're both fucking hypocrites. Dad, Maddi and I know about the cheating. All the lies. All the shit you put Mom through. You try to blame everything on her, when everyone knows it was your fault. She was a wonderful mom, and you did everything you could to break her," I say.

Dad's and Amber's faces change when I say this, but only for a moment. The smug smile Amber had fades. I can tell by looking at her that she hates me. She wants me gone, just like she wanted Mom gone.

"Charlotte, I don't know where you've been, but your mother was a full-blown alcoholic by the end. Whose fault was that? Certainly not your father's. You like to pretend she was so perfect, but she wasn't. She had problems too, just like you," Amber says. Her words sting, and it's all I can do not to pounce on her. Hit her hard. Scream in her face. Pull her hair out. But I don't. I just sit there for a moment. The room goes quiet.

Alcoholic?

Mom wasn't an alcoholic.

"What the fuck are you talking about?" I say. I picture Mom in the garden, sipping from her mug of tea, soaking up the sun. She had been acting different toward the end, but that wasn't because she was an alcoholic, it was because she felt sick. It was because she was dying. Because *they* were killing her.

Wasn't it?

"Amber, just stop, stop it! You're only making things worse," Maddi says. Her face going red and her hands shaking.

"This isn't about your mom," Dad says, "this is about Charlotte. And Amber is right. Your sister is out of control. Your sister is becoming delusional. I know you can see it, too."

What are they talking about?

What are they saying?

"This isn't how this was supposed to go, Dad. This isn't what we talked about."

When Maddi says this, my stomach turns and I feel bile hit my throat. I want to puke. I want to scream. That same headache that I keep getting comes back, and I feel my temples start to pulse.

Please, not her.

I try to stay calm, but I'm crying hard now.

"What are you talking about, Maddi? What did you tell him?" I point to Dad. Like talking to our father is the crime of all crimes. Because it sort of is. He's betrayed us. He broke our family up.

Why would she talk to him?

What would she discuss with him?

Maddi shakes her head and squeezes my hand again.

"I haven't. He's lying. They're both lying. I told him you'd go back and see Nancy again, that's it."

Maddi pauses for a minute, and then looks at Dad. "But I *never* said you should send her away."

Before I can respond, Amber chimes in.

"Don't lie to your sister, Maddi. Tell her that you think she needs help. Tell her that you're worried she's going to hurt herself just like your mom."

Dad reaches over and grabs Amber's hand and then gives her a look. I hear him say, "Stop," under his breath.

Amber has that smile on her face again.

I stand up and walk across the room and stand in front of her and stare. She scoots back a little bit but doesn't take her eyes off me. Before I can stop myself, I slap her hard across the face.

She cries out and falls against my dad. My hand stings and I hope the slap hurt her as much as she's acting like it did.

"You bitch. You lying bitch!" I scream. I reach down and pull her hair hard. Then I slap her again. "You murdering, lying bitch. You liar!"

Dad grabs me and pushes me away from Amber.

"Charlotte, stop! Please!" Maddi shouts. I run to her and she grabs me in a hug. "Let's go outside," she says.

As we walk out the front door, I can hear Amber crying like a fucking baby. I slam the door hard. Mom hated when I did that as a kid.

"What the hell was that, Maddi? What were they talking about?"

She's a traitor.

She's one of them.

She's trying to stab you in the back.

"What is going on? Have you turned against me too? Maddi, please tell me you haven't," I say. I try to fight the tears, but they still come. Maddi puts her arms around me and hugs me.

"Of course not, Charlotte. But they do want to send you away. And I'm worried. I'm worried for you," she says. "I begged him not to. But he thinks you're unstable."

We stand out on the front porch. Maddi is wearing a summer dress and no coat, and I can see the goose bumps on her arms. I'm so angry that I don't even feel the cold.

"What do you mean, you're worried for me? Where are they trying to send me?" I pull away from Maddi.

I breathe in the crisp air and try to calm down.

She looks at me and shakes her head. "Someplace in Boston. They think you've had a breakdown. They think you've lost it. What was that in there, Charlotte? You can't just hit someone like that—it only gives them more power."

When Maddi says this, I start to wonder.

"I don't know," I say. And it's true. I realize I don't know myself anymore. I'm so angry. Because of what they've done. "It doesn't matter. They killed our Mom. The proof is *everywhere*, yet somehow I'm being painted as the bad guy. I'm not the bad guy, *they are*," I say, pointing to the front door.

How are they spinning this back on me? Just because I'm angry doesn't mean I've lost it.

This is probably what Dad did to Mom. What they both did to Mom.

"I know. But, Charlotte, Dad has all the power. You can't have an outburst like that when he's on the verge of sending you away," Maddi says.

I know she's probably right. But that doesn't make it feel better. It doesn't change anything.

"And why was she calling Mom an alcoholic? Why do they

271

always have to blame Mom?" I say. Just mentioning her makes my heart ache more, and I know now why she was so sad. Everyone abandoned her.

"Charlotte, she had a drinking problem. The herbal tea she always drank was just rose-flavored vodka with tea in it. I thought you knew," Maddi says.

How many more secrets are they keeping from me?

Why can't everyone just be honest?

"I can't, Maddi. I can't take any more of this. The secrets, the lies, the pretending," I say.

"Forget the lies for a second, Charlotte," Maddi says. "This is serious. I can't let them send you away, but that's where this is headed. I guess Dad called Nancy. She thinks you need to come back. She thinks you stopped therapy far too early."

Nancy?

Did she talk to Dad before I talked to her?

Is she allowed to discuss my case with other people?

Underage.

"Nancy said that?" I ask. I try to picture Nancy turning on me, too. Even if I didn't stick with her, at least she understood my situation. At least she tried to help.

I should never have called her.

"According to Dad, Nancy was worried you were going to hurt yourself."

When Maddi says this, I feel my face go red.

Can Nancy read minds?

Did you tell her?

"That's bullshit," I say.

Maddi sighs and stares out beyond the yard.

"We have to figure this out. He can't send you away. I won't let him send you away. You just need to calm down," she says.

The sun is still out and glows pink and orange. A year ago I would have thought the sun setting on the snow like that was romantic. That the winter was romantic. But now I feel nothing.

Nothing but hate.

Hate for my father.

Hate for Amber.

Even for my sister.

But mostly for myself.

Charlotte

Mom walked into the kitchen. She was wearing a light pink dress with a low neck. I remember when she bought it. We'd been on vacation in Florida. She loved that dress when she picked it out.

I sat at the table and watched her. She looked like she hurt all over. Amber quickly grabbed a mug from the cupboard and set it down in front of the chair next to me.

"Sarah, I made you tea. Are you feeling any better?" She poured the tea into the creamy yellow mug.

The smell of rose and mint filled the air. It made the room feel calm and relaxed.

Mom shrugged. "My throat feels like it's gotten worse, but at least my stomach isn't hurting anymore."

Mom was getting sick more often around this time. Joint pains, migraines, but mostly really bad stomach pain. Dad said it was because she'd just lost the baby and that a lot of it was mental. But I wasn't so sure anymore.

"Is there something I can do for you?" Amber asked Mom.

The house was clean. The dishes were done. Mom was doing

a lot of resting and Amber was doing a lot of work. But that's what they paid her for.

"No. I'm fine. Just the tea, thanks." Mom took the mug and walked away.

After Mom left the room, Amber gave me a serious look.

"I'm worried about her. Something isn't right," she whispered. I scooted my chair a little closer to where Amber stood.

"Do you think it's because of the baby?" I asked.

Mom had lost the baby over three months ago. But she didn't talk about it. It looked like she was getting better. But maybe I was wrong. Maybe she wasn't better at all.

"I'm not sure, but I'm worried. I've talked to your dad about it and he hasn't really said much," Amber said. "Thinks that she's just grieving."

Mom was always quiet when it came to her emotions. Never told anyone what she was really feeling. Even when we'd have our girls' days together, she kept her problems to herself.

"I'll keep an eye on her. Try and talk to her," I said.

But I didn't keep my eye on her. I pretended like I didn't notice that she was hurting. I acted like she was over the death of the baby. I turned away when I knew she was going through heartbreak.

I let them kill her.

I let her die.

Charlotte

I walk inside. Dad and Amber are still in the living room. A blast of hot air hits me, and I'm glad I'm not wearing a coat. I'm still fuming mad, and the heat just makes it worse.

Waiting for us.

Waiting for me.

Why can't they just leave me alone?

Why can't they just let me be?

"Charlotte, this isn't finished. Do I need to call the police? You assaulted Amber!" Dad shouts. His voice is loud, and for a second I'm afraid. But I ignore him and go to my room and slam the door. I hear his shouts outside my door as I click the lock. My room is cold and dark. I crawl into bed and get under the covers.

She deserves it.

They both do.

Dad knocks on the door while my voice pounds in my ears.

Thiscantbehappenningthisisnthappeningthisishappening.

"Open the door. Open the fucking door or I'll break it down!" Dad shouts with every blow to the door. I can hear Amber in the background, and even Maddi. Her voice frantic and afraid.

"Let her be. Just leave her alone, *please*," Maddi says. Amber screams at the top of her lungs. She's screaming words I don't understand or care about.

Fix this.

You could fix this.

"Charlotte, I'm going to pick the lock if you don't open up!" Dad shouts. But I don't care. I put pillows and blankets over my head.

He can't hurt you anymore.

They can't do more than what they've already done.

We can fix this.

The shouts get louder, and I can tell by Dad's tone that he's madder than a hornet. Ready to strike at any moment.

But I don't care.

I don't care.

I can fix this.

I can fix this.

I can.

Charlotte

Mom and I sat on the front porch, we sipped tea and ate overly frosted doughnuts. The sun was rising, and at the time, I had no idea that this would be the last morning coffee I would share with her.

"Can I tell you something, Charlie?" It was the first time I'd seen Mom look happy, *really* happy, in forever, and suddenly I knew everything was going to be okay. She was getting better. She was finally healing. And maybe her heart was on the mend from the pain of losing the baby.

"Of course," I said. The breeze brought the smell of change, and I knew it had to be for the better. I was going to get my mother back.

Finally.

"Please, always promise to love me. Always promise to love your family, no matter what happens." Those last few weeks Mom was saying more and more strange things. Almost cryptic. I'd gotten used to it.

I nodded anyway. Maddi and Mom were my best friends. Amber and I were close, though we had grown apart over the last year. But even back then, family was the most important thing in my life.

"No, I need you to promise," Mom said. She reached over and grabbed my shoulder. "You're my baby girl. We have a bond, you and me. I've always felt it. Please never forget that."

My stomach fluttered with love. I wondered if Cat was close like this with her mom. Or if it was just me. Just me and Mom.

"Of course, Mom. I'll always love you guys. You're my family, and you're my best friend."

Mom smiled when I said this. An actual smile, like she meant it. I hadn't seen her smile like that in months, and it calmed my fears, my irrational thoughts, and I knew everything would be all right. Everything would be fine.

"I still remember the day you were born. We waited too long to get to the hospital, so I had you here in this house. Your dad was sure you wouldn't make it, but I knew. I knew you'd be okay. And you are. You're just fine," she said.

Mom had told me that story several times. About how her water broke and they didn't have time to get to the hospital. But she was okay with it because she didn't trust doctors. I came, and she knew I was her soul mate. Her special baby.

I knew she felt close to me because of it.

"I'll always love you. Don't worry," I said.

Charlotte

I hear my bedroom door open, and then Dad's voice. He's gotten in. Just like he promised he would. He probably picked the lock.

They can't hurt us anymore. Because we have a plan. A real plan. A plan that will fix everything.

The blanket gets pulled from over my head and Dad stands there, fuming. He couldn't keep that concerned father act going for long. Maddi and Amber are standing close behind him.

Maddi is still shouting at Amber. But Dad doesn't say a word, just stares at me.

"Leave me alone, just leave me alone," I say. I realize, looking at him, that I've broken my promise to Mom.

I will never love this man again. I stopped loving Dad a long time ago. And I believe that Mom probably did, too.

How could she have loved him?

Was he always like this?

"Charlotte. This has to stop. All of this will end today," Dad says. He grabs me by the arm. I let him pull me out of bed. He drags me back into the living room, and Amber follows. I feel like a rag doll. There's no point in fighting. He's too strong and I've lost all my energy.

"Dad, leave her alone. Just leave her alone. Please!" Maddi shouts. But he ignores her. Amber turns around and shouts, "Be quiet, just stop talking!" at Maddi.

Instantly I'm hit with rage again, and I want to punch her until my arms stop working.

Nancy was right to be concerned.

"Don't talk to her like that," I say. I jerk my arm, but Dad's grip is too tight to break free.

He pushes me into a chair.

"Sit, Charlotte. Just sit there, we're finishing this conversation. It will be quick and then you can go pack."

He's still trying to send me away.

He's the one that needs to go away.

"Okay! Just stop touching me. Tell me what you want to say and let's end this," I say. Maddi walks past Amber and sits next to me.

Dad takes two large breaths, all dramatic. It reminds me of when I was a kid and he'd argue with Mom. He was just as dramatic back then, too.

He sits on the couch next to Amber and she grabs his hand.

How do they not disgust each other?

"Charlotte, as I said earlier, I'm worried about you. That is why we're going to be taking you to the hospital tomorrow." He says this like it's no big deal, like he's just going to be dropping me off at school.

"You don't have to stay there for long, maybe six weeks. Just until you get stable again. We're all very worried about you. I've already talked to Nancy, and she has agreed to work with you again."

Worried about me.

When did he decide to be worried about me?

"Don't include me in this, Dad," Maddi says. "I don't agree with you at all. I just think she's stressed. All she needs is therapy, at the most."

Therapy didn't do anything for me.

Maddi knows that.

"Look, I've made my decision. Charlotte, you need to be ready to go tomorrow morning. That's final. That's that."

Dad stands up. He's still holding Amber's hand. I watch them walk into Mom's bedroom and close the door.

My heart feels empty, like someone squeezed all the life out of it.

"He can't do this," Maddi says, then she turns and looks at me. Her eyes talk to me, as usual. But this time they tell me something different.

They tell me she feels guilty.

They tell me she knew this was going to happen.

"How long have you known he's been thinking about this?" I ask.

"He told me today. The fainting at school was the last straw for him. He thinks you're having some sort of episode," Maddi says.

Episode?

Am I having an episode?

"How do you feel about all this?" I ask.

Has she completely forgotten about everything we discovered? About the letters? The affairs? The journal entries? The pills? The poison?

"I feel helpless, like there isn't anything else we can do. He's made the final call. He wants us gone. He may not say it now, but I'm sure I'm next."

At least Maddi's on my side. At least she still believes me.

"This is all Amber's fault," I say, "she's driven a stake through our family. She's ruined everything." I know it sounds melodramatic, but it's true.

She's the reason all of this started.

Mom's death.

The affair.

Everything is her fault.

Everything.

Charlotte

"Andrew. Andrew, hurry. Please!" I heard Mom shout from her bedroom.

I was lying on my bed talking to Stephen on the phone. He'd just sent me a new Spotify playlist that he thought I'd like. I wasn't even listening to it. I just liked to hear his voice on the other end of the line. The new music was a bonus.

"Can you hang on a sec?" I said into the phone.

I sat up and paused the music on the Bluetooth speaker.

"Andrew. Andrew, hurry!" Mom shouted. Only this time her voice had fear in it. She didn't sound like herself.

"I have to call you back," I said to Stephen, and hung up.

I hurried down the hall into Mom's room. It was dark except for a strip of light under the bathroom door.

"Mom? Are you okay?" I said.

I knocked on the bathroom door and then peeked inside.

"Mom, are you okay?"

Mom sat there on the floor, blood everywhere.

"Oh my God! Mom, what's happening?"

She was squished up against the side of the tub. She wore

a cream-colored dress, but it was covered with blood. Her face was pale and sickly. It looked like a scene from a horror movie. Only way worse. Because Mom didn't look like herself.

"Someone call nine-one-one. Hurry!" I screamed.

Mom had her hand over her pregnant belly, crying harder than I'd ever seen her cry.

"It's the baby. I know it's the baby," she said.

I got down on the floor next to her and put my arms around her.

"It's going to be okay. It's going to be okay," I said. But all that blood scared me. I wasn't sure if it was true or not.

"Dad. Hurry. Hurry!" I screamed.

Finally, after what felt like hours, Dad ran into the bathroom. His face was flushed like he'd been out in the cold.

"Sarah, oh my God, are you okay?" Dad came over to where Mom and I were and picked her up. She was so little compared to him. He held her like she weighed nothing.

"It's the baby," I said.

Mom put her arms around Dad and cried into his shoulder.

"I'm taking her to the hospital. I'll call you as soon as I can," Dad said to me. "Call Maddi and tell her what's happened. Amber too." It was one of the rare times that Dad was home and everyone else wasn't.

I just nodded as he spoke. I couldn't keep my eyes off Mom. The blood, her sobs. I wanted to help her, but there was nothing I could do.

I watched as Dad carried her outside to the car and they

drove away, and I knew that this was going to change everything for our family. For Mom. And when they called and told me she'd lost the baby, I was glad to know that Mom was safe. That Mom was alive. Because she was the most important person. And we couldn't lose her. Our family needed her.

There she is.

Asleep on Mom's side of the bed. I wonder if she thinks it's strange, lying in a dead woman's bed. Using a dead woman's pillows, sheets, blankets. Being with a dead woman's husband.

I stand next to her. She breathes so soft that the blankets don't move.

I wonder what she dreams about.

I wonder if she thinks about the awful things she's done to this family.

To Mom. Even to Dad.

Dad. Where is he?

Maybe drunk on the couch. I bet he needs that liquid courage to get into bed with her every night.

She sleeps, and I know I can't allow her to stay in this house.

She can't stay here.

She has to go.

She has to.

Charlotte

"Won't you please take me driving? I need to practice before the test on Monday," I said to Mom. She and Dad sat at the kitchen table. Dad sipped his coffee and read the paper. It looked so ordinary and normal, his doing that, even though it wasn't normal for him to be home.

Mom drank a cup of tea and read an old book called *Drowning Ruth*. She'd read it multiple times, but lately she was rereading a lot of her favorite novels. I wasn't sure why.

She looked up from the pages and shook her head.

"I can't handle it. You scare me when you drive, sorry, Charlie." She took another sip of her tea and I knew that was that.

She hated driving with me. I'd hit the curb one too many times, she said.

"How am I going to pass? Maddi won't take me either, and Amber is just as bad of a driver as I am." I sat down at the table next to Mom.

I reached over and took a sip of her tea. It tasted like bitter herbs.

"Gross," I said. "I can't believe you'd rather sit here drinking bitter tea than take your favorite daughter driving."

Mom laughed, then turned the page of her book and continued to read. Or at least pretend to read.

"I'll take you," Dad said. I glanced over at him and he smiled.

Dad and I didn't spend that much time together, so I was surprised.

"You will?"

He stood up and set his paper down on the table.

"Sure. Grab the keys, I'll meet you outside."

Mom looked up from her book again.

"You sure you wanna do that? Driving with this girl is a death wish."

Dad laughed and nodded. "It'll be fine. Let me just grab my wallet."

"Sweet! I'll go get my shoes," I said.

When I got outside, Dad sat in the passenger seat of his Porsche.

"We aren't taking the Volkswagen? I don't know how to drive a manual," I said. The Porsche was brand-new. Shiny black with a yellow interior. Mom called it Dad's Midlife Crisis Car.

Dad looked at me and smiled. "If you can learn to drive a manual you'll ace the test in an automatic. Hop in!"

I hesitated, but then got into the driver's seat.

He showed me how to ease the clutch out, and right away I stalled.

"Damn it," I said, and he laughed.

"Try again," he said. He didn't mention my swear word. Probably because he knew he wasn't one to talk.

I did what he said and went easy on the clutch and backed out into the road. I made it a few feet before I stalled again.

"That was better than the first time," he said. It made me feel less nervous, and I tried again. This time I made it all the way down the block and to the stop sign. When I finally did stall, Dad clapped.

"You're getting it," he said. He almost sounded excited, like maybe he was actually enjoying this time with me. I'd forgotten what it was like to spend time with him. He'd been traveling so much the last few years that I almost felt like we were strangers.

"Make a right up here," he said. Now I was cruising, and I was sure I wouldn't stall again. I gave the car some gas. We zipped forward and then the car died. Before I could say anything, Dad burst out laughing.

"You're doing better than Maddi, I can tell you that!" he said. "I'm trying to get us over to the snow cone shack, but at this rate, the sun will be down by the time we get there. Wanna swap seats and you drive on the way home?"

It had been years since I'd gone to the snow cone shack with Dad. But when I was little, he and I would walk there once a week. He'd ask me how my week had been. It was our father-daughter tradition. I couldn't remember the last time we had done it, or when and why we had stopped.

"For real?" I said.

Dad looked at me and grinned. His teeth were yellowing and he looked tired, but he seemed like he didn't mind being around me.

"For real," he said.

He hopped out of the car and we swapped spots. Dad drove the few remaining blocks to the shack without stalling once.

When we arrived, he parked but didn't get out.

"Listen, Charlotte, I've been wanting to talk to you," he said. "To apologize for how much I've been gone lately. I know it's been kind of difficult at home with your mother, but I promise, I'm going to be around more often." When he said this, I felt my face flush. I'd never known my father to apologize. Especially not to me or Maddi.

I glanced out the window and stared at a cyclist riding by. A young woman, with long dark hair. She looked free on her bike. Like nothing in the world could take her down.

"It's okay," I started to say, but Dad cut me off.

"No, it's not. I need to be better, for you and your sister. From now on, I promise I'm going to be here for you. I'm going to try harder." Something in his voice sounded sad, and I wondered if he really meant it. If he really was going to make an effort.

"I would like that," I said. Before I knew it, Dad leaned over and gave me a big hug. I could smell his aftershave and it reminded me of when I was little.

I so badly wanted him to mean it, so badly wanted him to be around, but I knew deep down that he wasn't going to be and that nothing would change.

Sometimes the only way to make things right is to take care of the problem yourself.

I wander into the living room. And there he is. Just like I thought.

Passed out on the couch. Dead drunk.

I snap my fingers in front of his face. He doesn't move.

Does he dream? Or is his mind gone to the world when he's in this state? Does he think about Mom? About his kids? Does he think that things could have been different if Amber hadn't come into our lives?

Would things have been different?

It didn't have to end this way.
It didn't have to end like this.
It didn't have to end at all.

Maddi

When I fall asleep, I dream I'm talking to Mom.

We sit on my bed, and she looks young and beautiful. Almost angelic. I've been waiting all this time. She can finally hear me.

"Is it really you?" I ask. My eyes are heavy, and everything in the room is dark and cold except her. She glows in the dark, and her body gives off heat. I can't believe it. Can't believe it's really her. I want to burst into tears of happiness.

Mom reaches out and touches my hand.

"I've missed you so much," she says. Her voice sounds different, but I don't care because I know it's her. I know she's been waiting for a chance to talk to me. It's been almost six months since I've seen her.

There's so much I want to say. So much I want to tell her. So much I want to explain. But before I do, I have to ask her what happened.

I need to know.

"Mom, I can't believe you're here. Can't believe it's really you." I scoot closer to her and notice that there's something by her feet. Something large and shiny.

"Did they hurt you, Mom? Were you murdered?" When I say this, I start to cry. Big fat tears roll down my face, and suddenly the despair, sadness, anger, and everything else I've been holding in come out.

Mom puts her arms around me in a tight hug. She doesn't smell like herself, but that's okay because there's something familiar about her hug. It reminds me of Charlotte. *She* reminds me of Charlotte. Oh, how I wish Charlotte could be here to see Mom. To see how beautiful she is.

Mom holds me for a few moments longer and then lets go. I realize she's wearing the necklace that I found in Alex's purse. It's the exact same one.

"Your necklace," I say, touching it. The sapphires shine bright against her skin.

"It's for you," she says. She takes the necklace off and puts it around my neck. "It looks beautiful on you."

"Oh, Mom, please stay with me. Stay forever," I say.

Mom smiles at me. Again, she doesn't look exactly like herself, but I know it's her. Know she's finally come back to me. Finally answered when I called.

"I have something else for you," she says. She reaches down by her feet and grabs the shiny object.

She puts a hatchet in my lap.

The same one that was out in the garden, all those weeks ago.

"You know what to do," she says. "You know what to do."

That's when I wake up.

Charlotte

"Oh my God. No. No! Charlotte. Charlotte, let me in. Let me in!"

I hear screams outside my bedroom door.

At first I think it's in my dream. The whole night I had nightmares. Terrifying nightmares. About Mom and the baby. About Maddi getting hurt. About Lana and Stephen.

I open my eyes and realize it's Maddi.

"Please, Charlotte, are you okay? Are you in there? Open the door!" she screams. I can tell by her voice that she's crying. More than that, though, I can hear her fear. It reminds me of the night Mom died. That horrible night.

I jump out of bed and unlock my door.

Who locked it?

You locked it.

I never lock it when I sleep.

Not since Mom died.

"What? Maddi, what, what's going on?" When I open the door, Maddi is standing there, covered in blood.

Blood everywhere.

"Oh my God, are you hurt?" I grab her. She starts shaking

and falls to the floor. Her face is sheet white and her eyes are huge. Like a lost puppy, trying to find its way home.

"What happened? Whose blood is this?" I ask.

Not again. Not again.

Please not again.

Who would do this to her?

I sit down next to Maddi and shake her shoulders. She stares past me, tears rolling down her face. I hug her and there's blood on her hands and on her neck and on her white night-shirt. There's a little in her hair, and some on her forehead.

So much blood.

"Maddi. Maddi! Where are you hurt?" I scream.

She shakes her head.

What will I do if I lose her?

I can't lose her.

I can never lose her.

My insides start to twist, and my world closes in. I want to fall over and scream. The fear pulsing through my veins makes my heart beat so fast that I think it'll explode.

Please oh please.

Not again.

Not my sister.

"Maddi! Tell me what's happened! Where are you hurt?" I scream. I don't recognize my voice. And my throat starts to close.

"I'm not hurt," she says. Her voice comes out in a hoarse whisper. I grab her hand and squeeze it. She doesn't try to grip mine. Her arms are limp, like she's dead. Like she doesn't have the energy to lift them.

I look down and realize that I'm also covered in blood.
What?

"What's happened? Please tell me," I say. Now I'm crying.
Big fat salty tears stream down my face.

Whose blood is this?

Is she going to die?

"Maddi! Please. Are you okay?" I shout. Her eyes look far away. Her body shakes and I can tell she's not with me. Mentally, she's checked out. She's left me behind to fight whatever's in this house.

Is she dying?

"Maddi!" I scream.

It's as if my scream wakes her up. She stares at me.

"She's dead," Maddi says. "She's dead."

It was a dream. It was all a dream.

  It didn't really happen.

  It couldn't have really happened.

  It couldn't have really happened, could it?

  No.

  No way.

But maybe it did.

Charlotte

"Don't go in there, Charlotte. Don't." Maddi grabs me. I look down the hall at Dad and Amber's room. The door is open a crack. I see blood smeared on the knob.

Maddi stands up, her whole body shakes. She tries to grip my arm, but mostly I hold her weight. We both stare down at the bedroom.

It reminds me of when Mom died. I stood there waiting for her to come out and she never did. I waited for what felt like hours, for what felt like years, even. Sometimes it's like I'm still waiting.

But she's never come back.

And now here I am. Staring at that door.

This house.

That room.

The blood on the doorknob reminds me of something. Something familiar, but I can't put my finger on it.

"It's horrible, Charlotte," Maddi sobs. "I'm afraid." She's crying so hard that it scares me.

She scares me.

"Don't move, Maddi. Just stay here." I walk down the hall and push the door open with my foot.

When I look inside, I feel my stomach drop to my feet. Vomit hits my throat, and I have to force myself to keep it together. To keep everything in.

The bed is drenched in blood. I take a step closer and see that Amber has fallen off the side. There's a pillow over her face, but the rest of her body is exposed. The skin on her arms is gray. Even without checking, I know she's dead. I take another step toward the bed, and that's when I see hair, blood, and something else.

I turn around and run back into the hall and slam the door behind me.

"Where's Dad?" I ask Maddi.

I glance down at my hands and see blood on my palms and some on my shirt.

Is that from Maddi?

Is it?

"I don't know. I don't know!" she screams.

"Maddi, go outside. Go outside and call nine-one-one. I'm going to find Dad," I say.

Maddi shakes her head. "No, what if whoever did that to her is still in the house? I can't leave you in here by yourself."

They are in the house.

This didn't really happen.

This couldn't have really happened.

I run to my room and grab my cell phone.

"Here, call nine-one-one. I'm going to check the garage," I say.

Why am I so calm?

Why are you so calm?

Maddi grips my arm as we walk toward the garage. We pass the door to the living room, and that's when I see it.

More blood.

How can there be more blood?

All over the couch, on the floor. There's even some splashed on the walls. But more than that, I see Dad. Lying on the couch. His eyes are half-open, and he almost looks alive. Except the top of his head and his neck have huge hunks taken out of them.

Oh my God.

"Maddi, look away. Go outside!" I scream. The vomit I've been fighting back hits my throat and I lean over and puke all over the floor.

He's dead.

Dad.

Not Dad.

Maddi lets go of me and falls to the floor again. She's crying so hard I don't think she'll ever stop.

"No. No. No!" she screams. She hits the floor over and over. I reach down and pick up my phone and dial 911.

Charlotte

The police come.

On my way outside, I see an envelope with my name on it. Next to the envelope is a suitcase and some bottled waters.

He really wanted me gone.

He really wanted me out of the house.

I grab the letter and go outside.

"Can you tell me your full name?" a police officer asks me.

An ambulance comes.

Two ambulances come.

Then a third, for Maddi.

She screams and cries and kicks and slaps as the bodies are taken out of the house.

"No. No! It isn't true. It didn't happen. It didn't happen!" she screams. I hold her tight, promising myself that I'll never let anything happen to her. No one will ever hurt her. No one will ever hurt my family again.

"She's in shock," someone says. He grabs at Maddi, but she slaps him away.

Suddenly the world is black, white, and red. Blood and darkness everywhere.

Maddi is sticky with blood.

How did she get blood on her?

Did she touch one of the bodies?

How did you get blood on yourself?

"That was one of the worst crime scenes I've ever seen," I hear someone say. A few people around me look sicker than I feel.

A medic throws up near the driveway.

All the while, Maddi continues to scream and cry.

Her screams frighten me, and chills run through my body.

Uncle Jake and Alex stand outside the guesthouse door. Both dressed in their pj's. I forgot they were here. Forgot that they were just a few feet from us.

How long have they been there?

Did they see anything?

Did they hear anything?

Was it them?

They speak to a policeman. Alex stumbles and cries when he tells her what happened. Jake looks pale and tired. He also looks scared. Not like himself at all. Not like the confident man I spoke to just days ago.

Everyone is scared.

I know I am.

When Maddi sees Uncle Jake, her eyes change. She stops crying and her sadness changes to pure hate.

"Murderer! You killed them. I know it was you!" she shouts, as Uncle Jake walks toward us.

"You killed them. How could you kill them? How could you kill my father?"

305

Uncle Jake and Alex ignore Maddi. Her screams don't seem to faze them.

Uncle Jake leans in close to the police officer. He's crying. Alex sobs too loud. I stare at Jake as he talks to the cop.

What is he saying to them?

What is he telling them?

Did he kill them?

Do they think he killed them?

"Maddi, it's okay. Maddi, stop," I say. I hold her, and that's when the paramedic comes over to us.

"She needs to go to the hospital," he tells me. He takes Maddi by the arm and this time she doesn't fight. This time she goes limp, like she's lost all power over herself.

I look down at her feet and see that she's not wearing shoes. Neither of us are. My feet are red and cold. Maddi's body is covered in goose bumps. The sun is starting to rise, but I know it won't warm anything up around here.

"We need to get her shoes," I say.

"What are your full names?" the medic asks as we walk toward an ambulance. The first two are gone. So are Amber and Dad.

Gone.

They're both gone.

"Miss. Miss, please. Can you please tell me your name?" the medic says. My thoughts cloud his voice.

All this time I've wanted them gone.

And now they're gone forever.

No more Amber.

No more Dad.

Gone.

Charlotte

The day is a blur. With questions and more questions. Questions about Dad, and Amber, and Uncle Jake.

They ask me about my relationship with Amber and how I felt about her sleeping in my mother's bed. How I felt about her relationship with Dad. About Mom's death. About therapy and my mental health.

They ask us everything.

After hours of questions, they tell us we can't go back to the house. Not for a long time.

It's a crime scene, and they need to gather evidence.

I hang on to the envelope that Dad left for me. I know it was him who left it because of the handwriting. The way he's written my name on the front of it. All slanty.

What does it say?

Open it.

I can't.

After they let Maddi leave the hospital, they put us both up in a motel a few blocks from school. Because Maddi is almost eighteen, they let us stay by ourselves. But we aren't really alone. A cop is almost always stationed outside our door. We aren't prisoners, but it sort of feels like we are.

The doctors say that Maddi had a panic attack and she's going to be okay. She's sent home with a bottle of medication.

Who will we stay with?

There's no one left.

My phone rings and beeps constantly. Messages from people I do and don't know.

Some of the messages are kind, and some aren't. I try not to read any of them.

Sorry to hear about your dad.

Sending my love.

Do you know who did it?

Who's next to go?

Uncle Jake calls over and over, but I ignore him. He texts me and tells me he and Alex won't be going home for a while.

Nancy calls. She leaves voice mails that I delete. I don't care what she has to say right now.

The hotel room they put us in is dingy and dark, with orange and red blankets and photos of the sea on the walls. I can't tell if it's supposed to be inviting.

The texts keep coming, but none of them are from Stephen.

Maddi takes her pills that night, and then cries in her sleep. I stay awake and stare at the ceiling.

How could it have happened?

It couldn't have happened.

Charlotte

I wake with a jerk, not sure if the banging I hear is in my dreams or if it's real. The last twenty-four hours have felt like a waking dream. Asleep when I'm awake, awake when I'm asleep. My brain is numb, and thoughts of Dad's dead body come in and out of my head. I try not to think about it. About his body. About his skin. The blood. His eyes.

His eyes.

He almost looked alive.

Oh, Dad.

The banging outside the hotel room continues.

"Charlotte? Someone's at the door," Maddi whispers. Our room has two beds, but Maddi and I lie close together in one.

She grabs my arms tight. There's fear in her voice.

Outside the door, I hear shouts. "Girls, open up, it's the police."

I peek at the bedside clock: 10:35 p.m.

The curtains are drawn and the room is dark and dismal.

They're back.

Why can't they just leave us alone?

"Give us a minute!" I shout.

Maddi sits up and flicks on the light. She looks horrible. Almost ghostlike. Dark circles under her eyes. Her skin, which is usually tan and healthy-looking, looks yellow. Her hair is dirty and sits flat against her head.

When I look at her I want to cry.

My poor sister.

This is your fault.

The cops come into our hotel room and talk to us. I don't listen. They scrape gunk from under our fingernails. They take swabs of spit from our mouths. They did all this right after they found the bodies but do it all again now. It's invasive and I don't understand why it has to be done.

Maddi can't take it. I can tell. But I don't try to fight them. I pretend it doesn't bother me.

At least we're together. We had to sit in separate rooms at the police station the first time we spoke to the cops. They grilled me for what felt like years. Asking questions about Dad and Amber. I don't know how Maddi got through it.

"What was your relationship like with your father? What about Amber?" They've asked us these questions already.

Maybe they think we'll say more if we're not at the police station.

Maddi doesn't have anything to hide.

Do I?

Do you?

Maddi doesn't answer. Just cries and shakes her head. I know it's my turn next.

"Listen, we need you to cooperate," a cop says to Maddi. His name is Officer Peterson. Every time the police speak to us, he's the first to talk.

I hate that stupid fucking name.
I hate that stupid fucking guy.
He needs to leave her alone.
She hasn't done anything.

"I loved my father. He wasn't perfect, but he was still my dad," Maddi says through her tears. Seeing her like this makes my skin crawl. Makes me almost hate Dad and Amber for dying.

After he's done with Maddi, Officer Peterson turns to me. He has a large belly and his hair is thin on top. The skin on his neck is red and patchy and I wonder if he's as mean as he looks.

"Charlie." He pulls up a chair and places it next to the bed. I can smell his aftershave, and it stings my nose. It doesn't smell anything like the stuff Dad used. It's sweeter, and it makes me sick to my stomach.

"It's Charlotte," I say.
Leave me alone.
We don't know anything.
We don't, do we?
No.

I stare him right in the eyes. His are blue and clear, and somehow they look kind. The rest of him doesn't, but his eyes have something about them.

He asks me all the same questions he did when they found the bodies. But then he gets personal.

"Charlotte, a few sources tell me you didn't get along with your father's fiancée. Is that true?"
Sources?
I won't lie to him.

"Uncle Jake, right? He told you that. I'll admit it, I hated

Amber. She tried to tear our family apart. But that doesn't mean I wanted her to die," I say.

Liar.

Shut up.

Maddi looks at me and gives me her "what the hell are you doing?" eyes.

"That's pretty harsh," Officer Peterson says.

"She treated my mom poorly," I say, "and she was sleeping with my father. I already told you yesterday at the police station. I don't know how I was supposed to care about someone like that." I soften the edges of my tone and look away from Peterson. If I was on TV, I'd ask for a lawyer. Tell the police I don't want to talk to them by myself.

But I don't.

"That would make someone very angry. It would make me angry," he says.

You know what he's doing.

I don't care.

"Like I said before, just because I didn't like her doesn't mean I wanted her to die," I say.

Officer Peterson nods and then sighs.

"Okay. Well, that's enough chatting for right now. We'll be in touch," he says.

The next three days go like that.

Cops coming in and out of our hotel room.

Pestering us. Bothering us. Questioning us.

The stress of it weighs on Maddi even more than it does

on me. She stops eating completely and doesn't get out of bed except for when Officer Peterson makes her talk to him.

She never once asks me what I think happened. Just lies in bed and cries.

Except for the third night.

That's when she finally talks to me.

"Charlotte," Maddi says.

We sit in our hotel room with the window open to let some air in. The place is dirty, and smoggy. We haven't let housekeeping come in once. Outside, snow falls. The sky is dark.

The outside world reflects the sadness I feel.

The snow tells me that things will never be the same as they were years ago, before Mom died. Before Stephen left me, before our family was struck by death and murder.

The numbness that had shelled my thoughts and body is starting to wear off, and reality is sinking in. My stomach aches when I think how I'll never see my father again. I take one of the pills they gave Maddi for her nerves, but it doesn't do anything.

"What?" I look at Maddi. She's sitting on the edge of the bed in a baggy shirt and leggings.

She'll never be the same, either. And how could she be?

Neither of us will.

Nothing will.

"Who killed them? Who killed them? And why?" She starts to cry again, but this time she doesn't scream. Just weeps, like she'll never stop.

I want to make her feel better, I want to say the right things, but I don't know what to say.

Because I don't know the answers to her questions.

Who did it? Why?

You know who did it.

Do I?

I sit next to Maddi and hug her. She puts her head on my shoulder, and I can feel her tears seep through my sweater. Her hair smells dirty and I wonder how long it's been since she washed it.

"Do you think they really wanted Mom to die?" She pulls away and looks at me when she says this. Her eyes are glossy from the tears.

I want to tell her that I know they did, but at the same time, I don't want to speak ill of the dead.

Of our father.

No matter how much I hated him, I didn't want him to die, too.

Did I?

"I don't know, I just don't know who would do any of this to our family or why."

Maddi gets up and walks over to the window where I just was. She looks outside. I wonder if she hates the snow as much as I do.

"It was them, wasn't it?" Maddi whispers. Her voice so hushed I almost don't hear her.

"What?" I say. But she ignores my question and just keeps staring off in the distance.

Winter never brings happiness.

When I was little it brought Christmas, and snowball fights, and New Year's Eve with its new beginnings. Now it just brings cold and sadness. Things I should be used to by now, but I'm not.

"Jake. It was Jake, wasn't it?" Maddi says. Now her voice is louder, and she sounds like she's trying to convince herself.

She doesn't look like my sister anymore. She looks like someone else. A stranger who I once knew better than I know myself.

Jake. Why would Jake come here to hurt our father?

To kill our father.

My stomach turns.

Money?

Jealousy?

He doesn't need money. And why would he be jealous?

"Why, Maddi? What would he gain from killing Dad?" I wait for her to respond, but she doesn't. Just continues to look out the window.

She stares and stares and stares. Like something out there is calling for her. Calling her name. And maybe something is.

"I know it. I can feel it. In my whole self. He killed them. He's the reason they're gone. He's the reason they're dead."

Charlotte

The police come back, but this time they don't bang on the door or holler at me and Maddi through the window.

It's been five days since they died.

Five days of us locked up in this hotel room.

Five days of texts and calls and knocks on the door.

Five days of us not knowing anything.

Until now.

I almost don't hear the knock on the door. It's just a tapping in my dream.

Tap. Tap tap.

Like a crow tapping on the window outside my bedroom.

Tap tap tap.

The same crow I saw in my sleep when they found Mom.

"Charlotte," the crow at the window says. Its voice is familiar. "Hello?"

Tap tap tap.

"They're back." Maddi shakes my shoulder. It brings me back from my half sleep.

I sit up and look around the room. It's dark, with slivers of light coming through the blackout curtains. Can't Fall River bring us an ounce of sunshine? Anything to get rid of this darkness. A moment of happiness.

"Why so early?" Maddi says. She gets out of bed and opens the door.

This is the first time she's opened the door for the police.

Maybe all the rest has helped her. Maybe she's starting to feel better.

Maybe she's going to get better.

She looks worse.

She's never going to get better.

Neither of us will.

She opens the door, and two policemen stand there. One is Officer Peterson, the other is a man I've never seen before.

They both have their arms folded.

"Can we come in?" Officer Peterson says. Only this time he doesn't have the angry tone he's had the last few days.

This time he sounds sincere, almost sad.

I get out of bed and walk to the door and stand next to Maddi. I'm wearing a sweater that comes to my knees and no pants. The cold air that comes through the front door gives me goose bumps up and down my legs.

"Sure," I say. "What's going on?"

Have they come for me?

Have they come for her?

What more could there be?

Maddi walks over to the window and opens the curtains to let the light in. I know that the room smells of BO and old food.

We've been holed up in here for days, and neither of us has given an ounce of effort to keep the room clean, nor have we showered.

"We won't stay long," says the officer I've never met. He has dark skin and soft features. He's probably just a few years older than Maddi.

"Do you think you girls could take a seat?" Officer Peterson says.

Here we go again.

I don't think I can take any more seats.

Maddi and I plop down on our bed. Maddi throws the blanket over her legs. The room has already dropped from toasty warm to cold.

The two officers sit on the bed across from us. They look out of place, uncomfortable. Officer Peterson clears his throat and looks at the other cop. Mr. No Name. Has it gotten to the point where we have no idea who we let into our home anymore?

This isn't our home.

You know what I mean.

"There's no easy way to tell you girls this, but we are getting ready to make an arrest."

Who?

They've come for me. They're going to take me away.

They aren't, are they?

Would they?

Why would they?

"What? Who!" Maddi jumps off the bed and steps close to Officer Peterson. "Please tell us what you know, please?"

I grab Maddi by the hand and pull her back down next to me. She looks at me and all I see is a shell of my sister. A broken shell. Filled with pain and heartache.

"We're here because we want to tell you before word gets out. We have enough evidence to arrest your Aunt Alex," the other cop says.

I feel gut-punched, like I'll never get air back into my lungs.

No way.

She couldn't have.

Could she have?

No.

"What?" Maddi says. "What? Did Jake have any part in it?"

She grips my hand tight.

I feel as if I am going to puke. Throw up my insides all over the floor of this shitty hotel.

It isn't right.

That isn't right.

Tiny Alex. How could that tiny, small-boned woman be capable of something like this? Of hurting someone? Of hurting anyone?

"We don't know if your uncle had anything to do with it. We're still investigating," Peterson says. "But from what we've gathered, it looks like your aunt acted alone."

We let her into our home.

We were there the whole time.

"What kind of evidence did you find?" I ask. Not sure if it's something you should ask, but I do anyway.

Officer Peterson looks down at his shoes. They're shiny and black with scuff marks on the toes.

"We . . ." He pauses for a moment and glances at Maddi. Like she might break at getting more news. Like knowing more than she already knows could make this worse. "We found a necklace on one of the deceased. There was DNA on it, and strands of hair that matched your aunt's. Our guess is the necklace was put on the body after the murders took place, but we're still looking into it."

Maddi shakes her head and then starts crying again.

How could she have any tears left? Do they ever end? Will they ever stop?

They went shopping together.

They were friends.

My head starts to spin, and I do everything I can not to focus on the headache I know is going to come.

"With this evidence, and the murder weapon being left at the scene, it's enough to hold her for questioning," Officer Peterson says.

"Oh," I say softly. I remember how Alex gasped when I told her that I thought Amber and Dad had killed Mom. How shocked she looked. How she cried.

"Why? Why did she do it?" Maddi says.

"She was best friends with Mom growing up," I say, more to myself than to Maddi. "She said that she loved her."

Is that a reason to kill someone?

Why does anyone do anything? Why did Mom die? Why did Dad have to change?

The other cop shakes his head. He looks uncomfortable, like he's never given bad news in his life. He fidgets and keeps touching his coat. He's too young to be here. He's too young to be involved with the pain that is our lives.

"Why?" Maddi screams. She stands and she reminds me of a child. Lost and confused.

"Calm down, calm down," I say.

Why are you so calm?

Why aren't you screaming?

You know why.

"Don't tell me to fucking calm down. Don't fucking tell me what to do. They're dead, Charlie. They're all dead. They've all been murdered. They're all fucking dead."

She screams and shouts.

And it's true.

She's right.

We're all that's left.

She and I are all that is left.

Charlotte

Lana calls me over and over and over.

Then she texts me over and over and over.

I ignore all her calls. I ignore all her texts.

Until she mentions Stephen.

Charlie, Stephen and I are worried about you. Please call me. Please talk to me. Tell me what's going on.

When I read his name, my body shakes.

How did I not see it before? How?

She's sleeping with him.

She's been sleeping with him the whole time.

I knew she wasn't your friend.

I knew it.

Do you want to meet up? I text.

I know I shouldn't. I know the smart thing to do is to let this go. I've already done and said too much. But I can't help myself.

Blame it on grief.

Blame it on pain.

She's the one who pushed me to the edge.

She's the one who really made me think.

Yes. Please! Where are you staying? I can bring you and Maddi food. What do you need? I'll come and get you.

She cannot come here.

She needs to stay away.

I'll come to you.

Charlotte

I meet Lana at the coffee shop a few miles from the hotel. The shop has about three inches of fresh powder snow on top of it, yet the inside looks warm and inviting. But I stay in the car.

I didn't want to leave Maddi, but I need to do this. I need to fix this.

You shouldn't leave your sister.

You shouldn't tell me what I shouldn't do.

I sit in my car and wait.

And wait.

Lana doesn't show up for at least twenty minutes. I don't know why I stick around, but I stay until a loud Subaru hatchback pulls up next to me.

It's started to snow again. Fat flakes, like cotton balls, pour from the sky. I wonder how long it'll be dark. How long the world will have a gray cover of cold over the top of it.

Lana rolls down her window. Her eye shadow and lipstick are done in red. Her hair hangs around her face and she's topped it off with a black hat. It reminds me of a witch.

That's because she is a witch.

A witch bitch.

I stare at Lana through the glass for what feels like a good minute before I roll my window down, just a crack.

"Charlie. Are you okay? Sorry it took me so long, my car slid on some ice," she says.

She's lying.

She's always lying.

How could I not see it in her? She's a liar.

"Get in," I say through the crack in my window. And then roll it up.

She turns her car off and comes around and gets into mine.

What now?

What now?

What now?

I lock the doors and start to drive.

"Are you okay?" Lana says. Her voice is shaking, like she's afraid. The confidence she usually has seems to be hiding somewhere. Maybe it was fake all along. Or maybe I imagined it.

"I don't want to talk about it," I say. I drive toward Stephen's house.

"What can I do for you? My mom keeps asking about you," she says. Her body language is different from usual. She's crouched up against the door. She holds her purse in front of her chest like a shield.

Or maybe I'm just imagining that, too.

"Why did you get in my car? If you're so afraid?" I say. I hardly recognize my own voice. But it's me. The real me. The Charlie that's done pretending. Done hiding.

Angry Charlie.

That's who I am now.

"What?" Lana says. I hear real fear in her voice now. Like she knows she's made a huge mistake.

"You heard me. Why did you get in?"

Why did you invite her in?

She came to make you look stupid.

She wasn't thinking, that's why.

"I'm not scared. I've been worried about you, that's all," she says. Her voice cracks a little when she says this. I watch her open her purse and pull out a piece of gum. She pops it into her mouth, and for a second she has that confidence back. But it doesn't last long.

I stop the car and stare at her. Her eyes are shiny and she looks like she's trying not to cry.

"Why did you lie to me? Why? I thought we were friends," I say.

Will she admit to sleeping with Stephen? Will she actually tell me why she stabbed me in the back? Was it a game to her? Would it be a game to me, if the roles were reversed?

Probably not.

Probably never.

"What are you talking about?" Lana says. But I know she knows what I'm talking about. She can't pretend. What's the point?

She knows exactly what she's done.

This was a game, and she liked it. She got off on it.

She probably lay in bed with Stephen and laughed at me.

Laughed at how desperate I was.

"Stop fucking lying to me. Just tell me why you pretended to like me. Why would you do that?"

I hit the steering wheel and Lana jumps like maybe I'll hit her next.

Or worse.

"Stop it, Charlie. Stop," she says. She pulls her phone out of her purse. I slap it out of her hand and scream.

"Why did you lie? Why why why! Just tell me the truth!"

I'm like an outsider watching myself lose my mind. I'm like someone I don't know.

"I don't know! I wrote the letters because I thought it'd be funny. I didn't do it to hurt you. I was just curious, I'm sorry," Lana says. She's crying now. Red makeup runs down her face like blood. Even now she's beautiful. But she looks younger. Smaller.

Oh no.

"What? What are you talking about?" I say.

She wasn't just sleeping with Stephen.

The letters.

Of course.

No.

No!

"You wrote those letters?" My stomach turns. I know this can't be true. But it is.

Suddenly it all makes sense. It's clear as day now.

Why would Mom tell a stranger that stuff? Why wouldn't Lana's mom go to the cops? Why was it all such a secret? But why did I believe Lana? Why had I believed her?

Why?

You were desperate.

I was desperate.

She wrote them.

She tricked me.

She tricked me!

"You wrote those letters? Do you have any idea what those letters did to me and my family?" I try to keep my voice calm, but every word comes out louder than the last.

"Your mom did write one of them. The one where she talked about how proud she was of you, how much she loved you and Maddi. That wasn't a lie. She knew my mom. They talked sometimes. But the other ones, I'm sorry, Charlotte."

I feel like I could tear her hair out. I feel like I could drive the car off a cliff, with both of us in it.

"How did you know all that stuff about Amber? And my dad? How could you have known?" I know the answer without having to ask. But I ask anyway. She has to say it.

Tell me.

"Stephen told me. He told me how messed up your family is. I'm sorry. We were just trying to fuck with you, I shouldn't have let it go so far," Lana says.

How could Stephen do that?

He's never cared about me. Never cared about my family.

We were weird. He told me so all the time.

I was just a joke to him. And so was my family.

I want to scream at the top of my lungs, punch out all the windows, I want this anger that's inside me gone.

But instead I cry.

Of course you don't have any friends.

Why would I?

I'm messed up.

But it's more than that.

Those letters were proof.

Those letters were proof of what they did to her.

Did to Mom.

Proof that Dad wanted her gone.

"I'm sorry. I'm sorry," Lana says. And maybe she is sorry. Maybe she feels more than sorry for me. Maybe she's sorry for what she's done. For what she's put my family through.

"I'm sorry, I really am sorry," Lana says again. Her voice shakes, and she grips her purse so tightly her knuckles are white. "I thought it would be funny. I don't know."

Why?

Why?

Why?

All the planning. All the fear of living in the same house as the people who murdered my own mom.

Dad.

Amber.

Mom knew.

But that wasn't Mom. That was Lana.

Why?

How could I have been so dumb?

That's when I hit her.

Hard, in the face. I'm like an animal. I pounce on her and slap and claw. I punch her in the chest.

"Stop. Stop!" Lana screams.

I could kill her.

I could kill her.

I could fucking kill her.

She screams and cries and I slap harder. I punch and scratch until there's blood on my hands.

Lana manages to get the car unlocked and crawl out.

"Help, help!" she screams as she stands up. The snow is coming down hard, and she slips and falls. Her ankle slides in an unnatural way, and she cries out in pain. She turns back to me, and then starts to hobble away from the car. Every time she puts weight on her foot, she flinches. I watch her for a moment and then get out of the car and follow her. It only takes me a few strides to catch up.

"You liar. You liar!" I shout, and then push her to the ground again. She falls with a thud and snow puffs up around her.

"Charlie, stop!" she screams. Blood is pouring from her nose, and her face is swollen. Her hair's a mess. She doesn't look like a real person anymore.

She's not a real person. Not to me.

I stand over her as she cries. Her eyes are frightened, like she's looking at a monster.

Before I can stop myself I kick her hard in the ribs. Then again on the thigh.

I could kill her.

I could do it.

I could.

"Do you have any idea what you've done? Do you have any idea what you've done to my family?" I shout louder than I ever have. Every ounce of my body shakes with anger and grief. My entire life, ruined, because of her. Because of the things she told me and Maddi. The things she showed us.

I kneel down next to her and grab her tightly by the hair.

"Do you realize what you've done?" I whisper through gritted teeth. I don't even recognize my own voice.

"I'm sorry," Lana says. "I'm so sorry." Then she slaps at me. Her nails dig into my skin, but I can't feel it.

I can't feel anything.

She slaps at me again, and I taste blood in my mouth.

Nothing she can say will change how I feel. What she's done.

End it.

Take care of her.

Finish this. End this pain.

"Charlotte. Stop. Stop." Arms grab me around the stomach and I'm pulled away from Lana.

Stephen pushes me to the ground, and Lana stands up and cries in his arms. I watch him hold her close and kiss her on the neck. She looks like she fits right into his arms. Right into his little world. The place I used to fit, just months ago.

I stand up and watch them.

He never loved me.

She was never my friend.

"You need help!" Stephen shouts. He looks at me like he despises me. Like I'm the most horrible thing he's ever seen. And maybe I am.

"Call the cops!" Lana screams. Stephen holds her tight. And I stand there, on the outside looking in.

"I think my ankle is dislocated," Lana says. But Stephen doesn't move. He just stares at me.

"I loved you," I say. And I did.

"You're fucked, Charlotte. I never loved you. You're a fucked-up person," Stephen says.

And he's right.

He's right, and I know it.

He never did love me.

Charlotte

I sit outside the hotel and hold the letter Dad left me. Blood is on my knuckles and under my nails. I have scratch marks on my face, but I don't care about any of that.

I know that someone is going to come for me soon. The police, Lana's family maybe, but someone's coming.

So I wait for whoever it is, with the letter.

Open it. Just open it.

I can't.

Why?

I'm scared.

The last thing my father wrote to me. Probably some of his last conscious thoughts, in this note.

Read it.

Charlotte Andrew Vreeland. He went to the trouble of writing my full name on the envelope.

Mom hated my middle name. Told me often that she wanted it to be Lily, but Dad got the last word. Because he wanted me to be a part of him, too.

He wanted me to be like him, Mom used to tell me. All the time.

I wonder how much I disappointed my father.

Or my mom.

Open it, Charlie.

Open it.

I rip open the envelope, pull out the letter, take a deep breath, and read.

Charlotte,

By the time you read this letter, I hope you'll be on your way to get help.

You've needed it for a long time. I knew you did, but I ignored it.

I ignored you. Just like I did your mother those last few months.

There's a lot I'd like to tell you, that I wish I had told you a long time ago. But I failed to do so because I was selfish. And I didn't want you to hate me more than you already do.

I know you've been struggling with your mom's death for a long time, and that you've had suspicions that I, or Amber, had a part in it.

And it's true. We did.

The day before your mother died, I told her that I was leaving her. That Amber and I were planning to have a child. To start a new life. It was the same week I found out your mom had ovarian cancer. She discovered she had it soon after the miscarriage but didn't tell me until the week she died.

She had no plans of fighting the cancer, and because of that, I was angry with her.

I know it was wrong of me, especially after the miscarriage, but I couldn't support her not fighting for her children, so it was the last straw for me.

Your mom had been abusing prescription drugs and alcohol. Amber and I had found so many pills in the house. Painkillers, opioids. Your mom was hurting herself, and I couldn't take it anymore. Amber and I needed a fresh start and your mom needed help.

I told your mother this. And she did not handle it well. I was stupid to think she would. I was selfish. I hadn't been thinking about her, or you, or your sister. I only cared about me.

The next morning, she died.

She took her own life, Charlotte.

She was depressed, and I ignored the signs. And because I did, she took all of her pills at once, she went into cardiac arrest, and she died. I know you probably won't believe me. But she left a letter. I didn't give it to you or your sister because I blamed myself for her death, and I couldn't stand the thought of you both blaming me, too.

I can't tell you how much I regret my actions. How much I regret the things I did. If I could go back and do it differently, I would. And going forward, I will.

I won't let this happen again to someone else I love.

I'm worried about you. I'm worried you're going to hurt yourself.

That's why I'm getting you help.

Please understand why I'm telling you this and know that I love you and hope to see you get better.

> *Much love,*
> *Dad*

Included in the envelope is a letter from Mom.

GIRLS,

I KNOW IT'S HARD TO UNDERSTAND AND I KNOW IT WILL TAKE YOU A LONG TIME TO FORGIVE ME, BUT I HOPE ONE DAY YOU'LL FIND IT IN YOUR HEARTS TO SEE THAT THIS WAS MY ONLY OPTION.

I'VE BEEN A BURDEN FOR TOO LONG. YOUR DAD CAN MOVE ON WITH HIS LIFE AND HAVE A BABY WITH SOMEONE WHO LOVES HIM. CHARLOTTE AND MADDI, YOU HAVE EACH OTHER. I CAN STOP HOLDING YOU BACK. PUTTING SO MUCH STRESS ON YOU. PLEASE LOOK AFTER EACH OTHER. I WILL MISS YOU BOTH,

BUT EVERYTHING WILL BE OKAY. EVERYTHING WILL BE BETTER NOW.

I LOVE YOU WITH ALL MY HEART. THANK YOU FOR LETTING ME BE YOUR MOM.

Bile rises in my throat.

My head aches and I don't want to believe what I've just read.

It has to be a lie. He has to be lying. He wrote this. Just like Lana. He's lying.

Lieslieslies! More fucking lies.

More lies.

But I know, I know he's not lying.

I know everything in the letter is true.

Your heart doesn't just stop.

Maddi

I sit by my mother's grave, dripping wet from the snow. I touch her headstone and wonder, would she have liked this? Would she have chosen this font for herself? The headstone wasn't here last time I visited.

"Would you have liked this?" I say to Mom. I know she must be listening. She's here somewhere. She hasn't left me after all.

"You would have liked this, wouldn't you?"

I'm feeling a lot better, but it's been a few weeks since I've been able to come here. I'm glad Mom finally has a headstone.

Eventually, the police let me go home. It's so lonely in that house by myself. But at least I know no one is trying to take it away from me. I do stay away from town, though. People don't like me coming around.

They are still investigating the crimes.

All of the crimes.

That's okay. I understand why.

My old friends, they don't talk to me anymore.

And, of course, they took my sister away. She's in a hospital now.

Getting better.

I hope.

I miss her more than anything or anyone. But she's in good hands. Nancy is there with her. And I get to visit once a week.

"I found your necklace," I say to Mom, touching the rose pendant made of rubies. It hangs around my neck like it's belonged there all along. It makes me feel closer to Mom. Knowing that it's no longer on that woman. Knowing it's the reason I got rid of that woman.

"I also brought your favorite dress." The headstone is cold and my hands are freezing.

I pull the dress out of my bag and look at it.

"You loved this dress," I say. "But now it's ruined."

It was pure white when Mom bought it for Charlotte. But it hasn't been white since everything happened.

Now it's red all down the front. The sleeves are brown and hard.

Dried blood.

It's her blood. That woman's blood.

It's like a dream, the memory of her blood. Splashed all over the room. All over my sister's dress. Everywhere.

She disgusted me.

The sight of her blood disgusts me.

You need to get rid of it.

Get rid of it.

Burn it.

Burn it, and no one will ever know.

Author's Note

When I was ten, I discovered a children's nonfiction book about the Borden murders. At the time, I had never heard of Lizzie Borden or her story. I skimmed through the book and discovered that there were crime-scene photos of Abby and Andrew Borden, Lizzie's father and stepmother. Lizzie Borden was the main suspect. She was arrested and tried for the crimes.

Even though the crimes took place in Fall River, Massachusetts—far from my own home—and in August of 1892, seeing those blurry photos scared me. The brutal way the Bordens were murdered was disturbing. And yet, I couldn't stop going back to that book.

Here are some of the facts: Lizzie was in the home when the murders took place. She burned a "paint-soaked dress" in front of the police. She had no alibi, and her story kept changing when she spoke to the police.

The Bordens' housekeeper claimed to have heard Lizzie laughing moments before the bodies of Abby and Andrew were discovered.

Despite evidence at the trial that pointed to Lizzie, she was acquitted of murder.

As I grew older, the Lizzie Borden story stayed in the back of my mind.

There was always that question: Did Lizzie *really* commit these crimes?

Some say that Lizzie's uncle John, who had been in town the week of the murders, may have played a part, or even killed the Bordens himself. Others just assumed that Lizzie, a woman who taught Sunday school every week and who came from a wealthy family, wasn't capable of something so gruesome.

Whatever the case may be, the crime is still talked about today.

Even though no one really knows what happened, I believe that Lizzie did commit murder.

But *why?*

Why did she do it? That's another question that haunts me and that inspired me to write *It Will End Like This.* In my novel, I chose to turn this story on its head. But either Charlotte *or* Maddi could have killed their father and soon-to-be step-mother. The powerlessness and anger they both experience in this story are what I imagine could have driven Lizzie to murder in 1892.

Resources

It Will End Like This is a work of fiction and it is important to note that it's statistically more likely for a person suffering from mental illness to be the victim of a violent crime than to commit one. However unlikely the events of this narrative might be, this novel does explore many real mental health issues, including depression, grief, substance abuse, and suicidal ideation. If you or a person you know is struggling with mental illness, you are not alone.

National Suicide Prevention Lifeline
800-273-TALK
suicidepreventionlifeline.org

Families for Depression Awareness
781-890-0220
familyaware.org

National Alliance on Mental Illness (NAMI)
800-950-6264
nami.org/home

Al-Anon and Alateen
al-anon.org

Smart Recovery: Self-Management and Recovery Training
smartrecovery.org

Substance Abuse and Mental Health Services Administration
800-662-HELP (4357)
samhsa.gov

Acknowledgments

Writing a book can be hard. That's why you surround yourself with people who make the work a little bit easier.

Here are my people—those I need to thank.

First is Stephen Fraser, for always talking me through the panic, and believing in my writing. You are an amazing agent and an even more amazing person.

A grateful thank-you to Krista Marino, the editor of my dreams. I never thought I would have the opportunity to work with someone who understood my writing as well as you do. You are outstanding, and you made the process of book writing absolutely wonderful.

Thank you to everyone at Delacorte Press who had a hand in making this book happen. Especially Elena Garnu and Casey Moses. You created one of the most gorgeous covers I've ever seen.

A thank you to Cait and Laura, for reading this book when it was still in the stages of "write drunk, edit sober," and giving feedback that helped me have the confidence to submit this novel to my agent.

Special thanks to my fabulous mother, who has always encouraged me to write no matter what.

And thank you to Kyle. You're a wonderful support and champion.

About the Author

KYRA LEIGH lives in Salt Lake City, Utah. When she isn't writing, Kyra spends her free time in the mountains with her husband and two dogs. She is the author of *It Will End Like This* and *Reaper*.

🐦